# MISS CHRISTIE REGRETS

GUY FRASER-SAMPSON

urbanepublications.com

First published in Great Britain in 2016 by Urbane Publications Ltd
Suite 3, Brown Europe House, 33/34 Gleaming Wood Drive,
Chatham, Kent ME5 8RZ


A CIP catalogue record for this book is available from the British Library.

ISBN 978-1-911331-80-3
EPUB 978-1-911331-81-0
MOBI 978-1-911331-82-7

Design and Typeset by Julie Martin
Cover by Author Design Studio

Printed and bound by CPI Group (UK) Ltd, Croydon, CR0 4YY

urbanepublications.com

*Miss Christie Regrets* is the second volume of the Hampstead Murders. Readers are invited to sample the series in the correct order for maximum enjoyment.

*Death in Profile*
*Miss Christie Regrets*
*A Whiff of Cyanide* (due summer 2017)

## PRAISE FOR THE HAMPSTEAD MURDERS SERIES

"Comfortingly old school crime fiction with a modern twist."

Chris Brookmyre

"Classy and sophisticated … if you thought the Golden Age of crime writing was dead, then read this."

Ruth Dugdall, CWA Debut Dagger Winner

# CHAPTER 1

Burgh House sits rather smugly in New End Square, as if well aware of the fact that it is both one of the largest and also one of the finest houses in Hampstead. On this damp and blustery afternoon its three floors of imposing brickwork seemed to be acting as a buttress against the gusts of wind blowing fitfully westwards from the Heath, carrying flurries of rain which burst upon the window panes every few seconds like handfuls of gravel.

The man and woman who were moving slowly through the first floor of the house with little apparent sense of purpose or urgency seemed as solidly elegant as the building itself. The man, slim, with blonde hair and round spectacles, was wearing a neatly tailored tweed suit of brown flecked with green, a yellow waistcoat and brown brogues. His companion's dark hair was worn in a bun secured with a tortoiseshell comb, and her grey wool pencil skirt displayed to advantage the fine curves of her figure. Set against the wooden floors and panelling of the house, they depicted perfectly a 1950s couple. This was however not the 1950s, but some decades later but, this being Hampstead, their anachronistic appearance would doubtless be dismissed by any casual observer as mere eccentricity, at once harmless and engaging.

"I did somehow expect," Peter Collins observed with mock grumpiness as he wandered languidly from one room to another, "that a Constable exhibition would consist of paintings by Constable."

"But there *are* paintings by Constable, silly," Karen Willis replied, grabbing his arm. "What do you suppose you've just been looking at?"

"Oh, there are one or two, I grant you," he replied grudgingly, "if you pass over the sketches of cows and trees, that is. They demand little attention, which is perhaps just as well, since I gave them little. But I was expecting more, much more."

"Well, I don't know about you," she said, "but I've learned lots of things about Constable I never knew before. That he lived in Well Walk, for example. Why, that makes us almost neighbours, if you ignore the difference of the odd century, that is."

"He was only there for a year or so," Peter commented. "There, you see, I read the notes too."

"Yes, he thought the spring water and clean air would be good for his wife's TB," she said. "How romantic!"

"Not really," he replied. "It wasn't. She died."

"Oh, Peter," she cried in exasperation, giving him a little punch in the side. "Anyway, what more were you expecting? This is only Burgh House, you know, not the Royal Academy."

"Oh, you know, wall to wall Constables, room after room

of the things ..."

His free arm waved in a grandiloquent gesture as if sketching out an imaginary vista consisting entirely of canvas and oil paint.

"A clutch of Constables, perhaps?" she suggested coyly.

"Oh, dear God," he groaned. "Surely not a Ngaio Marsh allusion so early in the day? Why it's only three in the afternoon. I do think you might have kept her for later, Harriet. I've always thought of her as much more of a gin and tonic sort of writer rather than afternoon tea."

"You're just sore that you didn't think of it yourself," she said in superior fashion, not displaying the slightest surprise at being addressed as 'Harriet'.

He laughed.

"I do confess it," he conceded.

"Now that's cheating, surely?" she demanded. "Is that a Shakespeare confession, or a Marlowe confession?"

"Oh, Marlowe, I think, don't you? After all, any Tom, Dick or Harry can quote Shakespeare. One does like to be different."

"I fear you place altogether too much trust in the modern educational system," she commented sadly, "but so be it. Then the line is 'I confess it, Faustus, and rejoice', I believe."

"It is indeed," he nodded in approval, "but, standing here looking at you in that wonderful outfit, I think I prefer the one before it."

She wracked her brains in vain.

"No good," she admitted. "Tell me."

"O thou bewitching fiend," he said with a grin.

She laughed and clutched his arm more tightly.

"Anyway, that's an end to our clutch of Constables," she said. "It looks like we're back among the normal exhibits."

"Which we have of course seen several times previously, since we live just around the corner," he pointed out unnecessarily. "An unhappy alternative is before us ..."

"Ah, now you're on much safer ground with Jane Austen," she said delightedly. "Though I never believed for a moment that Mr Bennet would really make Elizabeth marry Mr Collins. Isn't he just a wonderful father? Anyway, never mind, what particular unhappy alternative do you envisage?"

"Going out into the rain and getting wet, since we didn't bring an umbrella, or going downstairs for a cup of tea. In which case it might stop raining or, there again, it might get worse."

"An unhappy alternative indeed," she concurred. "Now, let me see ..."

Suddenly she stopped dead in her tracks, released his arm, and said "damn" abruptly and intensely,

"What is it?" he asked.

"I've just remembered the rest of that Marlowe line," she said quietly. "'Twas thy temptation that robbed me of eternal happiness."

"I know," he said wretchedly. "I realised my mistake as soon as the words were out of my mouth. I'm so sorry, my darling."

She stood still for a moment, but then shook her head and smiled brightly.

"Never mind," she said, taking his arm again, more tightly this time. "Let's go and have that tea."

At much the same time but in a different part of London, Caroline Collison was handing a cup of tea to her husband, Simon.

"Well," she said, "it's taken a bit of getting used to having you around the house these last couple of weeks, but I rather think I like it."

Detective Superintendent Collison reflected that this was undoubtedly intended to make him feel better, and decided to take it in good part.

"Thank you, dear," he replied dutifully.

In reality he was restless to the point of torment. The two weeks' leave had been forced upon him at the end of a senior leadership course at Bramshill, the police staff college, and he knew all too well that it was intended to give the powers that be a chance to decide on his future career options.

"Only three days to go, though," his wife continued, reading his thoughts. "Any news yet?"

"None," he said ruefully. "I was hoping that if they couldn't come up with anything else they'd let me carry on with murder enquiries, perhaps even back at Hampstead. But who knows?"

"Hm," she said, "but Hampstead doesn't rate a Superintendent, surely?"

"It doesn't quite work like that anymore," he explained. "There are three murder investigation units: East, West and South, each headed by a Chief Superintendent. Each has nine Major Investigation Teams, each headed by a DCI as Senior Investigating Officer. That's probably why they're having problems making up their minds. Technically I'm already too senior to be an SIO, but I don't have the experience or the seniority to be bumped up a rank – after all, I've only just been made a Superintendent."

He took a sip of his tea.

"There again," he said with a smile, "it may also have something to do with the fact that they think I'm a loose cannon and they're trying to think of a posting where I can do the least possible damage."

"That's not fair," Caroline protested. "You're by far the cleverest man in the Met, *and* you've already caught a multiple murderer in a case which baffled everyone else, *and* you were hailed as a hero in the papers."

"And quite right too," she added, as she reached for his cup and refilled it.

"Too clever by half, most would say," he commented. "it's very kind of you to be so supportive about things, darling, but I really caught that killer almost by accident, and I know that some of the ideas I had along the way frightened the willies out of the Assistant Commissioner."

He received back his refilled cup.

"No," he went on, "I think they've got a pretty little conundrum on their hands. They made a great play out of having developed a new type of whizz-kid graduate policeman, because they thought it played well with the press, but in reality they've just created a Frankenstein's monster. They've alienated a lot of the traditional coppers who do good, solid police work every day of the year, and they've put themselves in a hugely high risk situation if they give me another enquiry to handle and I screw it up."

"Oh bums!" she said savagely. "Why does everything have to come down to politics all the time? Why can't people just be straightforward?"

"It's bound to come down to politics," he pointed out calmly. "Every Police Commissioner wants to have a period in office unsullied by disasters or scandal. Every Deputy Commissioner wants to become Commissioner. Every Assistant Commissioner wants to become Deputy Commissioner, and so on. They've taken many years to build their careers to date, so you can hardly blame them for being preoccupied with not wasting all the hard work they've put in so far."

"And bums to you too," she retorted. "Why do you have to be so bloody reasonable all the time, always seeing the other person's point of view?"

"Because it's the truth, perhaps?" he enquired with a smile, as he tried to decide whether to have another chocolate digestive.

"Well then, if you think you understand what's going on so well, what do you think will happen?"

"Dunno," he admitted. "What I'm hoping is that like all

difficult decisions they select a potential scapegoat to make it. If they do, that can only be the AC Crime and his ability to transfer me out of Specialist Crime and Operations will be pretty limited because nobody else will want a maverick like me posted to their command."

"So that's good, isn't it?"

"Maybe, maybe not," he mused. "There are lots of other parts of SCO, you know. Homicide and Serious Crime is only one piece of it."

"Like what, for instance?" she asked.

"Well, there's the Crime Academy for a start," he answered, "and the ACC has specifically mentioned that to me in the past. Seems to think I'd make a good Commandant there."

"Which you would, of course," Caroline concurred, "but if it's not what you want, could he force you to take it?"

"Technically, yes. It would be a posting and I'm under his command."

"Oh, bums," she said again. "What else is there?"

"There's Traffic," he said mournfully. "Not to mention the Dog Support Unit or the Mounted Branch. How do you fancy me on a horse?"

"But you can't ride," she said.

"I'm sure training would be provided," he replied.

At this point his wife gave up and threw the tea towel at him.

The elegant 1950s couple were by now the only occupants of

the buttery in the basement of Burgh House. The rain, which was strengthening in intensity all the time, had presumably deterred other visitors.

Carefully, they carried their cups of tea to a table and sat down. As Karen Willis crossed her legs, the swish of nylon on nylon was clearly audible even over the driving rain.

"It seems we are to get wet after all," Peter Collins observed, gazing with disapproval at the rain running down the outside of windows which were already beginning to mist up on the inside. "Oh damn and blast, why didn't we bring at least one umbrella between us?"

"Well, if you remember," she said mildly, "you said that it was pointless trying to struggle with an umbrella on a windy day, and that anyway we'd need to hold on to our hats as it was."

"Which we did," he pointed out, indicating the brown trilby which he had placed carefully on a neighbouring chair. "So maybe it wasn't such a silly idea after all."

She smiled but said nothing. There was what should have been the sort of companionable pause which occurs naturally between well settled couples, but the memory of that line by Marlowe ran between them like a tripwire, and they both knew to which particular explosive device it was connected. The pause lengthened and became pregnant, but nobody seemed prepared to volunteer to act as midwife. She could not even pretend to sip her tea, as it was still clearly too hot.

"So," Peter ventured at length, "how is Bob?"

Karen sighed inwardly, with sadness but also with resignation. She was in the unenviable position of being in love with two men at the same time, and was all too well aware that such a situation was untenable. She knew that Peter was trying to nudge her towards a resolution, and while she found the prospect terrifying she knew that it had to be done. She knew that he knew it was the right thing for her to do, even though he was frightened too, and that knowledge made her love him all the more.

"He's well, I think," she replied with a sad smile, "I don't know for sure. I haven't spoken to him for a few days. I think today is his first day back after his leave."

"Poor Bob," Peter said. "He's been so very patient, hasn't he? It really isn't fair that the situation should have dragged on so long. If I hadn't been ill nobody would have felt the need to tiptoe around me for fear of bringing on some sort of relapse, and all this could have been sorted out by now."

She reached across the table and took his hand.

"Are you sure that's what you want, Peter? For it to be sorted out?"

"It has to be," he responded, gazing at her in surprise. "Surely you can see that? It isn't fair on any of us to carry on like this. It's eating me up inside, and I'm sure it is you too, not to mention Bob."

"Oh, Peter," she said sadly, "you're so very wise. I really wish you could advise me on this, but of course you can't, and that makes me feel so very much alone."

They gazed across the table, each knowing that the other

was in pain and that there was the potential for it to become a lot worse yet. Each needing to cry, yet beyond tears; each feeling just a dull emptiness where their insides should be.

"You're right of course, darling," she said resignedly at last. "I have to make a decision. I have to put us all out of our misery, though I'm not sure that it will. You see I have this awful feeling that whichever decision I make, one of us will be destroyed by grief, and the other two by guilt."

"Guilt is a powerful emotion," he agreed automatically.

"It's two problems really," she went on. "That's the first one, but the second is that it's an almost impossible decision to make. You and Bob, and the sort of life I'd have with either of you, are so different that it's almost like choosing between parallel universes."

"I see that," he nodded. "It certainly doesn't make things any easier for you, does it?"

"I knew you'd understand," she said warmly. "Our life together is so magical, Peter. Music, books, beautiful clothes, elegant dances, the opera, all the things I've ever wanted. But it's so magical that I can't quite believe that it's real, or that it will go on forever. You see, I have to live in the real world too, and I sometimes find that quite a schizoid existence. When I come home to you it's as if I'm opening the front door not just to a flat which we share together, but a secret door to some magical world of fantasy and beauty."

"Like going through the back of the wardrobe into Narnia, you mean?" he asked thoughtfully.

"Yes, very much like that. And it's truly wonderful, Peter,

it really is. But then I have to get up in the morning and go out and deal with all sorts of pettiness and ugliness. And that makes me wonder if I'm really just escaping into some sort of alternative reality with you, do you see?"

As if echoing her reference to the real world, a siren wailed. It sounded close, as if in one of the adjoining roads.

"Oh blast," she said in exasperation, "am I making any sort of sense at all?"

"Yes, you are, of course you are. If it's any help, I feel like that too. But with me it's a deliberate escape. Oh, I have academia and you could argue that that's not real life anyway, but it's more than enough reality for me. The world is such an ugly, mindless place that I don't see anything wrong with wanting to inject some elegance, and wit, and intelligence. It's just that I've never met anyone other than you who could understand that, and want to share it."

"I know, I know," she said miserably, "and I do love you very much, Peter, but then why do I feel what I feel for Bob? At first I thought it was some sort of infatuation, but it isn't, it's much more powerful. I just feel an overwhelming need to be with him. You know the old Greek idea of two lovers sharing one soul? It's like that. It's just like that. It's as if we used to be one, but then got separated and are now being drawn back together again. I've never experienced anything like it; it's exciting and disturbing all at the same time."

She felt herself starting to cry and said "oh sod" because she really did not want to upset Peter any more than she had already. He smiled gently, and passed her his handkerchief.

"I do acknowledge," he said carefully, "that I cannot advise you. Of course I can't, I'm an interested party, God knows, but I do have a suggestion. It's not exactly conventional thinking, and I have to admit that it's at least partly self-serving, but would you like to hear it?"

"More than anything," she replied. "Right now I'm stuck in a very dark place, and any light would be welcome."

"Ah, now that troubles me," he commented awkwardly.

He gazed at her miserably, wondering how to put what he had to say next.

"That's exactly why I was reluctant to mention it," he went on. "For fear that you might be so desperate for some solution, *any* solution, that you'd grasp at it without properly evaluating it. It might seem like a quick fix, but actually just cause you more pain in the long term if it turns out not to have been the right decision after all."

She thought for a moment, trying to be calm and to ignore the ongoing tear damage to her make-up.

"Go on," she urged him. "I promise to give it all the consideration I can, and not to make a snap decision. Tell me what it is."

The door of the buttery opened abruptly and a police constable entered and looked around, the radio attached to the front of his uniform making loud squawking noises.

"Good afternoon, ladies and gents," he said in standard Metropolitan Police 'there's been an emergency but please keep calm because everything is under control' tones. "We've been called to investigate a serious incident at this location.

There's no cause for alarm, but I'm afraid I must ask all of you not to leave the building until further notice."

Peter looked at Karen and she smiled back in resignation. She carefully wiped runny black mascara from under both eyes, and then stood up, rummaging for something in her handbag.

"I'm Detective Sergeant Karen Willis," she told the constable, holding up her ID. "I'd better take charge until another detective arrives. What's happened?"

# CHAPTER 2

As a police officer, Detective Inspector Bob Metcalfe had long ago learned to expect anything when he attended a call-out to a crime scene. However, never in his wildest imagination would he have anticipated being greeted by the woman with whom he was in love, dressed in a pencil skirt, seamed stockings and high heels.

"Hello", he said, feeling straightaway that this was a somewhat lame greeting. "What are you doing here? I thought you were still on leave."

"I was – I am," she replied, feeling equally awkward. "That is, I'm not here officially. I was visiting the place with Peter and we were just having a cup of tea when uniform showed up. So I thought I should take charge until somebody got here."

"Quite right," he nodded with approval. "What's up, then?"

"Looks like murder, I'm afraid," she said as casually as she could. "Man upstairs with his head bashed in. I only looked briefly. I thought it was more important to secure the scene."

"Of course. What have you done about that?"

"Two uniform showed up in response to a 999 call. I put

one on the front door and one on the back. They haven't allowed anyone to leave or enter."

"Great," Metcalfe said. "You've done exactly the right thing."

"Thanks," she responded, "but of course our perp could have been long gone before the call was even made."

"True."

He looked around the entrance hall.

"I see they have CCTV," he commented.

"Yes, I've asked about that," she said. "Front and back. They were required to have it installed in order to get insurance cover for the art exhibition they're mounting. It runs a live feed to two screens in the office, but nobody seems to know whether it also records anywhere. I've asked them to check."

"OK," he said. "Let's take a look. You lead the way."

Walking up the stairs behind her gave him a chance to admire the way she and her skirt seemed welded together, her hips appearing to pivot around a plane of infinite geometrical smoothness. It almost made up for not having seen her for some days.

At the top of the stairs he stopped and looked around.

"Not here," she said with a shake of the head. "These are the public rooms. We need to go up another flight."

These stairs were narrower and steeper, as was the motion of her hips.

"Up here," she said to him over her shoulder, "there are apparently two sets of rooms, one small and one large. The smaller set is used during working hours only. The larger set was used as a flat by the victim."

"So he lived here, then?"

"Lived here and died here," she replied, moving aside to let him go through the door first.

A man sat with his back to the door, slumped forwards over a desk. A mass of congealing blood covered the top of his head and had run down the sides onto the desk. Some had gone further, dripping onto the floor. What looked like a police truncheon lay on the floor slightly to one side.

"The murder weapon?" Metcalfe asked.

"I don't know – I assume so. I told you, I didn't spend any real time in here."

He nodded, and stepped gently around the very edge of the room to explore the rest of the flat. He opened doors into a bedroom, a kitchen and a bathroom, all empty. He stopped in the kitchen doorway to examine the murder scene from a different angle. This did not seem to alter anything, though from here he could see a little more of the victim's face, as it was turned slightly towards him. A mass of papers, folders and ring binders covered the desk and overflowed onto a chair and the floor.

"Do we know anything about him?" he asked.

"His name is Peter Howse, and he's apparently been allowed to live here for some years. He's the manager and the rooms go with the job."

"He looks more like a researcher or something – an academic perhaps."

"Yes, he does, doesn't he? Though strangely there is a real academic who works in the other rooms – a Professor, I believe."

"OK, we'd better get out of here and wait for SOCO," Metcalfe said. "Do you know how many people were in the building?"

"I can tell you how many there are now," she replied. "As I said, anyone could have slipped out before uniform got here. The only visitors were Peter and me. Then there is the assistant manager and his wife, someone who serves tea and cakes in the buttery, and the Professor I mentioned. I've got them all in the buttery downstairs."

"Oh, Peter's here, is he?" Metcalfe asked before he could stop himself.

"Yes," she said gently. "Like I said, we were visiting the exhibition. Just think, the murder might have been committed while we were actually wandering about one floor below. It was only because the rain had got worse that we decided to stay for tea."

"You didn't hear anything, I take it?"

"Not that I can remember, no. But judging by the way he died it was probably pretty quick, and I wouldn't have though that a truncheon hitting a head makes that much noise, would you?"

"I don't know," he admitted, "though there have been plenty of occasions when I've felt a strong urge to find out."

"It's strange," she said suddenly. "We were just talking about you, Peter and me, and the next moment here you are.

It's almost like synchronicity – you know, subconsciously willing something to happen."

"Well," he replied, "I do hope not, since it's taken a murder to bring me here."

"Oh, Bob," she said, pausing as she went down the stairs, "what an awful thought. You're right, of course, I just hadn't thought about that. Do you think it's possible?"

"Not for a moment," he reassured her. "It's just a very large coincidence, that's all."

"But perhaps there's no such thing as coincidence?" she asked. "Suppose everything happens for a reason, everything is connected but we just don't see it?"

"I should save that sort of discussion for Peter," he said with as genuine a smile as he could muster. "I'm just a policeman, remember?"

As they reached the ground floor they met Detective Chief Inspector Tom Allen coming in.

"Afternoon all," he said jocularly. "What's occurring, then?"

"Murder, guv, two floors up," Metcalfe reported. "The manager, Peter Howse, has had his head bashed in. There's what looks like an old police truncheon lying on the floor which could be the murder weapon. I made sure the flat was empty apart from the victim, and then cleared out to wait for SOCO."

"OK," Allen nodded. "Who secured the crime scene?"

"I did, sir," Karen Willis piped up.

"Willis? Aren't you on leave?"

"Yes, guv, I was here as a civvy, just visiting."

"Well, now you're here you might as well stay, I suppose," he said indulgently. "Occupants of the building?"

"Six including me", she informed him. "Assistant manager and his wife, a café worker, a Professor who studies on the victim's floor – he discovered the body by the way – and Peter Collins, my – er, boyfriend."

She felt awkward somehow saying 'boyfriend' in front of Metcalfe, but got the word out finally. Perhaps it sounded strange, as Allen stared at her curiously for a moment.

"Well, there's no point in disturbing the scene more than we have to until SOCO turn up," he decided, "so let's go and see these bodies downstairs."

As they entered the buttery five strained faces turned towards them. Allen surveyed each of them carefully in turn without speaking for a few moments. He could feel the level of tension rising, which was no bad thing, he reflected. After all, any one of them might be a murderer.

"Many thanks for your co-operation to date, ladies and gents," he said finally. "I'm sure you're all aware by now that a serious incident has occurred upstairs."

"Is it ... Mr Howse?" a woman asked, a handkerchief half pressed to her mouth.

"A man we believe to be Mr Howse has been found dead, yes," Allen said carefully. "Beyond that, I can't comment at present."

He looked around the room again.

"I am going to have ask each of you to give a statement

about what you did and where you went within the building this morning. Once you have done that, you may go, but please make sure that you leave us your full contact details as it is highly likely we will need to speak to you again."

From above, came the sound of people tramping through the entrance hall. Allen and Metcalfe looked at each other.

"I will ask DI Metcalfe and DS Willis to stay here and take your statements," he announced. "Presumably there are some other rooms we can use for that?"

"We have a flat down here," a man said hesitantly, "you could use the living room, I suppose, and there's a kitchen just behind there."

"Good," Allen said. "Bob, will you organise that? I must go and deal with SOCO."

He headed back up the stairs to find the duty forensic surgeon, Brian Williams waiting patiently in the hallway, his bag set down on the floor beside him.

"Hello, Tom," he said. "What have we got?"

"Afternoon, Brian. Corpse upstairs apparently. Bashed on the head Willis and Metcalfe say."

"Well, we shouldn't have to wait long," Williams assured him. "I think I saw one of the SOCO boys parking his van just down the road."

"Speak of the devil," Allen replied as two more police officers came through the front door.

He was glad to see that the senior of the two was DI Tom Bellamy. He had worked with him before and was happy that he knew what he was doing. Similarly with Williams.

He reflected comfortably that the investigation was in good hands.

"Crime scene upstairs, guv?" Bellamy asked.

Allen nodded. Bellamy looked dubiously at the staircase.

"I'd like to start the isolation process down here," he said dubiously, "but I expect people have been tramping up and down here already, haven't they?"

"Willis and Metcalfe at least," Allen confirmed.

"Then there's probably not a lot of point," Bellamy concluded, "but let's suit up anyway and then I'll lead the way, please."

His assistant was already distributing white boiler suits, overshoes, and surgical gloves. There was a pause while they put these on and then Bellamy led the way upstairs. He halted at the top and looked around.

"I see three doors, all open," he called back over his shoulder.

"Those are the public rooms, I think," Allen informed him. "We need to go up one more."

"Good," Bellamy mused. "That means we may at least be able to include the next flight of stairs within the crime scene. Please come up and stand on the landing, gentlemen."

"OK," he said as the others crowded behind him. "Tape please, Chris."

His assistant taped off the landing behind them while Bellamy carefully photographed the landing from three different angles, and then the upper staircase.

"Right," he said, "let's move on."

He took more photos as he led the way up the second staircase and then again they halted at the top.

"I see two doors from this landing," he called down. "One is covered in what looks like green baize and is closed. The other is a plain door and is open. The open door leads towards the back of the building."

"That's the one, I think," Allen said.

"OK, then let's stick to the process," Bellamy said. "I am now edging round the open door and can see what seems to be the victim sitting at a desk. He seems to have fallen forward over it but his head is slightly turned to one side."

Allen realised that he was recording all of this and nodded approvingly.

"Doctor," Bellamy called, "will you please enter the room, trying to touch nothing but the victim, and examine him for signs of life?"

Williams knew the procedure as well as anyone. He took three or four cautious steps into the room and placed a gloved finger on the man's neck. He waited a moment and then shone a flashlight into each of the man's open eyes in turn.

"Life is extinct," he recited formally.

"Doctor Williams pronounces life extinct at 1627," Bellamy repeated into his tape recorder, having taken a look at his watch. Then he turned to Allen.

"Right, sir, you're the SIO. Are there any fast track actions you wish to designate in relation to the crime scene?"

Allen thought briefly. Experienced senior detectives

often talk of the so-called Golden Hour principle, under which action might be taken in the very early stages of an investigation to secure evidence which might otherwise be lost or contaminated, but here there seemed to be little point in rushing. The scene was not exposed to the elements and, now that Bellamy was here, access could be strictly controlled.

"No, I don't think so, Tom. You and Brian take all the time you need. Let me know when it's OK for me to come in and take a look round, will you? I'll be downstairs with the witnesses meantime."

Confident that he could leave the crime scene in safe hands, Allen headed downstairs again. A bored looking uniformed constable was sitting in the buttery with the assembled occupants of the building. The assistant manager and his wife were missing, presumably having their statements taken by Metcalfe and Willis.

He sat down beside the man with fair hair and glasses.

"We haven't met," he said bluntly, "but I know who you are. You're Willis's bloke, aren't you?"

"We live together, yes," came the reply. "I'm Peter Collins."

"Aren't you some sort of profiler?"

Collins coloured slightly.

"Not exactly," he said hesitantly. "I'm a psychologist, but it's true that I have advised the police in the past."

"Simon Collison, wasn't it? On that serial killer? Strange, I thought you prepared a profile for him."

He stared at Collins in what seemed to the latter a slightly aggressive fashion.

"Were you involved with the case?" Collins enquired mildly. "I don't remember you."

"I'm Tom Allen," came the response. "It was my case before it was Simon's. The AC Crime in his infinite wisdom decided that it was all getting too much for me, and that the enquiry needed a new pair of eyes."

"I'm sorry if that's the case," Collins said calmly. "It must have felt like it was some sort of reflection on your abilities, even though I'm sure it wasn't intended like that. I'll warrant you've solved lots of other murders before and since."

"Eleven before," Allen confirmed, "five as SIO. Only one case since, though that's never going to be solved. It's that prison murder you know about, and the investigation went nowhere fast from day one. Any one of twenty or thirty people could have done it, alone or jointly, and there's a wall of silence as you'd expect."

Collins noticed that his hands were beginning to tremble and clasped them behind his chair awkwardly to try to conceal the fact. At one time he had believed himself responsible for bringing about that man's death and had suffered acute psychological illness as a result. It was not clear whether Allen knew this, and was bringing it up maliciously, or did not, and was merely being clumsy.

"I'm sorry to hear that," he said. "It must be a source of great frustration for you."

"Strange," Allen went on. "You've got people locked up

in there for all sorts of evil deeds, including murder, and yet the one thing they won't tolerate is a nonce. Putting a sex offender in with other prisoners is as good as a death sentence. Don't know what the governor was thinking of, really. He was bound to get a good cocoaing at the very least."

"A cocoaing?" Collins queried, trying to breath regularly.

"Yeah, last thing at night an urn of cocoa goes round, see? It's very hot, as you might expect, and it's amazing how often someone manages clumsily to tip the whole thing over some pervert or other. Amazing how none of the prison officers ever seem to have seen anything, neither."

Collins swallowed.

"I had no idea," he said weakly.

"I assume you're waiting to have your statement taken," Allen ventured, changing the subject abruptly.

"Yes, Bob and Karen decided to take the caretaker type and his wife first. So I'm just waiting my turn, as you say. Mind you, I don't think I'm going to detain them very long. Though I've wracked my brains I really can't think of anything I saw or heard which could be at all significant."

"Just tell them everything you can remember," Allen adjured him. "It's often some trifling little detail that turns out to be important in the end."

He got up and walked the few steps to sit beside the only other man in the room.

"Are you in charge?" he was asked before he could say anything.

"I am the Senior Investigating Officer, yes," he confirmed,

gazing at the other man, whom he found somehow familiar although he was sure they had never met. "I'm Detective Chief Inspector Tom Allen – and you are?"

"I am Hugh Raffen, Professor Hugh Raffen."

"I'm sorry to keep you waiting, Professor, but I'm sure you'll appreciate that thoroughness is everything in these matters. The first hour or so is particularly important."

"Yes, I dare say," Raffen said with no real show of emotion. "Though my experience of murder to date has been confined to fiction."

Allen said nothing for a moment.

"I understand you work upstairs?"

"I have a room there, yes. The Trust kindly allow me to work here. It saves me having to take the tube, which I detest. My other office is in town, you see. So that means that unless I'm actually teaching, which I do very little these days, I can just walk round the corner from the flat and get on with my work here."

"And what work would that be, sir?"

"I'm working on a book about Britain's vanished railways," came the reply. "Beeching, you know, that frightful fellow, he hacked away at the network in such a vandal-like fashion that today large parts of the country are left without any railway access at all. Not like France, oh dear me, no."

He looked hopefully at Allen as if in search of a fellow railway enthusiast. If so, he was destined to be disappointed.

"Would that be the room behind the green baize door on the upper landing?" he persisted.

"Yes, indeed. The Trust were very kind. They know that I have an almost pathological hatred of noise, and someone told them that soft materials soak up a lot of noise, hence the trouble they went to having the door covered with baize. In the event it's almost useless, since the door itself is thin and ill-fitting, but it was sweet of them nonetheless."

"So you could hear noise from the staircase and the landing?"

"Oh yes, indeed."

At this moment Karen Willis walked into the room exuding, in addition to the glamour of a fitted suit of a former and more elegant era, her usual air of quiet efficiency. Allen thought briefly of the daughter he had lost, and whether she might have turned out anything like Willis. As if reading his thoughts, she turned and looked at him questioningly.

"The Professor next, I think, Willis," he said. "Professor, please go with this officer and she'll take your statement."

# CHAPTER 3

Peter Collins crossed the room and sat down next to Tom Allen.

"Forgive me for mentioning this," he said diffidently, "but are you sure you want Karen involved with taking statements, or even with the case at all?"

Allen stared at him blankly.

"I'm sorry," Collins went on, more uncertainly still, "but have you considered that she is herself a witness? Every bit as much as I am, anyway. Isn't there a danger that she might unconsciously allow something she did or did not experience to colour her view of other people's evidence? Particularly if she is actually engaged in taking their statement in the first place."

Allen tried not to give vent to a rising tide of irritation.

"Thank you for your concerns, Mr Collins," he said coolly, "I will think about it when I have time. Just now, I'm rather busy."

"The Golden Hour and all that," Collins said as he nodded sagely. "Quite."

Allen stared at him, initially in disbelief and then with amusement.

"I venture to suppose, Mr Collins," he said with mock-formality "that whatever you know about the Golden Hour comes out of a book."

"I have studied criminology, yes," Peter replied, "and it's Doctor Collins, actually."

Allen felt a strong desire to have Peter Collins out of the building and away from his investigation as quickly as possible.

"Since there is no-one else available at present, why don't I take your statement now?" he suggested. "I can quite see that it wouldn't be right for DC Willis to do so."

"With pleasure," came the reply. "By the way, she's a sergeant now you know."

"A very recent promotion," he proffered from behind as he followed Allen up the stairs to the ground floor.

"Yes, I know," Allen said, breathing rather heavily although that may just have been from climbing the stairs, "I forgot. When she was working for me she was a DC. Let's sit down in here, shall we?"

They installed themselves in a small public room which Peter knew was sometimes used for exhibitions by local art groups, but which was currently empty and unused. He sat down and crossed his legs, exposing a pair of grey herringbone socks. The rain was easing off at last, but the single naked light bulb served only to throw the gathering gloom of the autumn evening outside into even starker relief.

"Now then," Allen said, opening his notebook, "let's start with name and address, shall we?"

"Of course," Peter said. "My name is Peter Death Bredon

Collins, and I live at 26 Christchurch Hill."

"Deyarth?" hazarded Allen blankly.

"Yes, it's spelt the same as Death," Collins explained, "and 'Breedon' has only one 'e'. My mother was a great fan of Lord Peter Wimsey, you see."

"Who was he?" Allen asked, "a friend of the family perhaps?"

"Not exactly," Collins said, struggling unsuccessfully to conceal his surprise. "He was a fictional detective from the Golden Age, created by Dorothy L. Sayers."

"Never heard of him," Allen said unrepentantly. "Now, let's try to restrict ourselves to the matter in hand, shall we? What time did you get here?"

"I think it must have been about three fifteen," he replied after a moment's reflection. "You see I glanced at my watch as we came downstairs to the Buttery and it was about three thirty, and I reckon we only spent about fifteen minutes upstairs."

"All right," Allen said as he jotted this down. "Now, please think about everything you did and saw and heard from the moment you entered the building onwards. The slightest little thing might be important."

"Very well," Collins said. "Let me think. It was raining a bit and we hadn't brought an umbrella. We both tried to dry our shoes off on that coconut matting inside the front door. Then we both went upstairs to the first floor, because we knew that that's where the exhibition was. We looked at the paintings for a bit and chatted. As far as I can remember we were the only ones there the whole time – I expect the rain kept people away and also the exhibition has already been running some time."

"Did you at any time go up to the floor above, or hear anything from upstairs?" Allen asked.

"No," Collins said, having considered the question carefully. "I really can't say that I did. I saw the bottom of the next flight of stairs as we went up and then down again, but I don't remember seeing anyone using them."

"Would you have been in a position to see anyone if they had been using them?"

"No, only on the way up and down, as I said, and while we were briefly on the landing deciding whether to go home or stay for tea."

"Would you have been able to hear anyone use them, do you think?"

"Probably not," Peter mused. "The next flight of stairs is on the other side of the landing, you see. Maybe if someone was running, but not otherwise."

"And once you were downstairs having tea, did you stay there the whole time? Did you go anywhere else? To the toilet perhaps? Did you hear anything?"

"No and no, I'm afraid," Peter replied. "We didn't see anyone, other than the lady who was serving tea. The only thing we heard that was at all unusual was a police siren and the only other person we saw was the constable who came in and asked us not to leave. Then the others came down. They said they'd been sent by Karen."

"You say you're a psychiatrist," Allen began.

"Not a psychiatrist, no," Collins corrected him. "A psychologist. You have to be a doctor to be a psychiatrist – a real doctor, I mean, a medical doctor."

"OK, whatever," Allen went on brusquely. "My point is this: did you notice anything significant or unusual about the behaviour of any of the other people at any time when they came into the room or afterwards?"

Collins thought for a few moments.

"No, I don't think so," he said slowly. "Both the ladies were visibly upset, but then the man you were just speaking to told everyone straightaway that there'd been a murder, so that's hardly surprising. I asked him how he knew, and he said that he had discovered the body. The other man seemed upset too – shaken anyway. But I didn't observe anything that I would describe as unusual."

"Focus on the man who discovered the body, if you will," Allen said. "Any particular impression of him?"

"He seemed calm and collected," Collins said, "but then shock can work like that. It can hit you hours, or even days later. I can't really comment beyond that. I'd have to know him, and I don't."

"Very well," Allen said, closing his notebook. "I don't think we need detain you any longer, Dr Collins. You might as well go home. We'll get this typed up for you and you can come into the station to sign it."

"What about Karen?" Collins asked uncertainly. "I suppose she'll be busy for a while yet?"

"I'm afraid so," Allen replied. "Shame that she's supposed to be on leave. You don't expect to go to an art show and end up securing a murder scene, do you?"

"You certainly don't," Collins agreed, picking up his hat.

Allen took him to the front door and nodded at the uniformed constable, who stood aside. Collins put his hat on, squinted unhappily at the rain which was still falling, though more lightly than before, thrust his hands into his pockets, and walked off up the road towards the Wells Tavern.

"Excuse me, sir," one of Bellamy's junior SOCO team members said as Allen came back through the hall, "but the doctor would like to speak to you."

"Right", said Allen and trudged up both flights of stairs.

Brian Williams was standing on the top landing, undoing his boiler suit.

"I'm finished here, Tom," he informed him. "Time of death probably between midday and one o'clock, but I'll be able to tell you better once I've done the PM. SOCO's not ready to release the body yet, but we're probably talking tomorrow morning now in any event."

"Thanks, Brian," Allen said. "See you tomorrow, then."

"I'm just about to start recording the scene, sir," Bellamy interjected, "but you can have a quick look from the door first if you like."

Allen nodded and stood reflectively in the doorway. He could see the victim slumped over his desk, the door open to the room beyond. He felt a distinct draught.

"Is the window open through there?" he asked.

"Yes, guv. Bob Metcalfe said it was that way when he made his initial inspection to check the victim was dead, and that there was nobody else on the premises."

"Did you point that out to the doctor? It might affect his estimate of the time of death."

"Yes, sir, he knows."

"Good. OK then, I'll leave you to it. I'll check downstairs with the others."

As he descended the stairs, he could hear a female and a male voice in question and answer mode. In a public room at the back, Karen Willis was taking Professor Raffen's statement. He hesitated and then opened the door and entered the room.

"Don't mind me," he said quickly as they both looked at him. "I'll pick it up as I go along."

The two previous occupants of the room were sitting on opposite sides of what was presumably a dining table in highly polished dark wood. He drew up a chair two away from Karen Willis so that he was looking at Hugh Raffen from a slight angle.

"We were just getting the timeline straight, Professor," Willis reminded him, as she crossed her legs with another audible swish. "You say that you arrived at work about ten o'clock, and worked in your office until about quarter to one. Did you leave the office at any time?"

"No, I had no need to. I have both a bathroom and a kitchen attached to my room, though I rarely use the latter. At about a quarter to one I left for lunch, as I always do. I walked up the road to the Flask, had lunch, did the crossword, and came back about two."

"While you were in your room during the morning, did you hear anything at all? Anyone coming up and down the stairs, for example?"

"From what I remember," Raffen said, puckering his eyes in concentration, "I think there were three journeys both up and down. I think that two of the trips were Howse. He makes a lot of noise on the stairs and I've had occasion to speak to him about it, as I find it disturbs my concentration. Of course it could have been someone else – Bailey for example – but I don't think so."

"And the other?"

"I'm pretty sure that was *not* Howse. For one thing it was someone with a lighter tread, and for a second I think I heard a knock at the door."

"What time was this, do you think?"

"About half an hour before lunch, I suppose."

"So, about quarter past twelve, then?"

"Yes, I suppose it must have been."

"Tell us everything you can remember, please," Allen cut in.

Raffen turned and looked at him.

"I heard someone come up the stairs and I'm pretty sure I heard a knock at the door. A little later I head Howse shouting as if he was having an argument with someone. Of course he could have been on the phone, I suppose;

I couldn't hear another voice. Then a few minutes later – perhaps five minutes or so – I heard what sounded like the same person going down the stairs again. I didn't think any more about it at the time."

"So, to be clear, Professor," Allen summarised, glancing at Karen Willis, who was writing quickly. "You heard someone enter the victim's room at about twelve fifteen and leave it again at about twelve twenty, and in the interim you heard the victim's voice raised as if in an argument?"

"Yes, but I can't be that precise about the time. I mean, I don't remember looking at my watch or anything like that. What time did he die, by the way?"

"I can't answer that, I'm afraid," Allen replied gravely. "Now, let's try to think about this a bit more deeply, shall we? Were you able to catch anything that the Mr Howse was saying?"

"I think it was something like 'why must we keep having this conversation?', you know in a very exasperated sort of way. But he only spoke really loudly for those few seconds. After that I could hear his voice, but not what he was saying. The other person must have been speaking very quietly because I don't remember hearing them at all."

"So you couldn't say whether it was a man's or a woman's voice, then?" Allen asked.

"No, obviously not."

"I see," Allen said moodily.

"Did you see anyone as you left the building, or when you came back, Professor?" Karen Willis enquired.

"You mean did anyone see me, don't you?" Raffen answered with a smile. "Corroboration and all that."

"Just answer the question, please," Allen interjected.

"I don't think anyone would have seen me leave," Raffen mused. "The house was very quiet today. But the barman at the Flask should remember serving me at about twelve fifty. I'm quite a regular there. If it helps to remind him, I had a glass of red wine and the steak and kidney pie."

"And when you came back?" Karen Willis asked.

"Yes. By chance the lady from the Buttery – I'm afraid I don't know her name – was just arriving for her afternoon shift. We said hello as we came up the path together. I saw her walking up from Gayton Road as I came back along Flask Walk."

Allen waited for Willis to finish writing.

"Tell us about how you came to discover the body," he suggested.

"It was sometime after three," Raffen said. "Again, I can't be precise about the time because I don't have a clock in my room, but I suddenly realised that I'd run out of cartridges for my fountain pen. As it was pouring with rain, I didn't fancy walking up to the High Street to buy some more, but then I remembered that Howse used a fountain pen too, so I tapped on his door and went in to ask if he could let me have one. I saw at once what had happened. He was lying over his desk with an obvious head wound. I said something silly like 'are you all right?' but of course he didn't answer. I felt at once that he was dead. It looked a very nasty wound."

"Did you touch him, or anything else in the room?"

"No, only the door I suppose, on the way in and out."

"Then what did you do?"

"Well, I know this will sound a bit stupid but I sort of didn't know what to do next. My father would most certainly *not* have approved, but then I've never been much of a man of action, you know. Well anyway, I just sort of stood around on the landing for a minute or two, not quite believing that I really had seen what I had just seen. Then I had a quick peek round the door again just to check that I hadn't imagined it all. That's when I finally went downstairs and banged on the Baileys' door. I told Jack that Peter Howse had been attacked in his room, that I thought he was dead, and that he was to call the police. I waited while he did it."

"Was Mrs Bailey there too?" Allen asked.

"She was in the next room, yes. I think she was doing some ironing. She came in when she heard what I said."

"How did the Baileys react to the news?"

"Poor Sue became hysterical pretty quickly. She flapped around for a bit, and then sat down and started crying. Jack took it quite calmly. He dialled 999, told them everything they wanted to know and then went outside to wait for the police. He asked me to stand guard on the landing to stop anyone going upstairs until the police arrived – which I did. Then when the policemen came they asked me to go down to join everyone else in the buttery."

"Do you remember seeing anyone else in the building earlier today – before the police arrived, I mean?"

"No, but then I rarely see people visiting the house since I'm right upstairs and visitors aren't allowed beyond the first floor. My impression is that it was pretty quiet today. The Constable exhibition is pretty much done, so anyone who wants to see it is likely to have done so already."

There was a pause during which Karen Willis wrote steadily and silently. Then she stopped and looked up.

"What can you tell us about Peter Howse?" she asked.

"Not a lot, I'm afraid. We've been working in adjoining rooms for three years now, but we both keep pretty much to ourselves."

"Did you dislike each other?"

"No, not at all. We just didn't have very much in common, that's all, and to be honest he wasn't an easy man to get on with. He could be very moody and withdrawn."

"Moody? What about? Anything in particular?"

"I'm no psychologist ...," Raffen began.

Allen gave Karen Willis a wry glance which she affected not to notice.

"But it seemed to me that he was someone who was very much disappointed with how things had worked out in his life. Felt he deserved better, that sort of thing."

"How so?" Allen asked.

"Well, this place used to be his family home, you know. He and his mother were the last people to live here. Unfortunately someone – his father I think – made a dreadful mess of the family finances. I think he was a drinker and a bit of a wastrel. After his father's death his mother had to mortgage this place to pay off all the debts. At the time she died the bank had been trying for some time to foreclose because she hadn't been able to keep up the repayments. Somehow Peter Howse managed to stitch some sort of deal together with the Trust and the bank whereby the bank accepted what little he had in satisfaction of their debt, the Trust took the property, and he was effectively given a job and a few rooms for life. So I think he took it very badly, being reduced to managing the house his family had once owned. Knowing the Trust, I'm sure his salary can't have been very much. The Baileys are on an absolute pittance too, I think."

"So what did he do here exactly?"

"He managed the property – you know, repairs, insurance, making sure there were enough volunteers to keep the place open, that sort of thing. But what he really enjoyed were putting the various exhibitions together. He could give himself airs and graces then, as if he were some sort of real curator, or even academic, God help us."

Raffen smirked mirthlessly.

"Gave himself airs and graces?" Allen echoed.

"Oh yes. If you look at the brochure for the Constable exhibition you'll see that he's penned a little programme note and signed himself 'artistic director' if you please. Don't get me wrong, he could be a very charming man when he was in the right mood, but that wasn't very often, and when he was in a black mood they could be very black indeed."

"Did he have any family still living?"

"Yes, I think he had a nephew whose father – Howse's brother I suppose – died quite young. In fact, I think Howse once mentioned being his guardian or something. He used to visit the house occasionally; I met them in the hallway once and Howse introduced me. I think his name is Alan."

Karen Willis held up her hand in a sign that she needed to catch up. That was fine with Allen as he needed time to think about how to phrase his next question. In the end he decided to ask it directly.

"Can you think of any reason why anyone might want to kill Peter Howse?" he demanded.

Professor the Honourable Hugh Raffen looked deeply uncomfortable.

"Oh dear, oh dear," he lamented. "I knew someone was going to ask that sooner or later."

# CHAPTER 4

Tom Allen and Karen Willis looked at each other.

"I think you'd better tell us what you know, Professor," Allen said firmly.

"Well, I'm not going to answer your question directly," Raffen said rather primly, "because it's not for me to say what anyone might or might not have wanted to do, but I will tell you what I know, or think I know, and then you can draw whatever conclusions you want."

"Very well," Allen said with a nod, in a tone of voice which clearly communicated the sentiment 'get on with it'.

"I'm almost certain that Howse was having an affair with Susan Bailey," Raffen said. "As I said he could be a very charming man when he chose to be. Unfortunately that wasn't very often, at least not with me at any rate."

"How do you know this?" Allen asked.

"Because a lot of it went on in his room, which as you know is adjacent to mine," Raffen said, pouting with mild distaste. "The sound of people making love is unmistakeable, even when they are trying to do it as quietly as possible. She used to come upstairs in the afternoon on a pretty regular basis. Once I happened to be on the first floor and, looking up the stairs I saw her open his door and go in without knocking. She was holding her shoes in her hand as if she wanted to make as little noise on the stairs as possible. She went in quickly too, as if she was anxious not to be spotted. That pretty much confirmed what I already suspected."

"When was this?"

"I suppose that must have been several weeks ago," Raffen said uncertainly.

"Can you think of any date or event which you could use as a reference point?" Allen suggested.

"Why yes," Raffen replied, the doubt clearing from his face. "It was just before the Constable exhibition opened. That's why I'd gone downstairs, come to think of it. The pictures had just been hung and I decided to have a little private sneak preview. I think the press launch was one or two evenings later."

"All right," Allen said, crossing the room to examine the events schedule on the wall. "For your notes, Willis, that puts it exactly eight weeks ago."

He paused and then came back to the table thoughtfully.

"You've been very straight with us about the basis of your belief," he said slowly. "So let's assume that they were in fact having a relationship. Did anyone else know about it, do you think?"

"Yes, her husband, for one. I think he found out a few weeks back. He went and confronted Howse in his room and they had an almighty row. Then he came out, slammed the door, and went storming off down the stairs. When I saw Susan Bailey a little later it was obvious she'd been crying."

"What happened then? With the relationship, I mean."

"I really have no idea, Chief Inspector. Come to think of it, I can't remember her coming upstairs much recently so perhaps there has been a cooling off."

"But you said that when you saw here that time eight weeks ago she had taken her shoes off."

"Yes, that's right."

"So isn't it possible that she could in fact have been creeping up and down quite often without you hearing her?"

Raffen thought for a moment.

"You're right of course," he said quietly. "Silly of me. I should have thought of that."

"Each to his own, Professor," Allen said with heavy irony. "You do railways, I do homicide."

"I do ancient history, actually," Raffen pointed out diffidently. "Railways are a bit of a sideline – oh dear me, no pun intended."

Karen Willis smiled.

"What can you tell us about the Baileys?" Allen said, ignoring the sally.

"Not much more than I have already. I've been here six months or so and they were already here when I arrived, but when they came I really don't know. I can't say I've ever asked them. I rarely have much occasion to talk to them, except when I want something. Other than that it's just a matter of saying hello when we pass."

"And their relationship with the deceased? In normal, day to day terms, I mean."

"I really don't want to spread any mischief," Raffen said hesitantly.

"Just tell us what you know, Professor, please," Allen urged him. "We'll decide whether it's useful or not."

"Well, I'm not sure I really *know* anything," Raffen temporised, "but it's always been my general impression that there was some bad feeling between Howse and Bailey, even before this business with Susan. I think Bailey believed that Howse should be doing much more of the day to day work of actually running the house rather than just swanning around playing the lord of the manor which, let's face it, he was quite inclined to do. I'm not sure Howse actually *did* anything at all in practical terms."

"Nothing at all?"

"Not really, no. For example, even when there was a shortage of volunteers he never came downstairs to man the desk and greet visitors. He left the Baileys to do it, and was even prepared for the door to be open and the desk unmanned for people to come and go as they pleased, rather than come downstairs and get stuck in. I believe he thought that sort of thing rather beneath him."

"Is that how things were today?"

Again Raffen pondered.

"Well, when I went to lunch there was nobody on duty, and nor was there when I came back so I suppose yes, just like today."

"You mean anybody could come and go?" Allen asked incredulously. "With a room full of valuable paintings upstairs?"

"There are TV cameras I believe," Raffen equivocated, "but other than that yes, I suppose so."

Allen pulled an incredulous expression while Karen Willis wrote quickly.

"So you're saying that there was bad feeling between Howse and Bailey?" she asked, having caught up.

"A certain amount of ill-will, certainly," Raffen concurred.

"And then he found out about his wife's affair," Allen commented. "That can hardly have made the atmosphere around here any less chilly."

"As I said, I keep mostly to myself," Raffen said, "but no, I don't suppose that it improved relations between them."

"Hm," said Allen, trying to think what to raise next.

"Do we have any further questions for the Professor, Sergeant?" he asked Willis finally.

"I don't think so, sir. I'll turn my notes into a statement for the Professor to sign."

"Yes, well I think we can let you go for now, Professor, but I'm sure we'll be wanting to see you again to follow up as things become clearer. By the way, you won't be able to use your rooms here for a few days, of course. The upper floor is now a crime scene. We'll let you know when you can come back."

"Can I just go up before I go to retrieve some notes and books?" Raffen asked.

"No, I'm afraid not," Allen responded. "Like I said, it's a crime scene and it's very important that we preserve it exactly as it is."

"That really is most inconvenient," Raffen said crossly. "I need to get on with my work."

"Your studies will have to wait for a few days I'm afraid, Professor," Allen said with an air of finality as he stood up.

He crossed to the door and called for a constable to escort Raffen off the premises.

"Now then," he said as he came back and sat down again. "What do you make of all that, young Willis?"

She thought for a moment.

"It gives Jack Bailey a motive for murder, clearly," she answered. "His wife too possibly, depending on the circumstances of the break-up."

"If indeed there had been one," Allen murmured.

"Yes," she agreed. "We need to find out about that."

"What else?"

"We know that probably anybody was free to come and go into and out of the building, so theoretically the opportunity was there for anybody to have access to the victim's rooms."

"Yes, though Raffen usually heard people coming up the stairs."

"Unless they particularly wanted to keep quiet," she reminded him. "Like Mrs Bailey."

"Yes, but probably more difficult for a man," he mused. "Heavier and clumsier usually, and less likely to slip their shoes off."

She was taken aback for a moment. It was the sort of insight she would have expected from Collison, but not Allen. She suddenly realised that perhaps she did not know him as well as she thought she did.

"But we do know for certain," she said, recovering her poise, "that people went upstairs on at least three occasions during the morning. We also know that the victim was heard arguing with someone between about twelve fifteen and twelve twenty, which we believe was between the upward and downward journeys of the third person."

"Third occasion," he corrected her. "Not necessarily the third person. Particularly if the first and second were Howse himself."

"Yes," she agreed, angry with herself for the slip. "Of course. The third occasion."

Allen sat silently for a while with his hands thrust into his trouser pockets and his legs stuck straight out in front of him.

"It will be interesting," he said with a rather savage smile, "to see exactly how forthcoming the Baileys are going to be about their dealings with Mr Howse."

"I've already taken the wife's statement," she said, flicking backwards through her notebook. "She said nothing at all about having any sort of relationship with the deceased except in the normal way of working together."

"Well, what *did* she say?"

"She was very upset, so it was difficult to get much out of her. I'd already decided that we'd probably need to bring her in tomorrow to question her some more once she'd had a chance to calm down. Just a basic timeline, that's all. According to her she was downstairs in the flat all morning apart from a couple of spells on the ground floor, first to do some polishing, and then to make sure all the windows were firmly closed when it really came on to rain."

"So she didn't go upstairs at all, or see anyone else do so?"

"No to both, but like I said, she wasn't making a lot of sense. Within about ten minutes it was pretty hopeless. She was just crying uncontrollably."

"Which if she was innocent is probably only to be expected," he mused, "but if she was guilty could have been putting on an act to avoid being questioned too closely."

He stood up suddenly, as if coming to a conclusion.

"Come on," he said, "let's go and see how Metcalfe is getting on."

He gave a quick rap on the door of the flat and they entered the little living room. Had the lights not been turned on it would probably have been a dark and rather depressing room, having only the one window, giving onto the back garden. Allen noted that, as with many London houses, the basement level at the front of the house was at ground level at the rear, the result of earth excavated from the foundations being piled up at the front during the building works.

Metcalfe was clearly just finishing taking a statement

from Jack Bailey. Karen Willlis sensed that there seemed to be a tautness in the atmosphere. Bailey's body language was closed and defensive; his chair was pushed back from the table and he had his arms folded tightly across his chest.

"I'm just finishing, sir," he said, looking up at them as they entered the room, "unless you have anything you'd like to ask?"

Allen looked around without saying anything. He noticed that the door into the kitchen was ajar. He crossed the room and closed it. Then he went up very close to Bailey and spoke quietly but distinctly into his ear.

"I have reason to believe that your wife was having an affair with the deceased, Mr Bailey. Did you mention anything about this to Inspector Metcalfe?"

The surprise on both sides of the table was palpable. Bailey stared hard at the table but said nothing. Allen looked quizzically at Metcalfe, who silently shook his head.

"Oh dear, oh dear," murmured Allen rather theatrically as he moved away and stood behind Bailey, looking over his head at Metcalfe. They waited for Bailey to speak, but still nothing came.

"Then I'm afraid that gives us a bit of a problem, doesn't it?" Allen said at length, without apparently addressing anyone in particular.

"Sergeant," he said to Willis, "would you please stay here with Mr Bailey while I go outside with Inspector Metcalfe?"

He beckoned Metcalfe outside and they closed the door behind them. They walked forward into the now empty buttery which stood in darkness. Allen switched on the lights and then closed the door behind him.

"Well," he asked, "what do we do now?"

He fumbled in his pocket for a cigarette and then thrust it back again with a scowl as he spotted smoke alarm on the ceiling.

"How did you know about Mrs Bailey and the dead man?" Metcalfe enquired.

"From the Professor – the bloke who has the other rooms on that floor. He heard them at it on various occasions apparently, and he reckons Bailey and our victim had a blazing row about it not so long ago."

"So Bailey may have had a motive for killing Howse?"

"Yeah, but come to that so might she. The Professor reckoned that Howse might have broken it off recently."

"Or even both together, then?"

"Yes," Allen said heavily. "It's early days, but yes. Hence the problem. If we leave them both here, we give them all night together to get their story straight. But I don't see that we have enough to take either one of them into custody, do you?"

"Probably not. What did the wife say, by the way?"

"Almost nothing. According to Willis she's not in any fit state to be interviewed. She broke down and became hysterical after only about ten minutes."

"Which could be very convenient, of course ...," Metcalfe suggested.

"Exactly what I said to Willis. But we have to deal

with the situation as it is. If Willis says she's not fit to be interviewed then I'm not going to second guess her. And we certainly don't have enough to take the wife in. So, the question becomes: do we have enough on chummy to park him in a cell for the night?"

"He had opportunity, but then so did anyone who was in the building at the relevant time. He probably had motive –"

"Why do you say 'probably'?" demanded Allen.

"Well, if Howse and Mrs Bailey had broken it off, wouldn't the motive be much less powerful?" Metcalfe asked.

"Possibly," Allen conceded grudgingly.

"There's another thing to consider too, guv," Metcalfe pointed out. "If we take him in then we have to treat him officially as a suspect, and tell him that's what we're doing just in case it isn't obvious anyway, which means bang goes our chance to interview him without a lawyer."

"And of course the clock would start running, so we'd have to charge or release him," Allen added gloomily.

"Why don't we have another go at him now?" Metcalfe urged. "If he won't answer our questions that might give us something that *could* justify our taking him in. That's why you left Karen in the room, wasn't it, so that he wouldn't have a chance to speak to his wife?"

"It was, yes," Allen acknowledged. "All right, let's give it another go."

As they went back into the room the mood was quiet but

expectant. Willis shook her head to indicate that Bailey had said nothing in their absence.

"So, Mr Bailey," Allen enjoined him, "why don't we start again, and this time you tell it like it is?"

"I did tell it like it is," Bailey replied sullenly. "I just left out the bit about him and Sue. I wasn't trying to hide anything, I just didn't think it was relevant."

"Leave us to judge what's relevant will you, please?" Allen said smoothly. "Just tell us what happened."

Bailey stared at the table and flushed.

"It all started a few months back," he said, "or at least I think it did. That's what Sue says anyway."

"We will have to re-interview your wife in due course," Allen commented, "since I assume she had a similar attack of amnesia when she spoke to Sergeant Willis. Just tell us your story. Tell us what you know."

"Sue goes upstairs a lot," Bailey began. "She 'as to, see? There's always cleaning and stuff to do on the upper floors. So I never thought too much about it. But a couple of times I went looking for her and couldn't find her, and putting two and two together that's when I realised she must be spending time in Howse's room."

"Did you ask her where she had been on these occasions?" Metcalfe interjected.

"Yeah, she admitted it all right, but said that he'd been giving 'er advice on an Open University course."

"Did you believe that?"

"Well, yeah, sort of, to begin with, though I'd never

heard her say anything about it before. She said she was just thinking it through – doing some kind of course, I mean – and that he was helping her decide which subject to choose."

"So, what changed?" Allen asked.

"There were a couple of times she was up there for a long time," Bailey said, "but that wasn't it really. It was more that she was – well different somehow."

"Different how?"

"I noticed that she was wearing high heels when she went up to see him, and that didn't make sense really, not if she was just running around the building doing cleaning and stuff. Make-up too, much more than she usually did. And she was just different, she seemed different, more cheerful somehow."

"Did you challenge her about the affair?" Allen enquired,

"Yes, one day I did. I caught her coming down the stairs. I noticed she was crying, which was odd, and holding her shoes in her hands, not wearing them, like. I asked what she was doing, and she said that there was something wrong with one of the heels, but I snatched them from her straightaway and saw that wasn't true. That's when I realised that she must have been creeping up and down the stairs more often than I thought, maybe when I was stuck on the reception desk, or when I was out."

"Go on," Allen said.

"Well, I got proper mad, didn't I? Wouldn't you?"

"She confessed, then?"

"Yeah, well, couldn't very well not, could she? Seems it

had all been going on for a couple of months. Howse had just ended it that afternoon, though, that's why she was crying as she came downstairs. Seems 'e said it was getting too dangerous, that people might find out."

"How did she take the news?" Karen Willis, asked, without looking up from her notebook.

"Dunno, you'd have to ask her, wouldn't you?"

"We're asking you," Allen cut in sharply.

"Not well," Bailey said heavily, with an attempt at a wry smile. "Not well at all. She was snuffly for days, the poor mare."

The trio of police offices stared at him without speaking. It was a poor thrust at levity, and felt badly out of place.

"Don't get me wrong," he said hastily, looking around. "It's just that she was a bit stupid, wasn't she? I mean, what would a man like him see in a woman like her? He was just after sex on the side, nice and convenient whenever he wanted it. Aren't we all? But she let 'im turn 'er head. She believed all that romantic crap he give 'er. That's all I meant by 'poor mare', you see."

There was a pause.

"I can see that we will need to interview your wife about all this at some length," Allen said presently, almost as if to himself, "but I realise that can't be this evening. Can I ask you both to come to the police station at two o'clock tomorrow? We'd like to go over what you've already told us and then ask you some follow-up questions. You know where it is? It's just down the road on Rosslyn Hill."

"Yeah, I know. We'll be there."

Allen nodded, Karen Willis put her notebook back in her bag, and the three of them trooped out of the room. They said nothing until they were upstairs, had gone outside and closed the front door behind them. It was still raining, but much more lightly now.

"What's your woman's intuition say, then?" Allen asked Willis.

She smiled uncertainly. It was hard to know if he was being serious or not.

"The husband's embarrassed to have to be talking about it. That's natural enough, I suppose. But it could be masking something else, a different sort of uneasiness. It's difficult to tell."

Allen nodded acknowledgement.

"Fair enough. Robert?"

The 'Robert' was a longstanding affectation.

"I agree with Karen, guv. I don't see we can do anymore until we have the wife sitting in front of us in a fit state to be interviewed."

"Fair enough," Allen said again. "OK, let's regroup at nine in the nick. First order of business is to get these statements typed up and signed. Willis, you do that; Bob will give you his notes. Bob, you chase for the forensics. See if you and I can attend at the morgue sometime in the late morning for Brian to give us a quick update over the body. Then we'll come together to see the Baileys."

They walked to the end of the path. Just before Karen

Willis turned away to head in the opposite direction to the others, up towards Christchurch, Allen said something else.

"In the meantime," he mused reflectively, "it would be helpful if you could both put your thinking caps on. What we need are some theories."

"OK, guv," she replied, and then called "goodnight" after them as they walked away up Flask Walk. She knew they were unlikely to get much further than the warm and inviting interior of the pub. She was wondering to what extent the wounds in their relationship might have healed. Unbeknownst to her, so was Bob Metcalfe.

# CHAPTER 5

The 1960s rabbit warren that was New Scotland Yard was ageing badly and hopelessly overcrowded, but the office of the Assistant Commissioner (Crime), as befitted the status of one of the five most senior offices in the Metropolitan Police, was on one of the topmost floors and actually commanded a view from its windows, albeit only of equally uninspiring offices on the other side of Broadway.

The ACC flexed his fingers across his midriff as he gazed at Collison in contemplative fashion. A silence had fallen on their conversation which had at first seemed like a natural pause for mutual reflection but which was now in danger of becoming intrusive. The younger man felt that he should say something, and drew breath.

"I really do appreciate your good wishes, sir, and the honour of being offered the command of the Crime Academy, but in all honesty I'd feel a complete fraud."

"You've got the best academic record in the Met, Simon," the ACC pointed out. "Who better to be in charge of a college?"

"That's all very well," Collison remonstrated, "but to have the credibility for a role like that I'd need to have everyone's respect as an experienced detective, and I'm not."

"You have a very high profile multiple murder enquiry to your credit."

"Credit?" Collison echoed wryly. "Come on, sir, we both know that a lot of things went wrong with that investigation."

"The outcome is all that matters," the ACC said briskly, "and after your blanket coverage in the press and on television you have a very high profile, whether you like it or not. I really don't see that you'd lack credibility for the job, even given your relative lack of experience."

"I'm sorry, sir," Collison said firmly, "but we'll have to agree to differ on that. I really wouldn't feel comfortable pontificating on detective methodology to experienced officers. Not yet, anyway."

There was another pause, this time markedly cooler than the first.

"So what are your own thoughts about your future?"

"I'd like some more real detective work, sir. Back in Hampstead, for preference. I know the team there now."

The ACC sighed heavily.

"I must say I'm disappointed, Simon. This Academy posting was my idea. It's a Chief Superintendent's job, you know. You could act up for a year and then get an early promotion. After that, who knows? We have plans for you, remember. It's people like you who represent the future of the force."

"Please don't think I'm not grateful for the thought, sir, because I am. It's just that I'd like to get some real detective experience under my belt first."

The ACC sighed again, and started counting objections off on his fingers.

"One, those postings are for DCIs, not Superintendents. Two, as you know we already have Tom Allen in place as SIO at Hampstead. Three, we don't really want anyone there at all because we've been trying to close the bloody place for years. Fourth, I'd need to persuade the DCS who runs the Murder Investigation Unit. Fifth, I'd have to explain to the Commissioner why you're not taking the Academy job."

Collison sat listening with a growing sense of frustration.

"I'd be happy to explain myself to the Commissioner myself if it would help, sir," he offered quietly.

This time the ACC's sigh sounded dangerously like a Nigel Gresley steam engine. He rose abruptly from his seat and went to stare out of the window.

"I don't know where you get your luck from, Simon, if luck it be, but there was a murder on Tom Allen's manor yesterday afternoon."

"I hadn't heard, sir."

"Hasn't made the news yet."

"But isn't Tom already working a case?"

"He is and he isn't," the ACC replied cryptically. "It's that prison killing, and we all know how much chance there is of cracking that particular nut. It's officially still an open enquiry, but we're only going through the motions now. We need to redeploy those resources."

"But even so – " Collison began.

"Yes," the ACC concurred heavily. "Even so that means

we have a single SIO at Hampstead who is officially already handling two cases. I actually had a call from the DCS this morning asking about some extra capacity. As it happens, I mentioned your name."

"And?"

"We can skip the actual conversation, but the outcome was that there's an opening there if you want it, as a sort of roving reserve SIO."

"I'm very grateful sir," Collison, but this time he really meant it.

"Hang on, Simon," the ACC said, crossing back to his chair; sitting down he gazed levelly across the desk.

"I want to make two things crystal clear," he went on. "First, this is a purely temporary posting which can and probably will be rescinded as soon as this short term capacity crisis is over. Second, you will be attached to the MIU, which covers all of West London as well as some of North-West. So, wherever a homicide occurs, that will be where you go – and, as I want to stress, only for the duration of the enquiry."

"Third," he said, holding up a hand to signify that he had not finished, "this posting will be entirely at the pleasure of the DCS. Upset him or disappoint him in any way and I can assure you he will be on the phone to me and your detective jaunt will be over."

"I understand, sir. I'm still very grateful for the opportunity."

The ACC waved towards the door to indicate that the meeting was over.

"Simon," he said as he stood up and shook hands, "why the hell don't you do something sensible with that bloody great brain of yours? Something becoming a senior officer."

"You mean like the Academy, sir?" Collison asked warily.

"Not necessarily, but something that will get you noticed. Why don't you put up a paper to the Board? I can see that it's given a fair wind."

"A paper, sir? I'd never really considered it."

"Then you should. The present Commissioner wrote his first paper while he was a DI with Vice. Can't remember what it was about, mind you."

"But what shall I write about?" Collison enquired, as much to himself as to anybody else.

"Anything you like, chum," the ACC responded as he opened the door. "Anything you like."

By midday Karen Willis had the various statements typed up for checking and signature by the relevant individuals. Forensics had however been less forthcoming than had been hoped. Their current estimate for a "rush job" was, despite Tom Allen's insistent urgings, "sometime within the next 48 hours". Though Allen slammed his phone down with a certain amount of venom, he knew that he was just going to have to get on with something else until the report was available.

"Well, there it is," he said in somewhat more philosophical mood to Willis and Metcalfe after lunch. "We're just going to have to wait, aren't we? But I can't see it telling us anything we don't already know. It seems safe to assume that the blow to the head was fatal and that chummy died sometime yesterday morning."

"Order of business then, guv?" Metcalfe queried.

Allen thought carefully.

"Obviously we need to get the statements agreed, signed and on file," he said. "In the meantime let's take a step back and consider where we go next."

"We were talking about re-interviewing the Baileys ...," Metcalfe ventured.

"Yeah, I know we were," Allen replied, "but given that they've already had a night and a morning to get their stories straight together I can't see that it does much harm if we have to wait a little longer."

"It might even be an advantage, guv," Karen suggested. "This way we'll have their statements down on record with their signatures on them, while the delay can only possibly make them feel more nervous."

"It's possible," Allen conceded. "All right then, Willis, you make it your task for the rest of the day to get everyone's signatures. Obviously don't discuss the case in any way, regardless of what they ask you."

"Obviously," she echoed, trying unsuccessfully to hide her irritation as she gathered up papers and bag.

"As for us, Bob," Allen continued as Willis strode out of the room amid a clacking of heels and a faint whiff of perfume, "let's sit and think through where we are, and where we go from here."

He walked up to the board, on which Karen Willis had already drawn a rough floorplan of Burgh House and the names of the victims and all the interviewees. He glared at this for a while, as if it was to blame for not instantly offering the identity and present whereabouts of the killer.

"So what do we know, then?" he asked at length.

"We know that Peter Howse could have been murdered by any of the people we spoke to yesterday," Metcalfe said slowly, as he considered the situation for himself. He wished that Karen was there; she was usually so incisive in her thinking.

"I'm assuming we can eliminate Willis's bloke," Allen said with a sour smile.

"I think that's a safe assumption," Metcalfe said carefully. "That leaves four that we spoke to, all of whom would theoretically have had an opportunity to go up and down the stairs during the period in question. As for the means, the weapon was lying ready to hand if we assume that it was indeed in Howse's rooms all along, which of course we should check."

"So we should probably focus on motive, then?"

"Yes, guv, and that eliminates everyone except the Baileys."

"Except," Allen said heavily, "that because of the lax – one might almost say non-existent – security, anyone at all could have wandered in off the street, bopped our victim on the head, and walked out again, unseen and unnoticed."

"That's true," Metcalfe said carefully again, "but right

now we only know of two people who had a real motive for killing Howse. I say 'real' because it seems he was a thoroughly unpleasant individual who was universally disliked, but we need to go beyond mere dislike and find someone who hated him enough to kill him; that's a big leap."

"I agree," Allen nodded. "OK, then."

He picked up a marker pen and wrote: 'Suspects: (1) Jack Bailey (2) Susan Bailey [together or alone?]'

Then he drew a line to Howse's name and wrote: 'Who else might have had a motive?'

He put the marker down with a sigh and turned back to Metcalfe.

"I suppose," he enquired, "there's no way we can find out who else might have entered the property during the time in question?"

"I don't see how, guv," Metcalfe replied. "Not in the absence of CCTV footage anyway."

"All right then," Allen said with a nod, "let's get on with finding out as much as we can about our victim. This doesn't feel like a random nutter. Somewhere in his past there is something that made somebody feel he was worth killing. Maybe it was just the Baileys, but maybe not."

"There's that nephew, for a start," Metcalfe mused.

"Exactly, Robert," Allen acknowledged. "Why don't you make that your afternoon's work? It's not exactly a DI's work, I know, but it looks like we've lost Willis for the rest of the day. And start thinking about tasks and priorities. By tomorrow morning we should have a full team together in the Incident Room."

"Right you are, guv," Metcalfe agreed, closing his pad and putting his pen back in his pocket.

He walked back to the office which was designed to be shared by eight detectives, but was currently occupied by only four as a result of the proposed closure of the station. By tacit agreement, two of them, an elderly detective constable and detective sergeant gently working their way into retirement, dealt only with local crime, which these days consisted largely of giving victims crime reference numbers for their insurance claims. Metcalfe and Willis were available for more serious crime, such as homicide, under the leadership of whoever was assigned as Senior Investigating Officer for the particular investigation.

He had always liked the extra space that this state of affairs gave; the four desks that were surplus to requirements were pushed together into one corner. However, as from tomorrow he would be moving back into the incident room that was always held available for serious crime enquiries. Already he could hear the technicians moving around in there setting up phones and computers. He would need to go and speak to them in a minute.

On balance it felt good to be back in harness. The enforced inaction since the end of his last case under Superintendent Collison had been supposed to be a rest, a recharging of the batteries, but in truth he had been left feeling not reinvigorated but rather flat and dull. When Peter Collins fell ill, Metcalfe and Willis had been on the verge of openly enlarging what was already a complicated relationship; complicated not only because they were colleagues, and of different ranks at that, but because this would involve her breaking with Peter, a man whom she loved and admired, and whom Metcalfe liked and respected.

These plans had necessarily been put on hold during the dark days when Peter's demons had threatened permanently to engulf him, and although she had told him briefly that she was hopeful Peter had made a full recovery, she had then gone on leave and they had not had any chance of further discussion. Inwardly, he was in turmoil. What if she had changed her mind but had not yet plucked up the courage to tell him so?

As he sat down, he noticed that there was a handwritten note on his desk.

*Bob, I'm back at Hampstead nick, at least pro tem. Do you fancy a tea and a chat? I'm in the home for surplus senior officers on the top floor. SC*

He smiled, partly from pleasure, for he liked Collison, and partly from quiet amusement: anyone else would have sent an email. As with Peter Collins, there was something of an English gentleman from a former time about Collison, though Metcalfe suspected that with him it was simply a level of natural courtesy which no longer existed (and certainly not within the Metropolitan Police), whereas for Peter Collins it had probably begun as exaggerated playacting but had somehow become part of the fabric of his reality. In normal times it was all very amusing to hear him slipping in and out of his Lord Peter Wimsey persona and calling Karen 'Harriet', but in abnormal times, when he had been consumed by guilt believing, albeit wrongly, that he had caused someone's death, it had become a place of refuge which had threatened to overwhelm him and shut him off from the real world forever.

He realised that he could kill two birds with one stone. He walked down the corridor and popped his head round the door of what was quickly re-assuming the appearance of an incident room. Karen Willis's floor plan and notes were already on the large board which was otherwise a large, blank, virgin expanse of whiteness. He recognised one of the IT technicians and they nodded in greeting.

"I've just got to say hello to someone upstairs," he announced, having to pause momentarily mid-sentence as someone suddenly operated some kind of power tool away in the corner. "I'll be back in a few minutes."

The power tool started up again, and so he pointed to the desk nearest the front and then patted his own chest. The technician nodded as if he understood, but just to make sure he took a piece of paper, wrote 'DI Metcalfe' on it, and wedged it firmly under the telephone. After a moment's thought, he then wrote 'DS Willis' on another piece of paper and placed it on the adjoining desk. By tradition, Allen, as SIO, would retain his own office and simply visit the Incident Room when he needed to. It had been one of the recommendations of the commission which had investigated the shortcomings of the Yorkshire Ripper enquiry that an SIO should hold themselves aloof from the daily nitty gritty of an investigation, the better to maintain their objective judgement, and to form hypotheses away from the groupthink which could so easily come to dominate a packed incident room.

He went upstairs and saw one of Collison's police business card which had been neatly cut to size to fit exactly into the frame for a name plate on one of the doors. He knocked and went in, finding Collison standing gazing out of one of the two sash windows of a large office, looking rather bored and restless. There was only one desk in the room, but it could easily have accommodated four. Space was not a problem at Hampstead police station; the Met had been attempting to close it for years and, as a means of gradually reducing its headcount, tried to avoid posting anyone there. Every so often an outcry by local newspapers and community groups would prompt a very public reinforcement by uniformed constables who would pointedly walk the beat and chat to local shopkeepers, but after a few weeks these would be quietly and gradually withdrawn, and the process of slow decay allowed to gather pace once more.

Collison smiled, a smile of spontaneous pleasure.

"Hello, Bob," he said simply.

# CHAPTER 6

"I can only stay for a few minutes, guv," Bob Metcalfe said as he sank into one of the easy chairs in Collison's spacious new quarters. "We've got a case on – just came in yesterday."

"Yes, I heard about it from the ACC."

"That was quick, then," Metcalfe told him. "It was only late yesterday afternoon. Somebody got himself knocked on the head at Burgh House. Karen was there with Peter at the time, funnily enough, visiting an exhibition. At the moment it's just her and me on the case – plus Tom Allen of course; he's SIO. The rest of the team will be coming in tomorrow."

Collison raised his eyebrows in mild surprise.

"You mean she's potentially a witness but also an investigating officer? Isn't that a little, well ... unconventional, shall we say?"

Metcalfe reflected on this.

"I suppose you're right," he replied at length. "I must say I hadn't thought about it."

"No reason you should, I suppose," Collison mused. "It's an issue for the SIO to consider. But it might be worth suggesting to Tom – just as a friend, mind – that he might like to clear it with the Chief Superintendent. Better to be safe than sorry, eh?"

"You're right of course," Metcalfe acknowledged. "Funny case, this one – "

Collison held up a hand.

"I'm not on the team," he said, "nor likely to be. I'm here to take charge of whichever homicide comes up next anywhere vaguely close to Hampstead, not this one. So don't tell me anything about the case. Tom can if he wants to, but nobody else, unless he authorises it. Remember, we've had this issue before."

They both smiled wryly. An unthinking slip on a previous case had ended one officer's career and damaged both of their own.

"Well," Metcalfe said slowly, "without telling you anything about the case, have you ever heard of a Professor Hugh Raffen? Finding out about him is my task for today anyway, so I can sit here with a clear conscience as long as we're talking about him."

"The Honourable Hugh?" Collison asked in surprise. "What's he got to do with all this?"

"He's a witness," Metcalfe informed him. "Not a suspect. We're just trying to gather some background on everyone who was in the house at the time. Karen's got the caretaker and his wife. I've got Raffen. What's all this 'honourable' stuff?"

"His father's a lord," Collison explained. "and most people wouldn't use the honorific today, but the Honourable Hugh does. He's always had a proper sense of his own importance."

"How come his father's a peer?" Metcalfe asked. "What did he do? Was he an academic too?"

"I don't think so," Collison. "I think he had some job in the Civil Service, though I'm not sure what. He inherited the title from Hugh's grandfather, an academic who was rumoured to have had links to the intelligence services as well. I believe he recruited agents straight out of Oxford, where he taught. Got the peerage for being Master of some college or other."

"Wasn't there some trouble about that?" Metcalfe enquired, struggling to remember something he had read. "Burgess and Maclean and so forth?"

"There was indeed," Collison replied grimly. "Many of them who were recruited back then in the thirties from Oxford and Cambridge became Soviet spies – like Burgess and Maclean – either at the time or shortly afterwards. But I don't think there was ever any suggestion of anything untoward where Raffen was concerned. If there was, he'd hardly have been given a peerage, would he?"

Metcalfe had his notebook out and was jotting things down.

"What about this Hugh character? What can you tell me about him?"

"I don't really know much more than anyone else, though I've met him socially a couple of times. Once at some ghastly dinner, and once at an equally ghastly drinks party."

"Why ghastly?" Metcalfe queried.

"Partly because, as I remember it, the Honourable

Hugh's chief topic of conversation is himself. He's pretty unbearable."

"I thought I recognised him for a moment when I first saw him," Metcalfe said hesitantly, "almost as though I'd seen him somewhere before."

Collison laughed.

"He did a television series on the Byzantine Empire a few years ago," he proffered. "You probably remember him from that."

"Oh, yes, of course," Metcalfe lied.

"Though I understand," Collison continued, "that he's a bit of a railway nut as well. Didn't he do some programme on steam trains recently?"

"That would make sense," Metcalfe confirmed with a nod, "he told us he was writing something about railways at the moment."

"Well, there you are then," Collison said, leaning back in his chair, "and there, I'm afraid, Bob, the Collison fount of knowledge runs dry."

"Well, thanks anyway, guv," Metcalfe replied as he closed his notebook. "I'm sure that's all useful background."

"I'm sure it's not," the other chuckled, "but thanks for saying so anyway."

"Actually," he went on quickly as Metcalfe rose to his feet, "you might like to help me out with something."

"If I can, of course," Metcalfe responded, pausing on his way to the door.

"Well, the ACC has suggested that I might like to write a

paper on something. Any ideas?"

"A paper? Good God – I mean, I'm sure that's a good idea, guv, but on what?"

"Ah," Collison thoughtfully, rubbing his nose, "that's where I'm a bit stuck. I was wondering if you might have any ideas."

"My mind's a complete blank," Metcalfe confessed. "The only thing I can think of is that thing the Met called in some management consultants to do a few years back – do you remember?"

"Vaguely," Collison murmured, looking the part. "Can you remind me?"

"It was a report into the future structure of police forces," Metcalfe said, looking suddenly uncomfortable, "but come to think of it, guv, I don't think it's the sort of thing you're looking for."

"Why not?"

"Well," Metcalfe replied awkwardly, "as I remember it, their main recommendation was that the rank of superintendent should be abolished."

Before they broke for the evening, the team reconvened, Karen Willis having returned from her errands, with a folder of typed and signed statements on the desk in front of her to prove it.

"Progress?" Allen asked simply.

"All statements signed and filed, as you can see, guv," Willis replied, nodding at the folder.

"And what about our friends Mr and Mrs Bailey?"

"I've provisionally arranged for them to come in tomorrow afternoon, guv. I thought you'd like to have the morning to meet with the troops, but I can easily change that if you'd prefer."

"No, that's fine," Allen replied. "Of course they'll have had a whole 24 hours to get their stories straight together, but we can't help that."

"I think it was the lesser of two evils," Metcalfe commented, almost as if trying to reassure himself. "If we'd taken them in to hold them separately we'd already have their lawyers hollering at us by now to charge or release them, and we'd have achieved nothing."

"I know," Allen scowled, "but it's hardly ideal, is it?"

"Little in life is," Willis murmured.

Allen started hard at her and she flushed slightly and busied herself with her notes.

"Talking of troops, guv," Metcalfe cut in quickly. "We should have everyone reporting at 0900 tomorrow, so perhaps we can fix a briefing meeting for 0930?"

"Who have we got?" Allen demanded. "Anybody from the last mob?"

"I've managed to get hold of Priya Desai," Metcalfe said proudly. "She'd just completed a children's course and was glad for a chance to get back on homicide."

Allen grunted noncommittally. He did not share their assessment of the detective constable's qualities. At the same time they were all acutely aware that one of his best friends,

Ken Andrews, who had served with them on their last investigation, had in the interim effectively been dismissed from the force in disgrace, although early retirement through ill health had, as so often, been used as a convenient fiction.

"As for the rest," Metcalfe went on, "it's a pretty motley bunch who just happened to be available at short notice at other nicks."

There was a collective lowering of spirits. They all knew that in such a situation every police station would seize the opportunity to post away their least valued detective.

"If we had a permanent team like in the old days," Allen said, voicing their thoughts, "we wouldn't need to go through this."

"Well," he went on after a pause. "You'll need to get the measure of them all pretty quickly, Bob. Learn who we can rely on and who we can't. Be careful when you give out the tasks, and don't necessarily assume that rank is any guide to ability."

"Present company excepted, of course," Metcalfe said with a smile.

"Naturally," Allen agreed gruffly, and then, unexpectedly, looking directly at Karen Willis, "*all* present company excepted."

The compliment surprised her, and she blushed slightly. She tried to speak, but found that she did not know what to say.

"Now," Allen said, "what about dear Professor Raffen? And what about this nephew of Peter Howse?"

"As to Professor Raffen," Metcalfe said rather smugly. "I found out quite a lot from a source upstairs – quite a lot about his family background anyway."

"A source upstairs?" Allen echoed. "What are you talking about? There's only one office upstairs, and it's mine. The others are all empty."

"Not anymore," Metcalfe informed him. "One of them now belongs to Superintendent Collison."

"Collison? What's he doing here?"

"He's been posted back, as a spare SIO as far as I can gather."

Allen recovered quickly and began spontaneously to mutter something about 'spare' being a fitting description. However, seeing that Karen Willis was beaming with obvious pleasure at Metcalfe's news, he stifled his interjection.

"All right then," he said with as good a grace as he could muster, "what did you find out?"

So Metcalfe told him, noticing him look increasingly irritated at the mention of dinner parties and peers of the realm.

"And the nephew?" Allen demanded as Metcalfe drew to a close.

"Ah," Metcalfe said diffidently, "not a lot of luck there, so far. I'm having problems tracing any close family at all, in fact. According to public records, both Peter Howse's parents are dead, which squares with what we thought anyway, and I've found one sibling: a sister. I'm assuming she's dead too, but we won't know for sure until we can trace her married name and cross-reference with deaths. Presumably this nephew is her son."

Allen looked unhappy.

"Well, we'll have to make that a priority, Bob. And we need to find out about a will, as well."

"I asked the Professor about that when he was signing his statement, guv," Karen Willis interjected. "He didn't know who Howse's solicitor might have been, or even if he had one, so I suppose we'll have to look out for that when we go through all his papers."

"The room's still sealed, I hope?" Allen queried.

"Yes, guv, I checked when I was there."

"OK," Metcalfe said, jotting down some action points. "That's going to be a job for some people with brains in their heads, people who can think about what they're seeing and decide whether it's relevant and whether it needs following up."

"Let's hope they send us some, then," Allen commented gloomily.

They looked at each other bleakly. They all knew this was unlikely.

"I think," Allen decided, "that the two of you had better be responsible for that, unless something more important comes up. I'm sorry, Bob, I know it's not the sort of thing a DI would normally be asked to take on -"

"Don't worry, guv," Metcalfe said quickly. "I agree completely. Our problem at the moment is that we know almost nothing about our victim, and the easiest way to address that is to go through everything of his that we can find."

"Mm," Willis agreed. "It's going to be a tough job, though. According to Professor Raffen, Howse was preparing an exhibition on the Isokon, so there's going to be a lot of stuff which may be very relevant to that but completely irrelevant for our purposes."

Metcalfe and Allen looked puzzled.

"I don't remember seeing that in the draft statements," Metcalfe said uncertainly.

"No, sorry, you wouldn't have because it wasn't there. It just occurred to me that it was something it would be useful to know, so I asked Raffen when I was with him. He told me."

"Who or what is the Isokon?" Allen enquired.

"It's an iconic block of flats on Lawn Road," Willis explained. "A lot of people think that they were designed by Walter Gropius but they weren't, although they were inspired by his work, of course. Actually they were designed by an Englishman, whose name I forget for a minute, who was always a bit miffed that he didn't get enough credit for them."

"So you mean that Howse's room are likely to be stuffed full with documents about a block of flats?" Metcalfe asked.

"That's about the size of it, yes. Not just any old block of flats, of course. The Isokon was very special. Had lots of famous residents as well: Agatha Christie for one."

"Oh, gawd," Allen groaned theatrically.

"Are you 'oh gawding' about the idea of detective fiction, or the idea of having to go through dozens of boxes which almost certainly have nothing to do with our enquiry?" Metcalfe asked with a smile.

"Both!" Allen replied firmly. "But seriously, Bob, the two of you will have to decide pretty quickly what we need to look at and what we don't. Concentrate on anything which mentions relatives, or his financial affairs. So far we don't have any idea of a possible motive apart from jealousy on the part of Bailey, or the pangs of rejection on the part of his missus."

"His wallet was on the desk, and I could see that it had cash in it," Metcalfe proffered, "so I'm assuming we can rule out theft."

"Sounds reasonable," Allen concurred. "From what we hear he didn't have anything worth stealing anyway."

"That may narrow our search in more way than one," Willis suggested.

They looked at her enquiringly.

"Well," she said, "what I mean is: I'm sure we've all considered the possibility of some passing stranger making their way upstairs for some reason and killing him, but if we rule out theft, what other motive could they have had? They'd have been likely to have been an opportunistic thief, attracted by the open front door and lack of security, so surely they'd have taken the cash?"

"They might have been a random nutter," Allen said sourly. "There are a lot of them about in Hampstead. I had one nattering away to himself sitting next to me on the bus the other day."

"Possible but unlikely," Willis countered. "Think of the odds – how likely is it that a 'random nutter' would choose that particular time to wander into that particular house? Or that they would find their way to Howse's door? Or even that they would be capable of murder in the first place? Most of these people are quite harmless, you know."

"A possibility, nonetheless," Allen maintained.

"You know, there's something else about this that we need to consider," Metcalfe said suddenly.

"Go on," Allen prompted him.

"Well, if the wallet was there on the desk with money in it, that means that whoever murdered our victim had the perfect chance to make it look as if theft *was* the motive, for example by taking the cash and throwing the wallet on the floor."

"True," nodded Allen, "but where does that take us?"

"I'm not sure," Metcalfe admitted, "It's only just occurred to me."

There was a long pause and then Allen sighed and looked at his watch.

"I wonder if it's too early for a beer?" he asked.

# CHAPTER 7

As the investigation team was still arriving the next morning in dribs and drabs, Tom Allen decided to delay their initial briefing meeting until the afternoon, which left the morning free to interview the Baileys. This was done separately, Allen and Willis interviewing Susan Bailey, since Karen had taken her initial statement, and Metcalfe and Priya Desai Jack Bailey, for the same reason.

"Now then, Mrs Bailey," Allen said without preamble once the preliminaries were over and the tape was running, "why don't we just ignore what you told DS Willis and start again from the beginning?"

Susan Bailey bit her lip, glancing nervously from Allen, to the tape recorder and then at Karen Willis, who had the original typed statement in front of her.

"Well," she said nervously, "it was just like I said, wasn't it? Just like I told the lady here."

"Oh, really?" asked Allen.

He picked up the statement and studied it theatrically for a minute before tossing it down on the table in from of her.

"I don't think so," he countered. "You seem to have forgotten to mention a few points, don't you? For example, that you were having an affair with the deceased, and that your husband had recently found out about it, and that you were very unhappy with the deceased for dumping you, and that your husband had recently had a flaming row with the deceased ... Shall I go on?"

Susan Bailey shook her head silently, gazing down at the table.

"So, like I said," Allen continued after a pause, leaning back in his chair and wishing desperately that he could have a cigarette, "why don't we start again, and this time let's have the truth, shall we?"

She nodded jerkily, but still said nothing.

"Come on, Susan," Willis said gently, "talking of starting at the beginning, why don't you tell us how your relationship with Peter Howse began?"

"I don't know really," she replied helplessly. "It was just one of those things. He was always so charming to me – a real gentleman, you know? – and when I told him one day that I was thinking of studying something he suggested the Open University straightaway, and we got talking, and when I had to go back downstairs he said I should feel free to come and see him whenever I wanted."

She fiddled with the thick green porcelain teacup from the station canteen.

"And I did," she said simply. "I started popping in for a chat once or twice a day, and staying for a cup of tea, and without really knowing why I found myself really looking forward to seeing him, and making an effort to dress up when I went upstairs – you know, a bit of make-up, that's all – and then one day he just suddenly kissed me, and I kissed him back, and that was that."

Karen Willis had recently taken the advanced interrogation course and knew that in most cases staying silent was more effective than prompting the witness, so she said nothing. Allen, who had not, grew restless and was searching for the next question when Susan Bailey drew a quavering breath and went on.

"I don't know why I did it, really," she said again. "Like I said, it just happened. But suddenly it became the most important thing in my life, the *only* important thing, really. Oh, I know it wasn't fair on Jack, but it was just so different with Peter. He made me feel special, he made me feel that I really mattered to him. That's why I was so upset when he ended it. I couldn't believe that he'd said all those things without really ever meaning them at all, just stringing me along."

She looked up and gazed fixedly at Karen as if desperate for understanding, her eyes filling with tears.

"Can you describe your feelings when he ... ended it?" Allen asked, having searched all too obviously for a gentler version of what he had been about to say.

"I suppose I should have hated him, really. When Jack found out he said he'd just been using me, and asked how I could have been so stupid, but I kept hoping that he'd somehow realise that he'd made a mistake."

She paused and choked quietly.

"... and I suppose I thought," she went on wistfully, "that maybe it was just Jack finding out that had frightened him into not seeing me, and that in a little while everything would be OK again, and he'd ask me back."

"And would you have gone?" Karen asked curiously. "Would you have left your husband for him?"

At this point the tears which had been threatening for some time totally engulfed Susan Bailey and she sat before them weeping helplessly.

Karen pushed a box of tissues forward and Susan Bailey dabbed with a handful rather ineffectually, saying "I'm sorry", over and over again.

Eventually Allen gave up.

"This really won't do, Mrs Bailey," he said. "You know perfectly well that we still have lots of questions to ask you, and sooner or later you will have to answer them. For the moment, interview suspended."

In a different room, Metcalfe and Mehta were attempting a similar exercise.

"Mr Bailey," Metcalfe said formally, "I think you should be aware that we are very unhappy that the statement which you gave us on the day of the murder was so incomplete. We have asked you here today so you can set the record straight."

"I didn't tell you about my wife and Peter Howse," Bailey said straightaway, "because I didn't think it was anyone's business but our own."

"It was Peter Howse's business," Metcalfe pointed out.

"Peter Howse is dead," Bailey replied.

"And therefore anything which is relevant to him could be relevant to his death," Metcalfe continued smoothly. "Something which you ignored. In fact, not to put too fine a point on it, you deliberately concealed from a police murder enquiry something which could be a key part of the investigation."

"Look, I can see how it might look," Bailey said, more accommodating now, "but I knew that however he died it had nothing to do with Sue and me."

Metcalfe stared hard at him and waited, but it was clear that Bailey was not in a mood to do anything except volunteer short answers.

"Let's go back over the timeline of that morning, shall we?" Metcalfe asked.

"I already told you this yesterday," Bailey responded mulishly.

"Tell me again," Metcalfe directed him curtly. "I've already made it clear that we are not impressed with your statement yesterday."

"I opened the front door as usual at nine thirty, and I sat on the desk for a while because there was nobody else to do it. I don't like to leave the door unattended, though it does happen quite a lot."

"Why?" asked Priya Mehta.

"It's difficult to find volunteers to fill the rota, particularly around school time, and there's no money to pay people to do it. So usually it's just me, Sue, and occasionally Lord high and mighty Howse."

"Why only occasionally?" she probed.

Bailey snorted.

"Thought it was beneath him, didn't he? Oh, he was happy enough swanning around at drinks receptions, but he didn't fancy the real work of making the place run every day. Couldn't handle it, he couldn't. He could never forget the fact that the place used to be his home. Never let nobody else forget it, neither."

Metcalfe made a show of consulting his notes.

"It was my understanding," he said, "that Mr Howse was in fact engaged in research work upstairs. Something to do with the next exhibition which the House was planning to run."

"He might have been."

"Well, was he or wasn't he? Surely you must know."

"He had loads of papers up there any rate," Bailey conceded grudgingly. "Though how much actual work he was doing I couldn't say."

"Well, if he was doing research work," Metcalfe persisted, "and, for what it's worth, Professor Raffen says he was, then surely that would have been a perfectly valid reason for him not to spend time sitting on the front desk, wouldn't it?"

"What's it matter?" Bailey asked truculently.

"Why it matters," Metcalfe replied. "Is that a jury might just wonder whether your reluctance to accept that Mr Howse was in fact genuinely engaged in paperwork of a fairly demanding kind, and that this gave him a valid reason not to spend long periods of time away from his office, was suggestive of some malice on your part towards him."

"Where are you coming from with this talk of 'malice'? I've already said I didn't like him. Why should I? He was screwing my wife."

"Which is really where we came in, isn't it? Surely if a man is murdered then the fact that someone in the same building bore him ill-will is a relevant consideration?"

He paused to let this sink in.

"Let's go back to half past nine that morning," he suggested at length. "You opened the door. Do you know if anyone else had already come into the building?"

Bailey thought for a moment.

"I didn't have to switch the alarm off," he said, half to himself, "so yes, someone else was definitely already up and about. A little while later I heard someone moving around upstairs, and I'd been sitting on the desk since I opened the door, like I said. I assumed it was Howse."

"Any particular reason?" asked Priya.

"Yeah, Raffen never gets in before ten at the earliest."

"It might have been your wife," Metcalfe proffered.

Bailey shook his head.

"Nah, she didn't go upstairs all morning."

The two detectives exchanged glances.

"How can you be sure?" Metcalfe demanded. "Were you with her the whole time?"

"No," he admitted, "but from where I was sitting you can look out into the hallway -"

"The hallway, yes," Metcalfe cut in, "but not the stairs,

surely? They face the other way. If someone was approaching them from the stairs to the basement level then you wouldn't be able to see them, would you?"

"I was going to say, before you interrupted," Bailey continued with heavy sarcasm, "that you can hear anyone going up the stairs, or down them for that matter. They're bare wood, and the house was quiet."

Metcalfe made another show of consulting his notes, though partly to conceal a sudden sense of excitement.

"We have evidence," he said carefully, "that your wife sometimes used to take her shoes off and creep upstairs in her stockinged feet so as not to be heard by anyone."

For the first time, Bailey looked shaken.

"Evidence? What sort of evidence? Who from? Who says she did?"

"Never mind about that. We have evidence, that's all. Now, let's try to get things straight, shall we? If your wife had taken off her shoes and been very careful not to make any noise, she could have crept upstairs without you hearing her, couldn't she?"

"Nah," Bailey replied stubbornly. "I'd have heard. Like I said, it was very quiet."

Metcalfe allowed another pause to build, but nothing was forthcoming.

"What time did you come off the front desk?" he asked finally.

"After about an hour," came the reply. "Nobody came in, not a dicky bird, and I was getting fed up, so I left the desk empty like Howse said it was OK to do from time to time."

"From time to time, yes," Metcalfe countered. "But surely not for hours at a time? From what you say and what we already know, anyone could have come in through the front door and gone upstairs unobserved from about ten thirty until lunchtime."

"Yeah, well, I thought Sue could do it for a while and then I'd do some more before lunch, but it turned out she was busy with stuff downstairs, and I sat with her and we had a cup of tea and time just sort of drifted away. You know how it is."

Metcalfe and Mehta looked at each other glumly.

"Well," Priya Mehta asked with a sigh, "did you see or hear anyone go upstairs after you were no longer on the desk?"

"Hard to say. Most of the time I was downstairs with Sue. I had a window to fix at the back and it took longer than I was expecting-"

"Was that outside the building or inside?" Metcalfe cut in.

"Both really, but I was outside for quite a while – maybe forty minutes or so. Like I said, it took longer than I was expecting. And from outside you couldn't hear anyone even on the ground floor, let alone if they were going upstairs."

"So that would have been – what? From about eleven to about eleven forty, say?" Metcalfe mused.

"That I was outside, I suppose, yeah."

"And what did you do between then and lunch time?" Priya quizzed him.

"Well, I usually have me dinner at about twelve, with Sue, so that one of us can go and sit on the front desk at one o'clock if there's nobody else to do it."

Again Metcalfe made a show of consulting his notes.

"But that didn't happen, did it? According to everyone we spoke to that afternoon, the desk, and thus the front door, had been left entirely unattended, presumably from when you went off downstairs at about ten thirty. So, what happened?"

"Dunno. I suppose I thought Howse would do it."

Metcalfe looked deeply unconvinced.

"But if you were ready to go on the desk if you were needed at one, or even a bit before, wouldn't it have been natural to go up and take a look?"

"Or even," Priya Mehta added as Bailey hesitated, "go right upstairs and ask Peter Howse what his plans were for the rest of the day?"

"I never went upstairs that day, I tell you," Bailey burst out, his face reddening. "Anyone who tells you different is a liar, see?"

"So what happened, Mr Bailey?" Metcalfe pressed him. "What were you really doing around lunchtime, and how come the front door was left unattended all that time?"

"There are volunteers that come in ..." Bailey proffered uncertainly.

"But surely there must be a roster for that, isn't there?

Otherwise you'd have different people turning up at the same time, and things like that."

"Yeah, I suppose so," Bailey concurred.

"So in that case you would have known that nobody was due in until after lunch, wouldn't you?"

There was a pause and the officers deliberately let it lengthen. Then, at long last, Bailey spoke.

"Well, if you must know," he said sullenly, "I was having a row with my wife. She ran off and shut herself in the bedroom and I was sort of waiting for her to come out."

"Oh come on, Mr Bailey," Metcalfe said wearily. "You and your wife have had all this time to put a story together; is that really the best you can do?"

"What do you mean?" he asked belligerently.

"What I mean is that your story is full of holes, as you must be able to see for yourself. With the exception of your wife, there is nobody who can vouch for even a part of your movements that morning. Now, come on. Why don't you tell us what really happened?"

"I have," Bailey said flatly. "Everything happened just like I said."

He looked meaningfully at the clock.

"Very well, Mr Bailey," Metcalfe said, "if that's the way you want it. But let me ask you one final question. What was your wife doing while you were outside mending the window?"

"She was ironing. I could see her through the window. She had a huge load to do, and because she ran off into the bedroom she never finished it, neither. She had just started doing it again when the professor came down to tell us he'd found Howse dead upstairs."

"Very well," Metcalfe acknowledged. "Interview terminated."

# CHAPTER 8

"That was a good idea of yours, Bob," Collison said as they sat over an early morning coffee the following day. "I've got hold of a copy of that management consultancy report you mentioned. I can see why the top brass didn't care for it much; it basically says they don't know how to run the Met."

"That's pretty much the way I remember it, yes," Metcalfe replied, "though I never actually read it myself. I just saw it summarised in the papers. Like I said, the bit they really got hot under the collar about was the proposal to abolish one of the two Superintendent ranks."

"Yes," Collison concurred. "It all seems to have been put out to grass and forgotten about. I was speaking to a mate of mine who's doing an MBA and he reckons that most consultancy reports suffer a similar fate. It's all very well knowing how an organisation *should* be run, but convincing the people who do actually run it on a daily basis that you know better than them must be quite a challenge."

"So what's your plan?" Metcalfe asked curiously. "You do have a plan, don't you, guv?"

"I'm not sure that I do," Collison responded with a smile. "Not yet, anyway. But I'm reading myself into the subject. My friend has lent me a few books on operational management and organisation structure. I must say that I never even dreamed that people got excited about such matters, let alone wrote books about it."

He took a sip of his coffee and paused reflectively.

"However," he continued, "I'm willing to bet that nobody in the Met has ever read anything about it either, so it's an area where a little knowledge might go a long way, particularly if dressed up in some business school jargon."

"In the land of the blind, eh?"

They both broke off as Collison's mobile rang.

"Sorry, Bob," he said as he answered it.

He listened intently for a couple of minutes and then said curtly "right, I'm on my way."

"Trouble, guv?" Metcalfe asked as he put the phone back in his pocket.

"Depends what you mean by trouble. I've got a body."

"Suspicious death?" Metcalfe enquired.

"Well, apparently it was found in a suitcase, so that sounds pretty suspicious to me. People don't usually crawl into a suitcase to die."

"Nor lock it from the inside," Metcalfe agreed.

"I'll have to be going I'm afraid, Bob."

"Of course, guv, no problem. Well, it'll be nice to have two murder enquiries being run from the same nick, won't it?"

"Interesting, certainly," Collison observed drily. "Presumably I'll be competing for resources with Tom Allen."

By the time Collison arrived at the block of flats in Lawn Road, Tom Bellamy and his team were already on the scene.

"Good morning, sir," he said in answer to Collison's introduction.

"What do we have, Inspector?" Collison asked formally.

"Some builders broke down a wall in the basement and found an old storage room. It contained three old suitcases and two larger pieces of luggage. The small ones were empty apart from a few old newspapers. Of the larger two, one contained books and the other a body. I'm just waiting for Dr Williams now – ah, speak of the Devil."

Brian Williams appeared in the entrance lobby, clutching his bag in one hand and a takeaway coffee in the other. He glanced at the huddle of curious builders on one side of the hallway and the small knot of police officer on the other and headed for the latter.

"Morning, everyone," he called briskly, "can't shake hands, I'm afraid. Hello, Tom."

"Morning, Brian. This is DS Collison, he's the SIO."

"We met on your last case, Superintendent."

"So we did," Collison acknowledged. "Good to meet you again."

"Of course, you've become quite a celebrity since then," Williams observed mischievously.

"Don't know about that," Collison said awkwardly. "Anyway, shall we go and take a look?"

"I don't think there's much chance of disturbing any evidence," Bellamy said, "particularly as the builders have been stomping around down there and knocking walls down, but it is a crime scene so let's observe the proprieties. Follow in my steps please, gentlemen, and stop if I say so."

"Why did they knock the wall down?" Collison asked curiously as he followed Bellamy downstairs.

"According to the foreman, sir, the architect noticed that the basement was smaller than it showed on the original plans. He measured the outside and the inside, put two and two together, and worked out that some space had been bricked off at some stage."

The storage space contrived to feel both damp and dusty at the same time. A bare lamp bulb hung unlit from the ceiling. An inspection light, presumably erected by the builders, blazed across the room casting stark shadows. Collison noticed that in some places not just the wallpaper but the plaster too had peeled off the wall.

"That's a cabin trunk," he said, looking at the piece of luggage. "Haven't seen one for years, except in junk shops."

He stopped and stared at the floor.

"From the marks in the dust, Inspector, I assume that the builders found it over there in the corner, and dragged it into the centre of the room before opening it?"

"So I understand, sir. I've got the uniform PC who called it in taking their statements one by one. As you might expect, they weren't very coherent to start with."

Bellamy beckoned them forward as he stood over the open trunk, shining a powerful torch inside. Stepping up and leaning over, Collison could see that the body was largely skeleton, although some leathery skin remained around the skull.

"Oh dear," Williams murmured at his side, "you really should have called me earlier, Tom. I might have been able to save him."

It was an old joke, and grew no funnier from retelling.

"Will you certify life extinct please, Doctor?" Bellamy enquired unsmilingly.

"With the greatest of pleasure, dear boy," Williams replied, "and may I say that I have never been more sure of any diagnosis."

Collison eyed him calmly.

"Initial thoughts, Doctor?"

Williams shrugged, but continued to scrutinise the body intently.

"Young male, probably twenties or thirties. No obvious factures. No obvious cause of death. No sign of any clothes, which I suppose suggests that he was dead when he was put into the trunk, but that's your department, of course."

"How long has he been dead?"

"Decades," Williams replied briefly. "Best I can do for you now, based on initial impressions, is at least forty or fifty years. "

He turned to Bellamy.

"There's nothing I can do here, Tom, so feel free to move the body as soon as your chaps have finished here."

He nodded to Collison and moved towards the stairs. It

had all been so fast that he had not even had a chance to sip his coffee.

Bellamy looked dubious.

"Is it really all as simple as that, guv? I've never done one of these 'long dead' jobs before."

"Not have I," Collison said, truthfully since this was only his second homicide. "Let's make sure we have the whole place well photographed, and then I'd like the whole room thoroughly searched, please, just in case there's anything lying around."

He watched as Bellamy beckoned to the photographer and then moved back to the doorway and surveyed the scene. There really didn't seem to be anything he could do here, so he went back upstairs, where a uniformed constable was going through the motions of taking statements from four builders, none of whom seemed to speak much English. The foreman was a better candidate, he reasoned.

"Your men aren't British, are they?" he asked, stating the obvious.

"No, they're Polish," the foreman replied. "So I am I. Jan Kubis at your service, sir."

He held out a hand. Collison shook it, feeling the rough skin of a professional builder.

"How did you get this job?" he enquired.

"From the architect, Mr Lazlo," Kubis replied. "You need to talk to him, maybe? He just arrive. That's his car now."

A well-dressed man stepped rather languidly out of a

silver grey Audi and moved towards the building. Collison intercepted him on the steps outside.

"Mr Lazlo, sir?"

"Yes, I understand there's a problem here," Lazlo said uncertainly. "I'm the architect."

"Are you supervising these men?" Collison enquired.

"Amongst other things, yes. That's only a small part of what I do, actually. I have a brief to completely refurbish the building. It's been unoccupied for years, you know."

"No, I didn't know," Collison responded.

He glanced up at the sky. It was starting to rain and the signs did not look good for it easing up.

"What is wrong? I understand the police have been called. Are you a policeman?"

"A body has been found in a bricked-off part of the basement," Collison said shortly. "I'm Detective Superintendent Collison, by the way."

Lazlo looked suitably shocked.

"Rather than getting wet here, Mr Lazlo," Collison said before the other could reply, "might I suggest that we meet up at Hampstead Police Station at three o'clock this afternoon? That will give me time to make the necessary arrangements with some colleagues to take your statement properly."

"Yes, of course," Lazlo said and then, uncertainly, "is there anything I can do here?"

"You might as well tell the men to go home for the rest of the day," Collison suggested. "Our Scene of Crime Officers are likely to be busy here for several hours."

"Very well, Superintendent," Lazlo nodded. "And I'll see you later at three."

The rain was already getting heavier and Collison realised to his dismay that he had neither raincoat nor umbrella. Fortunately, at this juncture the uniformed officer emerged from the flats and started walking towards a small car distinguished by some checked markings and a blue light.

"Have you finished in there, Constable?" he enquired.

"Yes, sir," the other replied. "Unless there's anything else you'd like me to do, that is."

"There is," Collison averred, starting to run towards the car. "You can give me a lift back to the nick."

Collison's efforts to have a spare detective assigned to him came to nothing, despite a personal plea to the ACC. So it was that when Viktor Lazlo arrived at the station the only additional police presence which could be summoned to sit beside the Superintendent was a uniformed Constable, looking stiff and uncomfortable.

"I understand that block of flats is something rather special in the architectural line," he said by way of a conversational gambit.

"Oh yes, I should say," enthused Lazlo. "Why they're positively iconic. Have you heard of the Bauhaus movement?"

"Yes, something to do with German architecture between the wars wasn't it? Function over form, that sort of thing."

"Exactly," nodded Lazlo. "The real guru, after Le Corbusier of course, was Walter Gropius. The problem was that he was Jewish, as were most of his associates, so it was convenient for the Nazi establishment to attack their work. He's intimately associated with the Isokon."

"The Isokon?"

"Sorry, yes, the Lawn Road Flats, as they were called, have always been better known in architectural terms as the Isokon Building."

"Did Gropius design it?"

"No, it was designed by an English architect called Wells Coates, though the real brains behind it was a man called Jack Pritchard, but Coates was hugely influenced by the Bauhaus School, and when Gropius and his friends were driven out of Germany a lot of them ended up living in the Flats. In fact, Jack Pritchard used to offer untenanted flats as temporary accommodation to Jewish refugees from Germany and Austria right through into the early part of the war."

"And how did the basement, or that part of it, come to be bricked up?" Collison asked, "and when was it done?"

"I can't answer either of those questions with any certainty," Lazlo said. "In fact, nobody can."

"Well, tell me what you know," Collison said with a smile.

"The basement came to be a restaurant and a bar," Lazlo replied. "The idea of the Flats, was that nobody would need to employ any servants as things like laundry and housework were provided on a service charge basis, and meals could be taken in the restaurant. In fact, there was actually a social club which carried on operating even during the war, which aimed at providing good food at reasonable prices."

"You said 'came to be'," Collison pointed out. "What was it originally?"

"Apparently the initial idea for the basement was that it would be a communal kitchen," Lazlo explained, "but it turned out that people didn't really fancy cooking their own meals; remember most people had at least one household servant back in those days. Then someone came along who wanted to operate a restaurant and a bar, so Jack Pritchard had the basement converted. A lot of the relevant papers were lost during the war, but that was probably sometime around 1937 or so."

"I see," Collison murmured, looking over the Constable's shoulder to check that he was getting all this down correctly.

"For what it's worth," Lazlo proffered, "my best bet would be that the storage area was bricked off and papered over then."

"Why?"

"Well in the early part of the war, say about 1939, an air raid shelter was created down there, and I would have thought that they would have wanted to free up as much space as possible, particularly since, as I said, the restaurant carried on operating. So my guess is that the air raid shelter – it was mostly just sandbags, really – was built by amateurs, perhaps even some of the visiting refugees, and they ignored the bricked-off area because they simply didn't know about it."

"Hm," Collison said noncommittally.

"There's something else as well," Lazlo went on hastily.

"Go on, please."

"Some time after the war the Isokon was sold, first to the New Statesman magazine and then later to the local authority. At some stage, in the late sixties I think, the basement was converted into flats. That's the only other time that any major works were carried out down there and it simply wouldn't have made sense to brick it off then. Again, they would have been looking to create as much space as possible."

"But wouldn't they have done what you did?" Collison mused. "Wouldn't they have measured inside and out and discovered the discrepancy?"

"You're talking about the 1960s, Superintendent," Lazlo said with a sad smile, "an era when cowboy builders were ripping the heart and soul out of houses all over London. Most projects didn't even have a surveyor or architect in charge of them. No, my bet is that they would simply have looked at the plans on file at the local council, if indeed they even did that, and because this work had never been documented they never knew about it or worked out the true position."

"And what's the reason for the work now?" Collison asked, changing the subject.

"The flats became derelict because the council wouldn't spend money on them," Lazlo said bitterly. "Imagine! One of the most important buildings in the country and they just sat back and let it fall apart. Things became so bad that they had to evacuate it. The council just saw it as a huge white elephant, and they finally managed to offload it as a wreck to a Housing Association. It's in the process of being re-opened as housing for essential workers and as part of the process we're renovating the basement flats and checking out the various services that run through there. Needless to say, we weren't prepared for what we found."

"That's all very helpful, Mr Lazlo," Collison said absently. "Tell me, is there anyone at all you can think of who might be able to help throw any light on the identity of the deceased?"

"I'm instructed by the Housing Association," Lazlo replied. "I can't believe they'll be very much help, but I really don't know what else to suggest."

"I see," Collison said with a rising sense of despair. "Well, thank you very much, Mr Lazlo."

After showing the architect out of the building, Collison went in search of a strong coffee, dreading the coming phone calls importuning colleagues to release staff for a new murder enquiry team. His expression obviously told its own story, for as he met Bob Metcalfe coming the other way through some double swing doors the other stopped dead.

"Hello, guv," he said, "you look cheesed off. What's up?"

Collison allowed himself a wry smile.

"If you fancy a coffee I'll tell you all about it," he moaned theatrically. "I've got a body at the Isokon Building which has been dead for several decades, no apparent cause of death as yet, a crime scene that's been rendered useless by Polish builders, and a strong chance that we may never even be able to identify him."

He became aware that Metcalfe was staring at him rather oddly.

"Did you say the Isokon?" he asked.

# CHAPTER 9

"So just what the hell is this all about?" Tom Allen asked.

Collison drew breath. It was clear this situation would have to be handled very carefully, as indeed would Tom Allen. However, before he could launch into an explanation, Bob Metcalfe spoke up.

"Mr Collison has a new homicide enquiry, guv, which may be related to our own."

"Yes, you've already told me that," Allen snapped, "but I really don't see how."

"May I make it clear before we go any further," Collison broke in, "that Bob has not divulged any of the details of your enquiry to me. He simply reacted when I mentioned the Isokon Building and suggested we should talk."

Allen pinched the bridge of his nose. One of the many things he found irritating about Collison was the way he used words like 'divulged' in ordinary conversation.

"Simon, just because there's a coincidence doesn't mean there's a connection," he pointed out.

"I quite agree," Collison concurred. "Correlation is not causation, as they say. But I'm in a difficult position, you see. Without knowing exactly what the Isokon element is in your investigation I can't form a view as to whether it may be relevant or not."

"That's for me to say, anyway," Allen stated obstinately.

They all knew this was not true. It would be for the Detective Chief Superintendent in charge of the Murder Investigation Unit for West London (which, bizarrely, also covered much of North London) to take a view, and before doing so he might well seek the advice of the Assistant Commissioner (Crime), particularly as it involved a high profile rising star who was known to be the ACC's protégé.

"I'm sure none of us want to have to start going through proper channels unless and until it's clear that it's necessary," Collison said, carefully avoiding contradicting Allen's last statement.

"What does that mean?" Allen demanded, reaching, as he often did these days, for a non-existent cigarette.

"It means, Tom, that if you could take me into your confidence sufficiently to give me the whole story about the Isokon angle – nothing else, mind, just that – then we can at least have an informed discussion about it."

Allen stared at the table and scowled.

"After all, " Collison went on calmly, "it may well be that once I know whatever there is to know I'll be able to see at once that in fact there is no meaningful connection whatever. It may be just, as you say, a coincidence."

"All right," Allen conceded grudgingly. "Tell the Superintendent what he wants to know, Willis."

"Of course, guv."

"I'll have to give you a little bit of the background as well, sir," she said, turning to Collison, "or you won't be able fully to appreciate the context."

They all looked at Allen, who gestured at her helplessly to continue. Why was it that all his team were starting to sound like Collison?

"Our deceased is a Peter Howse," Karen said, moving on briskly. "He was the manager at Burgh House, where he also lived. In fact, it was his family home when he was young, and he was kept on as part of the deal when it was handed over to a charitable trust. He was found dead shortly after lunch two days ago, cause of death a blow to the head with a blunt instrument, almost certainly an old police truncheon which was found near the body; no fingerprints, I'm afraid."

"What was he, or anyone else for that matter, doing with a police truncheon?" Collison enquired.

"That's part of the Isokon angle, guv. At the time of his death Peter Howse was working on curating the next exhibition at the house, which was to have been on the Isokon Building. During the war the roof and basement were used for a variety of purposes including fire-watching but for a while there was also a temporary station there for police, mostly special constables, patrolling the streets and assisting with air raid measures. The truncheon had apparently been used by a Hampstead 'Special' during the blitz."

"So it was going to be an exhibit?"

"Yes, it looks like there was going to be a little stand called 'the Isokon at war", or something like that. Gas masks, sandbags, ration cards, that sort of thing."

"So if the murder weapon was lying around at the murder scene, that would suggest an opportunistic killer," Collison mused, "or even someone who killed suddenly and unexpectedly on instinct."

"Hang on, Simon," Allen cautioned him at once. "I said you could hear about the Isokon angle, not start working on the bloody case."

"Quite right," Collison acknowledged, holding up his hands. "Well, Karen, what else do we know about this Isokon exhibition?"

"Not a lot, I'm afraid," she said, "apart from the fact that he had a hell of a lot of papers he was working on. They filled his living room, more or less. Piles and piles of them."

"What sort of papers?" Collison asked at once. "From what period?"

"I'm afraid we can't really help you there, guv," Metcalfe cut in awkwardly. "We've been putting them all to one side without really looking at them."

Collison looked first surprised and then confused. He looked enquiringly at Tom Allen.

"We were naturally assuming," Allen explained with heavy irony, "that whoever bashed chummy on the head did at least have some valid motive for doing so, some *personal* motive, that is, rather than just a difference of opinion between architects or historians, or whatever. That's why I asked Bob and Karen to concentrate on his personal papers rather than getting bogged down in loads of stuff that wasn't relevant."

"I can see how you might have thought that," Collison replied, "you weren't to know that within a couple of days a homicide victim was going to get dragged out of the Isokon basement."

"Even now we do know that," Allen challenged him, "I still don't see there's any connection. From what I hear about your victim, he's been dead for decades. Are you suggesting that my victim was killed by the same person, now presumably at least a hundred years old?"

"No, of course not," Collison said. "What I am saying, though, is that you have a man murdered while working on an exhibition concerning the Isokon Building before and during the Second World War, and then a few days later a further murder discovered at the Isokon which seems to date from the same period. As coincidences go, that's a pretty long one, Tom."

"But coincidences do happen," Allen muttered doggedly.

Collison allowed a pause in the conversation to develop. Allen glanced at first Metcalfe and then Willis, but neither would meet his gaze. He was feeling increasingly that he was not going to win this argument, and his sense of irritation was growing, particularly without the calming effect of nicotine.

"I'll tell you what, Simon," he said suddenly. "If you want to recommend to the DCS that the two investigations are merged then I won't oppose it."

"Thank you," said a relieved Collison. "I'm sure it's the sensible course-"

"Hang on," Allen interrupted him. "I haven't finished yet."

"I'm sorry. Carry on."

"I won't oppose it, as I say, but I will recommend that the new investigation be brought under the same team as the existing one."

Collison hoped his consternation was not obvious to the others. Thus was not a development he had anticipated.

"After all," Allen went on, warming to his task, "we have a team in place, an incident room, officers who have already interviewed key witnesses ... It would be downright crazy to start all over again from scratch."

He smiled at Collison for the first time in the conversation, and put his hands together. It was as if he had said 'your move'.

"You must do as you think fit of course, Tom," Collison replied, largely because he couldn't think of anything else to say. "You make your recommendation, I'll make mine, and we'll let the DCS decide."

"So what do you think will happen?" Karen Willis asked Bob Metcalfe later as they stepped out of the Incident Room for a coffee.

"I'm intrigued," he admitted, as he held a door open for her. "The DCS is an old mate of Tom's; when he was a DCI, Tom was a DS and worked as his bag-carrier on quite a few cases. So if it was up to him he'd probably give Tom what he wanted."

"But will it be up to him, do you think?" she enquired, her heels clacking on the concrete floor of the stairwell.

He shrugged.

"In theory, yes, but I can't believe he won't even bounce it off the ACC, seeing how high profile Collison is at the moment."

"Well, we'll soon know," she concluded as they stepped out onto Rosslyn Hill, "I heard Allen arranging a meeting with the DCS just now."

"Now that is a meeting at which I'd like to be a fly on the wall," Metcalfe commented with a grim smile.

Had Bob Metcalfe indeed been a fly on the wall, he would have observed DCI Tom Allen and DCS Jim Morris sitting comfortably together in Morris's office like the old friends they were, but having a less than comfortable conversation.

"Dammit, Tom, I dislike the man as much as anybody," Morris was explaining. "He's been promoted too far too fast, he's got almost no proper investigative experience, and he's got all sorts of fancy ways."

"But?" Allen prompted him sourly.

Morris laughed, but there was no real humour in it.

"But," he acknowledged. "But he's been all over the press and the telly, he's obviously been fast-tracked for promotion to a senior rank – possibly a very senior rank – and he's the darling of the ACC. I hear on the grapevine that he wanted to put him in charge of the Crime Academy."

Allen looked startled.

"Commandant of the Academy? But that's a Chief Super's posting, isn't it?"

"It is indeed," Morris said grimly, "and usually an automatic stepping stone to Commander at the very least. Now perhaps you understand why we need to tread very carefully."

Allen nodded sullenly.

"So what are you going to do?" he asked abruptly.

"I am going to do what any good senior officer would do, Tom. I'm going to pass the buck. Or rather, I have passed the buck. I asked the ACC for his advice and he rang me a little while ago, just before you arrived, actually."

"And let me guess: he plumped for his little pet, Collison."

"He did," Morris said heavily. "The two investigations will be merged, with Collison as SIO."

"And did his Lord High bloody Almighty give any reasons as to why I'm being passed over?" Allen asked.

"Yes, two reasons, actually. The first is that he apparently promised Collison the next homicide that turned up at Hampstead nick. I didn't think much of that, as you can guess, since that's supposed to be my call, not his."

"Bloody typical," Allen grunted. "And the second?"

"The second one made a lot more sense, to be honest, having read the files. It's his sort of case, Tom, not yours. Professors, exhibitions, history, architecture ... need I go on? It's all the poncey intellectual stuff that he does well because he understands it, and we probably wouldn't."

"He also pointed out," Morris added wryly, "that your

report on that prison murder you were working on was overdue. Given the sensitivity of that case he was 'anxious for you to focus on that', as he put it."

"Damn!" Allen growled angrily. "I was going to finish that over the next week or so, but then this lot came along."

"Well, there you are, then. I hate to admit it, but he's got a point on that too. You're recommending closing an unsolved murder enquiry. It's vital that your report says exactly the right things. By the way, on that point, I think you and I had better work on it together, once you've got a draft ready."

"It seems to me," Allen observed bitterly, "that from now on I'm going to spend whatever is left of my career stepping aside for that posh bastard Collison, and then cleaning up after him when he makes a mess of things."

"Well, we all know what happened last time," Morris replied uncomfortably, "and to be fair, Tom, I think there were arguments on both sides."

Allen simmered visibly but did not respond.

"Talking of making a mess of things," Morris went on with a sudden smile, "that brings me to *my* main reason why I think this is a good idea."

Allen looked at him enquiringly.

"As I said, I've read the files," the DCS went on, "and it seems to me, Tom, that both of them are bloody tough nuts to crack. In one case you have a man murdered in an insecure building which any nutter off the street could have wandered into. In the other case you have a long dead corpse which it's going to be a struggle even to identify, let alone solve a murder which happened sixty or seventy years ago and must have been committed by someone who is now likely either to be pushing up the daisies or dribbling down his bib in an old people's home."

Allen reflected on this, and felt his mood improving.

"You mean ...?"

"I mean why don't we just sit back and watch Collison make a mess of it? After the enquiry has dragged on for a few months, doubtless at great expense, and has gone precisely nowhere, I can express my regrets to the ACC that the SIO doesn't seem to be up to the task, and suggest replacing him."

Allen thought about this idea and realised that he found it appealing.

"I hadn't thought about it like that, Jim," he admitted.

"Then think about this as well," Morris continued. "The Met wants to close Hampstead nick, as you know. They won't want a major murder investigation dragging on there indefinitely. So sonny boy will find himself under pressure for quick results from all sides, won't he? And speaking as an experienced officer with many successful investigations under your belt, Tom, how would you rate his chances of achieving any quick results?"

"Absolutely bloody zero!" Allen crowed. "My God, Jim, now I see why you're a DCS. There I was pissed off because I thought I was missing out on something, but now I see that in fact I've dodged a bullet."

"I think so," Morris concurred, nodding happily. "Now

let's get that report of yours finished toot sweet, shall we? That way, when the ACC does agree to replace the SIO, you'll be ever so available and, having worked on the case already, you'll be the obvious choice to replace Collison."

The DCS rubbed his hands delightedly.

"And you know what the best part of all this will be, Tom?"

"What?"

"Showing the ACC that he ruddy well isn't the only one who knows how to play office politics."

# CHAPTER 10

"OK, everyone, good morning," Allen called over the dying hum of conversation in the Incident Room. "For those of you who haven't met him before, I'd like to introduce DS Collison, who will be taking charge of this investigation as SIO."

There was a puzzled buzz around the room and Allen held both of his hands up to silence it.

"The DCS has decided that our enquiry will be merged with another one, one which DS Collison is already heading up. This new one seems to have one or two issues in common with the Burgh House case you've been dealing with. "

"So," he went on airily, "with no further ado I will love you and leave you. Simon, your meeting."

"Thank you, Tom," Collison replied levelly as Allen strode from the room. "Good morning, everyone. I'd like to make it clear before we go on that the team will remain exactly as it is now, with DI Metcalfe organising all day to day operations. In other words, we will be investigating two murders instead of one, but with no additional team members. I'm pressing the DCS to let us have a few extra bods, but for the time being we'll just have to manage."

There was a predictable grumble at this news, but he

ignored it and went on.

"You may have noticed," he continued, "that the briefing note on the new case, which we're calling the Isokon murder, is very short. There's a reason for that. We really don't know very much about it."

It was a poor attempt at a joke and nobody laughed, though Metcalfe, Willis and Desai smiled dutifully.

"We don't even know who the victim was, and that's obviously our first priority by the way, but we are assuming that people do not crawl naked into cabin trunks and die of their own accord, and thus that he was indeed murdered. Nor do we have a cause of death as yet, but we'll hopefully know more after we receive the post-mortem report."

He perched on the edge of a table, swinging his legs.

"So much for what we don't know," he said. "Those of you who have worked with me before will know that I'm a firm believer in identifying exactly what we do know, and working from there to try to come up with some workable hypotheses. And our starting point here is that a man who was working on curating an exhibition relating to the Isokon Building was murdered a few days before the long-dead body of a man who clearly died in suspicious circumstances was discovered at the Isokon Building. That's either one of the most bizarre coincidences in history, or there's a connection and we need to find out what it is."

"This is all in your briefing note, but I'll summarise for you anyway what we know about the case, and then I'll ask DS Willis to do the same for the Burgh House situation."

He crossed the room to stand by the white board. This had been altered overnight to leave a complete section free on one side of the board with the word "Isokon" as its heading.

He wrote 'who' and then 'how', each followed by a question mark. He did the same for 'where' and then turned to face the room.

"I know it's highly likely that our victim was killed at the scene," he explained, "but until we know that for sure I'd rather leave this blank. After all, if you carried a corpse into a block of flats inside a large suitcase today, would anyone challenge you? Probably not."

He turned back to the board and wrote 'when?'.

"As you'll see from the briefing note," he said, "we have some clear possibilities here. From what the architect knows of the history of the building, it's likely that the area where the body was found was bricked off sometime around 1937. That would fit with the initial forensic impression that the body had been dead for some decades. I'm afraid none of this is anywhere as precise or reliable as I'd like it to be, but I think it makes sense to adopt this as a working hypothesis unless and until it's disproved. Does anyone disagree?"

He looked round the room but unsurprisingly nobody was about to challenge the opinion of a Superintendent they had never met before. So he wrote '1937?' after 'when?' and then stood back to look at it.

"Well, that's about it for the moment, I'm afraid," he commented ruefully. "As I said, our immediate priority is to identify the victim. Since DI Metcalfe and DS Willis have been involved with the Burgh House case from its very beginning – indeed, DS Willis was actually there when the body was discovered – I don't think it makes sense to take them away from what they're already working on, so, Bob, I'd like you to free up DC Desai please, and she and I can take a crack at this together. Priya, can you see me when this meeting is over, please?"

Desai nodded, smiling.

"Ok, so much for the Isokon," Collison said briskly. "Karen, let's hear about Burgh House."

He went back to sit with Metcalfe while Karen crossed the room to the whiteboard holding some notes. Those male officers who were new to Hampstead police station, and one or two who were not, found themselves watching her legs as she did so, and thinking of something far removed from a suspicious death at Burgh House.

"Peter Howse was found dead early Monday afternoon," she reminded the team. "Cause of death was a blow to the back of the head from a police truncheon."

She smiled thinly.

"The truncheon in question is said to date from around the Second World War. I was attending Burgh House while off duty. So far as I am aware, I saw nothing of relevance to the enquiry and I'll just have to ask you to accept my word that I'm not the murderer."

Again, there a few smiles but no laughs.

"The layout of the House is as follows: a basement, which

has a café called the Buttery at the front, and accommodation for a married couple, the Baileys, at the rear. A ground floor which has rooms used for a variety of purposes, concerts, weddings, that sort of thing. The first floor, which is used for exhibitions, and the second floor which has two small suites of rooms: a large one, where the deceased lived and worked, and a much smaller set of room where a Professor Hugh Raffen came to work during the day; he lives elsewhere."

She looked down at her notes.

"Professor Raffen says that he heard three sets of footsteps come up and down the stairs to the second floor that morning. He believes that the first two were Howse, as he used to make a lot of noise on the stairs. If all that were true then it would imply that the third visitor, who he thinks came up at about 12.15, was the murderer, a hypothesis supported by the Professor having heard sounds of an argument immediately afterwards."

"If only it were that simple," Metcalfe observed mournfully.

"As DI Metcalfe says," Karen echoed, "if only it were that simple."

She sat on the table beside the whiteboard and crossed her legs. Again, a noticeable frisson ran through the male occupants of the room like an unexpected breeze rippling the leaves in a wood, an image reinforced by a spontaneous collective sigh. As if oblivious to the effect she had caused, she stared around the room and went on with her summary.

"Unfortunately Professor Raffen cannot be sure about

exactly what he heard, or indeed when. He admits that he didn't look at his watch when he heard the third set of footsteps, so 12.15 is only a guesstimate on his part. Also, we know that at least one occupant of the building was able to go up and down the stairs so quietly that nobody heard her doing so."

"Furthermore," she said grimly, "despite the fact that an exhibition of very valuable pictures was taking place – that's why I was there – the front door was left unsecured and unattended for at least the last two hours before lunch, and possibly longer, so access by a random stranger or indeed anyone else was entirely possible."

"The passing tramp," Collison murmured.

"I'm sorry, guv?" Willis queried.

"Nothing really," Collison said with a smile. "It's just that the so-called passing tramp is a regular device in Golden Age detective fiction. You know, a bit like the locked room."

He glanced round the room but saw only bewilderment.

"Go on, please," he urged her quickly.

"We have two possible suspects so far," she noted. "Mrs Bailey had been having an affair with the victim, Howse. Mr Bailey had found out about it and confronted Howse who promptly broke it off with Mrs Bailey. Both have been left understandably upset, albeit for different reasons. So, each of them has a motive, and both seem to have had opportunity to go upstairs that morning since their alibis are each other, and even then they're not exactly cast-iron."

She uncrossed her legs, slid off the table, and pointed to

the word 'nephew?' written on the board.

"It seems that the deceased had no close family except a nephew, who occasionally used to visit him at Burgh House. It is possible that the relationship had financial implications as well as family ones. We need to identify him, find him and interview him. The first has now been accomplished. We have the name Alan Howse from the victim's personal documents, plus an address in Hackney, but no telephone number, at least, not yet."

"I was planning to go over there this afternoon, guv," she proffered.

"Good," nodded Collison, "thank you, Karen."

He stood up and walked back to the front of the room, thinking as he did so.

"I'm open to suggestions as always," he said as he turned back to face the team, "but it seems to me our priorities on Burgh House are as follows. Number one, find the nephew, which is already being taken care of. Number two, put out an appeal for anyone who visited the building on the morning in question, particularly between about twelve and one, to come forward and be interviewed. Number three, try some house to house enquiries in the surrounding streets just on the off chance that somebody did see something or someone suspicious: a passing tramp, for example. Number four, check the Professor's alibi at the Flask public house; I don't doubt he's telling the truth, and I know he doesn't have a motive, but we may as well do our basic police work anyway. Number five, we need to go through every one of the files and papers in the victim's rooms with a fine tooth comb. Bob, you'd better have a think about the best way of going about that."

He looked around the room.

"I'm sure you've all had an opportunity to form your own preliminary views on the case," he proffered diplomatically, "but at the moment I see four different possible hypotheses. One, this was a *crime passionel* committed by one of the Baileys, in which case the other may well be covering up for them, or by both of them acting in collusion with each other. It's difficult at the moment to see how best to proceed with this line of enquiry other than by continuing to test their evidence. There's an obvious practical issue there, which is that if we want to interview them again then I think it has to be officially as suspects with lawyers present, and we don't want to start that process unless we have to."

He took a sip of his tea, which he had parked on the table earlier. It was now cold, and he grimaced.

"Two, our man was killed for some personal motive which was unconnected with his recent affair with Mrs Bailey. We need to find the nephew and eliminate him from our enquiries. We also need to find anyone we can who can tell us more about Howse's private life. From what we know already, he clearly had … er, all the usual instincts, shall we say?"

"Three, what DCI Allen tends to refer to as 'a random nutter', but for which I prefer the term 'passing tramp'.

Different phrases for the same possibility. How likely is it? Not very, I'd say, not least because the motive for such an attack is usually theft, particularly being discovered in the course of stealing something, and we know that the deceased's money and credit cards had apparently not been disturbed. Of course, it's always possible that the attacker was startled to find someone in the room, struck him instinctively and then panicked and ran, I suppose ..."

He looked quizzically at Metcalfe, who nodded absently and jotted down a note.

"No," he went on more decidedly. "It really doesn't feel right to me. Why go all the way up to the second floor, for a start? But it's a possibility because of that wretched unlocked door and, like all possibilities, we have to do everything we can to eliminate it. Of course, if only they'd had their bloody CCTV cameras switched on and recording then we wouldn't be put to all this trouble."

He stopped and sighed. The sheer scale of the case was beginning to cast a shade over the glow of his initial excitement. It was as though some invisible hand was silently but determinedly putting every possible obstacle in the path of those seeking the truth.

"Four, is of course the Isokon angle, which has only just sprung into view. If our victim was killed because of some connection with the Isokon Building, then what on earth could it have been? It takes a pretty powerful motive for murder to survive for seventy or eighty years. Could Howse's family have been involved in some way with the earlier murder, and Howse himself the victim of some long delayed act of revenge? That seems fanciful, but I'm struggling here. Any thoughts?"

"He may have discovered something about the Isokon during his research, sir," Desai suggested. "Something that somebody wanted kept quiet."

"Quite right, Priya," Collison acknowledged. "Though it's difficult to imagine something that happened so long ago being worth killing someone today. But, yes, let's make a note of that."

He looked around the room again, but it was clear that no further ideas would be forthcoming.

"Alright, thank you, everyone. I'll leave it to DI Metcalfe to give out your individual tasks. Priya, can you come to my office in ten minutes, please?"

He left the room and went upstairs to his office. Given the station's long-delayed closure, the corridor had the feel of a bankrupt hotel awaiting the arrival of the auctioneers. Every room was empty except two: his own and Tom Allen's.

As if on cue, Allen emerged from his office carrying a couple of large ring-binders.

"Ah, there you are," the latter hailed him heartily. "Best of luck with the case. I'm off to write my report on the Gary Clarke murder. Nasty business, that."

They both knew that the death of Gary Clarke was a sensitive issue. Allen's implied criticism lay heavy in the air like a whiff of stale cigarette smoke.

"I'm glad I've caught you, Tom," Collison said calmly.

"There's something I wanted to mention. Have you got a minute?"

He opened the door of his own office and ushered the other man inside. Allen dumped his files on one of the chairs and sat down cheerfully on another. Collison did not sit at the desk but instead went to window and then turned back to face into the room, leaning slightly against the window sill for support. It was not very comfortable but that didn't matter, he thought; this need not take long.

"Tom," he said abruptly, "I know that in the past I worked for you, and I hope you know that I'm very grateful for all the help and guidance you gave me."

He paused but Allen sat impassively and said nothing. All right, Collison thought, so he wasn't going to make this easy. Well, damn him then. He had something to say, and say it he would.

"But I really must ask," he went on, "to show me the respect due to my rank when junior officers are present."

He felt stupidly nervous. He realised that Allen would think he was making himself look ridiculous, but there was no going back now. He fought to control his breathing.

"What on earth do you mean?" Allen queried, with what seemed like genuine bewilderment.

"What I mean is this. When we are alone together I am very happy for you to call me 'Simon', but not when junior officers are present. It's not right, Tom, and you know it. You've been a copper a lot longer than me, after all."

"So this is all about me having to call you 'sir', is it?" Allen demanded with a smile. "Oh, Simon, I always thought you were a bit of a prig, but has it really come to this?"

"The Met is a police service," Collison replied, realising to his dismay that this really did sound rather priggish, "and within the service there is a hierarchy. There are rules, Tom, and you know it. I didn't make them, but it's in everybody's interests that they be followed."

"Sometimes it's harder than others," Allen responded wryly. "I have been a copper a lot longer than you – you said it yourself. I will obviously have to get used to your meteoric career."

He stood up.

"Well, I'm glad we've had this little chat, sir," he said brightly. "I look forward to watching you exercise command in the future."

"Oh, don't be silly, Tom," Collison said awkwardly. "Of course I don't expect you to call me 'sir'. Why not just use 'guv' like everybody else?"

"You know," Allen said conversationally, "I reserve 'guv' for guvnors I admire and respect. All in all, I think you're much more of a 'sir', Simon."

With that, DCI Allen picked up his files, nodded calmly but contemptuously, and left the room.

# CHAPTER 11

Peter Collins and Karen Willis lived in Christchurch Hill, a road which took its name from the neighbouring church. It was in that part of Hampstead known as New End; 'new' by Hampstead standards that is, since it dated from only the eighteenth century.

When Bob Metcalfe rang the bell of their flat he was in a state of high anxiety and nervous anticipation. He and Karen had been in love almost from their first meeting, but it had taken time for them to confess this to themselves, and then to each other. First there was the mutual hesitancy brought about by Karen already being part of an established relationship. Then there was the awkwardness of working together on a daily basis as close colleagues. Finally, as Bob had been the first to admit, there was sheer disbelief on his part that anyone as intelligent, attractive and glamorous as her might possibly be interested in anyone like him.

Then Peter had fallen ill, seriously ill, before they could go public with their news, and they had agreed to carry the secret with them until he was better. Then, after he had recovered, Karen had deemed a period of convalescence advisable, declaring that Peter, whom Bob liked and respected, was still not strong enough to handle such a traumatic blow, and fearing that the shock might spark a relapse.

Bob had chafed at the bit but acquiesced in her wishes, but suddenly out of a clear blue sky had received a cryptic text message from her while she was on leave after their last investigation had closed. 'Peter knows'. He had waited for the expected call, but none came, and when he tried calling her, her phone was switched off. Quickly, impatience turned into concern, and concern morphed into an alarm bordering on obsession. Had she had an attack of guilt? Had she changed her mind, but was too distraught to tell him? It seemed the likeliest explanation. Then work had closed around them again, literally from the moment of their next meeting, when she had greeted him so unexpectedly at the crime scene at Burgh House.

Now a summons to a drink with them both at their flat. What did it mean? What *could* it mean but that she now regretted the whole affair (though 'affair' was hardly the right word, since they had remained almost ostentatiously chaste) and needed Peter's moral support to break it to him? After all, how could 'Peter know'? They had been so careful not to arouse any suspicions. No, she must have told him.

She opened the door, looking as nervous as he felt, and kissed him quickly and awkwardly on the cheek. He had last visited the flat in very different circumstances, when Peter had been in the full grip of his illness, and Metcalfe and Collison had joined together with Karen to assist her with a controversial course of therapy. Now as he came into the living room he saw Peter Collins sitting very upright in an armchair, apparently fully recovered.

"Bob," he called across the room, standing up. "How good to see you again."

He stretched out his hand and they shook, each looking into the other's eyes for a moment but seeing only a mirror of their own insecurity.

"Glass of wine, Bob?" Karen asked.

"Yes, please," he replied, seeing that the bottle on the table was already half empty.

"Sit down, won't you?" Peter said, gesturing vaguely towards the sofa.

"Bob," he went on while Karen was pouring wine into various glasses, "Karen told me what you and Simon Collison did for me while I was ill. I don't actually remember much of it myself, but you didn't have to get involved, and you both risked getting into trouble because of it, so I'm very grateful."

Metcalfe nodded awkwardly, unable to think of anything to say in reply.

"I also told him," Karen said quickly, "about you and me, Bob. I explained that it was something that, well, just happened, that's all."

"Actually, that's not true," Peter cut in. "She didn't tell me, Bob. I guessed."

She opened her mouth to speak but Peter raised up a hand from the arm of his chair with a smile.

"Much better if we're all honest with each other," he

observed. "Karen didn't break your confidence, Bob. It's important you should know that."

"Thank you," Metcalfe said, as if in a daze. This whole scene seemed to be happening to somebody else, as though he was watching actors play it out on stage.

As if in furtherance of this image, there was now a highly theatrical pause. Peter continued to smile indulgently at Karen. She looked expectantly at him. Metcalfe looked from one to the other, sure that something was supposed to come next, and wondering what it might be. Peter Collins became conscious that Karen's gaze was becoming beseeching rather than expectant, and seemed to come to with a start.

"Yes, well ...," he began, and then stopped.

"Bob," Karen said hesitantly. "Peter has an idea as to how we might all be able to ... move forward, as it were. Please understand, it's just an idea. He, well *we* actually, just wanted to know how you might react to it."

"OK," Metcalfe said slowly, "what is it?"

Karen looked at Peter Collins again. He gripped the arms of his chair as if for support, and began to talk.

"I suppose you might have wondered," he said conversationally, "how a lowly lecturer manages to live in a nice flat in an expensive part of London."

"Not really," Bob responded. "After all, it's none of my business."

"Well actually, it might be," Collins relied rather cryptically, "or rather, I'd like to make it your business, because it bears directly on what I'd like to talk to you about."

"Alright."

"Well, I'm an orphan. My parents both died when I was ten – in a car crash actually. I was brought up by one of my aunts, my mother's sister. Her family – my mother's I mean – were pretty well off. My grandfather had built up an electrical company and he sold it off when he retired. He put quite a lot of that money in trust for me, and that's what I live on, mostly. That's how I can afford this place, for example. Apparently there were some patents too, which he kept as they didn't seem worth very much at the time. But it turns out that they are something to do with a technology which can be used in mobile phones, and my grandfather's trustees have just sold them for rather a lot of money."

He paused and took a sip at his drink, gazing reflectively out of the window.

"By coincidence, just as the sale of the technology rights was being finalised, my aunt died. It was all a bit of a shock, as she hadn't seemed to be ill, but there you are. The result is that, since she left everything to me in her will and my grandmother died some time ago, I'm the only remaining beneficiary of Grandfather's trust – including all this new money that's now coming in."

"Well, I'm very happy for you, of course," said Metcalfe, "but I don't see how any of this concerns me, Peter."

"Well, it struck me that this was one of life's little ironies," Peter continued with what seemed a rather bitter little smile, "or rather, one of life's bloody big ironies."

"In what way?" Metcalfe asked.

"I mean that at the same time as I am handed a very great deal of money, enough to live very comfortably on for the rest of my life, something gets taken away from me which is worth more than all the money in the world, something which I would gladly give up all my worldly possession for if there any chance at all of keeping it."

He grimaced as if embarrassed at such a display of feeling, and Karen said "oh, Peter" quietly in the background.

"I don't remember very much about my parents," Collins said, as if setting off down a totally new path. "Strange that, how memories fade, don't you find? I have quite strong memories of things that happened at school when I was eight or nine, but not about what I did at home with my parents. Perhaps it has something to do with the fact that I wasn't very happy at school, whereas I was at home."

"I remember, though, that they used to give dinner parties all the time. Every weekend they'd be either off at a friend's house for dinner or entertaining themselves. Not just dinner parties, either. Lunches, drinks parties, all sorts of things ..."

He tailed off and realised that the others were looking at him in confusion and with something like concern.

"Sorry," he said, "I'm rambling, aren't I? What I meant to say is that I distinctly remember one thing in particular about those days, something I didn't really understand at the time -because I was so young, I suppose – but which I do now. You see, there was one couple who used to come that wasn't a couple at all. It was three people, not two."

"How do you mean?" Metcalfe enquired, puzzled.

"What Peter means," Karen broke in, as if anxious to put Collins out of his misery, "is that this couple had a woman who lived with them. She was only about thirty, but her husband had died very young and everyone said how kind this couple were to take her into their home and look after her."

"My mother used to complain like anything," Peter commented, "because it used to put her numbers out at dinner. I used to get roped in to make everything come out evenly around the table. They went everywhere as a threesome, you see, on holiday, out to dinner, to the theatre, everything. It was only later that I realised that they must have been a ménage à trois."

Metcalfe gaped. He looked at Karen, but she had gone red and was staring at the Chinese rug.

"What I mean is," Collins went on, launching himself desperately into the unwelcoming silence, "is that I could afford to buy us all a house in Hampstead, a big house, a really big house. God, we could have a whole floor each if we wanted to. And we could all live there ... together, as it were."

He finished and looked at the others for some sign of reaction. In Karen he read awkwardness. In Bob Metcalfe, shock. Gloomily, he took a long drink of wine.

"Whose idea was this?" Metcalfe asked quietly.

He looked at Karen but she could not meet his gaze.

"Oh, Bob," she began, but Peter stopped her.

"It's my idea," he stated firmly. "Entirely mine. Karen had nothing to do with it, except that I suggested it to her and she agreed that I could put it to you to gauge your reaction. I do realise that it's completely off the wall, but I was hoping that you'd at least agree to think about it."

Metcalfe continued to look at Karen. Softy, he called her name and she looked up, her eyes brimming with tears.

"I need to know where you stand on this," he said, feeling very lost. "I mean, are things still the same between us?"

She nodded. Then she held out her hand to Collins for a large white handkerchief, with which she blew her nose very vigorously.

"I'm so sorry," she said briskly after a little pause. "This is all my fault."

"No it isn't," Collins cried at once. "It's my idea, Karen, you know it is."

"Yes, but it's me being cowardly, isn't it?" she countered fiercely. "It's me trying to see a way of not hurting people, and pretending that everything can somehow go on being the same, and it can't, can it? Because I've bloody well screwed things up, and hurt the only two people I care about."

Both men looked at her with concern. Her pain was so obvious that it cut them both to the quick.

"If it's anyone's fault, it's mine," Metcalfe interjected. "I knew you and Peter were very happy together and I should have kept my mouth shut. Everything would have been alright if I hadn't spoken up. I'm sorry, both of you; I had no right to interfere in your lives like this."

"Oh, do shut up, Bob" she said with a sad little smile. "I knew how you felt long before you said anything to me, and I certainly knew how I felt."

To fill the pregnant pause which now ensued, she got up and poured the last of the wine into their glasses.

"I know what you want to know, Bob," she said calmly as she sat down again, "and the answer is yes. I will leave Peter and go away with you – come and live with you, if that's what you want. Peter knows that. I haven't changed my mind. I just agreed to him putting this crazy idea forward because I thought he deserved every chance ..."

"That's OK," Metcalfe assured her. "It's OK, Karen, please don't be upset."

"Upset?" she snorted. "You make it sound like I've spilt wine on the rug. No! I've already broken the heart of one thoroughly decent man, and now I've deeply offended another – and both of them did nothing wrong except falling in love with me. It's me who should apologise, me who should beg forgiveness, not either of you. You're just victims, both of you, all because I'm in a situation I can't handle."

There was another long pause during which everyone glanced dismally from one to another. A strong sense of unreality hung over the room, as if in the immediate aftermath of car crash.

"So, let me get this straight," Metcalfe said at length,

struggling to find his bearings. "If I say no to this idea, Karen, then you and I are still where we were when last we had a proper chance to discuss it – you'll leave Peter and we'll make a life together?"

Silently, she nodded vigorously.

"Hopeless," Collins murmured, leaning back in his chair and gazing at the ceiling, "bloody hopeless."

"Peter," Metcalfe began awkwardly.

"Don't concern yourself, old man," Collins replied gently, dropping naturally into the Lord Peter Wimsey mannerisms in which he took refuge in times of stress, "it don't signify, it really don't."

"I really am sorry about all this," Metcalfe tried to explain. "It never occurred to me how much pain I'd be causing."

"And it never occurred to me, old fruit," Collins said, lowering his gaze from the ceiling and fixing it benignly on Metcalfe's tortured features, "just how bally stupid my idea was until I trotted it out just now, don't you know?"

Karen Willis crossed the room, knelt by his chair and seized his left hand folornly in both of hers.

"Harriett," he tried to say jauntily as black despair overwhelmed him, but then his voice faltered.

# CHAPTER 12

The next morning found Collison, Metcalfe and Willis closeted upstairs in the former's office.

"Is it just me, guv," Metcalfe was asking, "or is this investigation just hugely complex? It's almost as though you don't know where to start. There are so many different angles."

"It's not you being fanciful, Bob," Collison replied gloomily. "I've been wrestling with that very point – the complexity of it – all night. In fact, I didn't get much sleep."

Abruptly, he brought his fingers down sharply on the desk, like a call to action.

"But that sort of thinking will get us nowhere," he went on. "It's just a matter of identifying the different lines of enquiry and then breaking each one down into a small number of manageable tasks. We made a start on that yesterday, so let's review where we are. Karen?"

"I've found the nephew, guv, and had a quick chat over the phone. He's coming in today to give a formal statement, but he sounds like a non-starter. He says that he has visited his uncle at Burgh House from time to time, but not that often as they don't get on. The deceased was the main trustee of a small family settlement – the other was the family solicitor – and it sounds like Alan Howse was the only beneficiary, so they had to see each other about financial matters. But it sounds like that's as far as it went. Once again, our victim isn't scoring highly as a warm and cuddly individual."

"Well, he may be able to give us some background on his uncle's private life, anyway," Collison said, "and if nothing else we should be able to eliminate him from our enquiries, and that's useful."

He ticked off a point on his action list.

"Now, what about the Isokon papers at Burgh House?" he asked.

"There's an awful lot of it, guv," Bob commented unhelpfully. "To tell the truth, I'm not sure where to begin."

"Excuse me, sir," Karen interjected, "but I've been thinking about that."

"Go on," he nodded.

"Well, I had a chat with Peter about it. I didn't tell him anything about the case, of course, nothing that he didn't already know, anyway, just the nature of the task which was facing us. He reckoned that if Peter Howse was doing a proper job as an archivist, and there's nothing to suggest that he wasn't, then he'd be listing the documents as he came across them, and then cross-referencing for whatever sort of cataloguing system he'd come up with."

"Sounds reasonable," Collison agreed. "So what do we do? Look for the list?"

"Exactly, guv. We know from the Professor that Howse

had pretty much completed the job. When Bob and I first looked at the task it seemed almost hopeless. But that's because we were assuming that the boxes of documents were all waiting to be gone through. What if we were wrong, and the boxes are actually part of the cataloguing system?"

"You mean," Metcalfe said thoughtfully, "that instead of the documents having just come in and waiting to be read, they've *been* read, and have been sorted into some kind of order?"

"Exactly," she repeated. "It should be easy enough to check. They key is the master list. If we find that, and if Peter's right, then it should be indexed with the names, or perhaps numbers, of different boxes."

"God, let's hope he's right," Collison said with feeling. "Alright, Karen, I think you'd better get on that today. Somebody else can take the nephew's statement; it sounds as though it's pretty much routine anyway. Just get them formally to ask him where he was on the morning in question, when he last saw his uncle, all that sort of thing."

"OK, guv. Can I take someone along to help? It's still going to be a big job."

"Yes, by all means, take two or three if you like. I can't see that there's much else for them to do is there, Bob?"

"There's all the house to house stuff, guv," Bob reminded him a little huffily.

"Mm," Collison said reflectively, "I suppose so. To be honest, Bob, I'm not really expecting anything to come of that. If it wasn't for that wretched open door I wouldn't take the passing tramp idea very seriously, but as it is we have to at least go through the motions. The papers are important, though, so you'll just have to juggle responsibilities as best you can."

"What about Priya, guv?" he asked without much hope.

"No chance," Collison rebuffed him firmly, "she's with me on the Isokon victim. In fact, we really need a whole team just on that, but my pleas to the DCS for more bodies seem to be falling on deaf ears."

"Well," Metcalfe said ruefully, "if you wanted to pick one person who could do the work of a whole team then you couldn't do better than Priya. She's bloody good."

"I know she is," Collison assured him, "that's why I chose her."

"What about the Isokon, guv?" Willis asked. "I mean, are you sure there has to be a connection? Coincidences do happen, after all."

Collison gave a short laugh.

"Believe me, I spent a lot of time thinking about that last night, Karen. I know we've discussed synchronicity in the past."

"That's my point, guv," she said eagerly. "Jung said that coincidence is all around us but that most of the time we don't realise it. We only notice when it becomes extreme."

"He went rather further than that, if you remember," Collison reminded her drily. "He put forward a hypothesis that human will, or perhaps unconscious desire, could play a part in bringing it about. Coincidence as wish fulfilment, if you like. That's what I got to wondering about last night."

"How do you mean, guv?" asked Metcalfe, who always found himself growing uncomfortable when the others started behaving as if they were in a university tutorial.

"Well, I freely admit that I wanted another homicide to investigate, yes and quickly too before the ACC had a chance to ship me off to some other posting. What if that desire somehow triggered the discovery of the body at the Isokon? Or suppose it's inducing me to give more meaning to it than it really merits? In other words, am I seeing it as a connection because that's the way I want it to be, rather than because it really is? DCI Allen thought it was a coincidence, and he has a nasty habit of being proved right."

"A very long one if so, as you said yourself, guv," Metcalfe maintained.

"Agreed absolutely," Collison concurred, "but just because something is very improbable doesn't mean that it can't happen. At the back of my mind there's this nagging fear that I'm leading us all up the garden path. After all, we have two strong suspects for the Burgh House killing. If I'm right about the Isokon connection then they can't possibly have done it; their motive falls away."

"Oh no it doesn't," Bob countered stoutly. "It doesn't mean that the affair never happened, or that Howse's rejection of the woman never happened. Of course they have a motive, regardless of whether or not they did it."

Collison thought for a moment.

"Sound common sense, as ever, Bob," he said with a smile,

"and well done. You've actually developed my thinking on the Isokon angle, though I'm not sure it helps a lot."

"How?" Metcalfe asked blankly.

"You've made me realise that there are two possibilities I hadn't considered. One: there is an Isokon connection but it's not of a nature to provide a motive for modern day murder at Burgh House. Two: there is, but nobody acted upon it. In either case, the Baileys are still in the frame."

"Oh dear," Willis said drily.

Yet as the meeting broke up, her thoughts were already elsewhere. There was a young Constable in the Incident Room on secondment from uniform who was not expected to show any great promise as a detective, but who looked as though he might come in very useful for box carrying and stacking purposes. She hurried away on busily clacking heels to secure his services before Metcalfe could send him out to knock on doors in Flask Walk.

Collison moved onto new business, ringing down for Priya Desai, who arrived looking briskly efficient in trim black slacks and sweater. He waved to her to sit down.

"Hi, Priya, any luck?" he ventured without much hope.

"Actually yes, sir," she replied brightly, "after a fashion, anyway. After I'd searched on the Isokon and Lawn Road for a while I came across the name of a bloke called Tim Murfitt who's writing a book on the history of the building. I've had a quick chat with him already. It seems he was miffed with Peter Howse because he offered his help with the exhibition and Howse turned him down flat."

"Hardly a motive for murder," Collison observed with a smile.

"No, but it gels with Howse having been a difficult man to deal with," Desai replied, having apparently taken his answer seriously.

"Well, it sounds like he could be just the man we need to speak to, anyway, so well done for finding him, Priya. After all, our chances of finding anyone who was actually living or working at the place in the 1930s are pretty slim."

"You're right, guv, I've been checking."

She consulted her notes.

"Wells Coates, the architect, died way back in 1958. Jack Pritchard, the sort of brains behind it, who I understand from Murfitt ended up running the building, died in 1992. The same is true of everyone else too. When he started researching his book he couldn't find anyone who could help him with any sort of first-hand account."

"So what was he working from, then?" Collison asked.

"He started off by using publicly available sources like old newspaper articles, but of course they only took him so far. Then he had a stroke of luck. One of Jack Pritchard's descendants gave him a load of old files he found in a garage, or an attic or something, which turned out to be all the original papers from when he was building the place and then running it."

"Was there a list of residents?" Collison enquired hungrily.

"I asked him that and he said yes, sort of. It seems the

residents of each flat could change frequently as some people just passed through for a few months. Apparently that was particularly so during the war, because people were getting bombed out of their homes, and getting posted away and so forth. But he says it is possible to put together a list of residents for each flat from what he's got. In fact, he's done it. It's all handwritten as part of his research notes, but he says he can bring in it for us to copy."

"I think we need to look through everything he's got, Priya, not just the list he's extracted. After all, we have no real idea what we're looking for."

"By 'we', guv, I assume you mean me?" she asked pointedly.

"Yes, at the moment anyway," he responded apologetically. "To tell you the truth, Priya, there's nobody else on the team I could really trust with this – apart from Willis or Metcalfe of course, and they're already busy with other stuff. I need someone who's intelligent enough to spot when something maybe relevant, or even important."

"Flattery will get you everywhere, sir," she commented archly.

A sudden smile transformed her face, making her eyes look black and sparkly. He realised with a start that this was a very attractive woman sitting in front of him. Strange that he had not noticed it before.

"Let's suppose that Murfitt's list is accurate and complete," he said slowly, forcing himself to concentrate on the case. "How should we proceed?"

"I'd say a good first step would be to cross-index for anyone reported missing," she suggested after a moment's thought.

"Agreed, though we need to be careful. Everything back in those days was kept on card index files and there's no guarantee that they were all indexed similarly or computerised properly later. Do you know the story about the Yorkshire Ripper case?"

She nodded; everyone heard that one during training. Because a hammer which the serial killer had been carrying when arrested for an earlier incident had been categorised as 'builder's tools' a key connection had been missed. Computerisation had made such mistakes less likely, though they still happened.

"Of course, there's nothing to say that our body was a resident, guv," she pointed out. "It could even be that someone who wanted to dispose of a body knew the builders who were doing the work and had the trunk slipped into the basement at the time."

"Yes, I thought about that too," Collison said gloomily. "That would leave us really up the creek because we'd have absolutely no way of trying to trace the guilty party. Why, it might even be someone who just knew about the works taking pace, carried the trunk in there one day bold as brass and dumped it. It's quite possible that nobody would even have challenged them, since we know that residents were coming and going all the time, and it would have been standard practice to have your trunk delivered in advance."

"I've considered that too," Priya countered, "but I think it's unlikely."

"Oh? Why is that?"

"Well, think it through, guv. The builders were about to brick off an area of the basement. No matter how cussed they were, they wouldn't just deliberately brick up somebody's luggage, would they? They would have asked about it, or even moved it to an area which was going to remain accessible. So, whichever way you look at it, whoever did the works had to be involved."

"You're right of course," he admitted. "I should have thought of that. Not that it takes us very much further."

"It's a lead," Desai persisted. "Maybe a very difficult one to follow up, but a lead nonetheless. After all, it may be possible to tell from Murfitt's papers who did the works."

"It should be," he nodded, "but anyone who was swinging a sledgehammer in 1937 is unlikely still to be around to be interviewed, so I'm not sure where it takes us."

Priya Desai frowned gently, as if disapproving of such negative thoughts.

"I'll ask Murfitt if we can go through his papers, then," she concluded, shutting her notebook. "Would you like me to bring him in for a chat, guv?"

"Yes, please do, Priya. I think we need to soak up all the background we can."

"That's good," she replied with another one of those sudden sparkly smiles, "because I've already asked him in for 2.30."

# CHAPTER 13

There was an awkward silence between Willis and Metcalfe as they picked their way up Rosslyn Hill through the wandering shoppers and mothers with prams towards Flask Walk. It was only as they turned right and went past the second-hand bookshop that they were able to walk level with each other for more than a second or two.

"I'm so sorry about last night, Bob," she said at once. "Somehow when Peter first laid out the idea to me he made it sound almost reasonable. It wasn't until I saw the look on your face that I realised just how crazy it really was."

She slipped her hand through his arm, just for a moment, but he felt a sudden thrill nonetheless. It was as if she had said 'I belong to you, and only you'.

"Actually," he said wryly, "it *is* almost reasonable. After all, everyone would get some or most of what they want. That's Utility-something, isn't it? The greatest good for the greatest number ...?"

"Utilitarianism," she prompted him. "Yes, I remember that from University."

"Well then," he said as they went past the Flask, "there you are, you see; not really crazy at all."

"Oh, Bob," she said fondly. "Anyway, thank you for

behaving so well. Most men would have blown a fuse and walked out."

"That would hardly have been very fair, would it?" he replied. "Peter was clearly very unhappy, and that's mostly my fault, no matter how decent he tries to be about it. If I'd kept my nose out of your private life then you'd both still be very happy together, instead of which he's now got this huge black cloud hanging over his head."

"I would still have felt what I did when I met you and got to know you," she countered, looking straight ahead as they walked, "and by the way, I seem to remember that it was me who made the first move, not you. In that restaurant just back there, wasn't it?"

She jerked a thumb over her right shoulder in the direction of La Cage Imaginaire.

"It was," he concurred, "as if I could forget ..."

She squeezed his arm briefly again before they had to move into single file on the raised narrow pavement to allow some Chinese tourists to pass. They seemed to be following some sort of pre-planned trail, as they were gazing at pieces of paper and looking bewildered. It occurred to Willis that this could provide a fitting image for the afternoon which they had ahead of them.

"Isn't that whatshisname, Evans, standing outside Burgh House?" Metcalfe asked suddenly.

"It is indeed," she replied, "I thought he had the ideal sort of physique for humping boxes of documents around, so I grabbed him to work with us."

"What's wrong with my physique, then?" he asked only half humorously as they approached the sturdy form of Constable Evans.

"Nothing at all, but there are those who are made for carrying boxes, and those who are made for examining their contents. I was assuming that we would both wish to fall into the latter category."

"Good point," he conceded, "and well done."

"His name is Tim," she hissed, as they were now very close.

"Hello, Tim," Metcalfe said easily.

"Guv," Evans nodded in greeting.

"Timothy Evans: that's an interesting name for a murder investigation," Metcalfe observed playfully.

Evans looked blank.

"Not with you, guv."

"Never mind," Metcalfe said sadly. "Come on, let's go in and get to work."

The house had been closed since the murder had been discovered, and Willis pulled out a key with a scene of crime tag dangling from it with which to unlock the front door. The hall was dark as it received little natural light. Flicking the light switch revealed police tape still obstructing the way up the stairs. Metcalfe pulled off one end and the refastened it behind them as they went up.

The deceased's living room was still piled with boxes, although on a previous visit Metcalfe and Willis had attempted to go through them to ascertain which papers were of a personal nature. Perhaps fortunately, in view of the direction the investigation now seemed to be taking, the answer had been none, a couple of folders in the bottom of a cupboard seeming to have done service for Peter Howse's private filing needs.

Metcalfe tugged a couple of chairs into place around the small dining table.

"DS Willis and I will sit here," he decided, taking off his jacket and draping it over the back of his seat. "Tim, you bring us the boxes one at a time. Make a note of whatever names or numbers are written on each. We will go through the contents of each and make a list of what is there. When we're finished with each box, you can take it and put it in the bedroom through there. That way we'll know exactly which boxes we've dealt with and which we haven't."

"Fair enough, guv," Evans said resignedly. He had already been in the police force long enough to know that murder enquiries were usually far from the glamorous affairs they were portrayed as being on television.

"What are we looking for, by the way?" he asked.

"Initially," Willis answered, turning through the pages of a ring binder which she had found in a drawer of the desk, "we're looking for some sort of master list. It may not exist, but we're hoping that it does. If Howse was nearly finished his work, and had been archiving things properly, then it should be here somewhere."

"Unless of course the murderer nicked it, sarge," Evans suggested brightly.

"Very funny," Metcalfe muttered uncomfortably. It hadn't occurred to him that perhaps it was the master list itself which the killer had been after.

"But fortunately not," Willis said, thumbing back to the beginning of the folder. "I think this is it. How easy was that?"

"Really?" Metcalfe asked, coming to peer over her shoulder.

Without warning he inhaled the smell of her hair, shot through with hints of perfume. For a moment a murder investigation in Hampstead seemed a very long way away.

"Yep," she confirmed confidently, "this is it all right. Look, the list itself is here at the front and then there's a section for each box listing its contents. Some have only two or three entries, while others have a dozen or so."

"Thank God for that," Metcalfe said with feeling. "That makes life so much easier. All we have to do is to check at the end whether there are any boxes which he hadn't got around to. If that's the case, then they'll be here in the room but won't appear in the folder."

"OK, Tim," Willis said briskly, "let's get started. How about that one over there?"

Back at Hampstead police station, Collison and Desai were hearing about the Isokon Building in mind-numbing detail from Tim Murfitt, an unkempt individual whose general untidiness was matched only by his unbounded enthusiasm.

"So, how do you come to have Jack Pritchard's papers," Collison asked, "and what exactly do they comprise?"

"Well, at the time Jack Pritchard died, it was very sad because the Isokon had been terribly neglected by the local authority and nobody was very interested in it," Murfitt explained. "Fortunately, his children decided to hang onto all his papers. When I came calling I think they were actually quite relieved to be able to get rid of them with a clear conscience."

"I'm surprised some university didn't want them," Desai observed.

"Yes, you would think that, wouldn't you?" Murfitt replied. "But, as I say, the flats had fallen into disrepair and it was politically inconvenient to say how hugely significant they were from an architectural point of view because nobody wanted to have to pay to restore them. In fact, there were a lot of people, even people who lived right here in Hampstead, who had never even heard of the Isokon."

"So, you got hold of his papers," Collison urged gently, anxious to move the conversation along, "but what are they precisely?"

"Nothing personal or private really," Murfitt said with evident disappointment, "which is a shame, because he knew some hugely important people, including of course all the Bauhaus movement. There are a few letters left, that's all. No, most of it is day to day stuff from the period when he was managing the flats, which would have been right up to 1968, when they were sold to the New Statesman."

"So that would include the period just before the War?" Collison queried.

"Yes, certainly. In fact, a lot of the most interesting stuff is from that period," Murfitt enthused. "Pritchard was very prominent in getting Jews and anti-Nazi refugees to England, and sometimes, as with Gropius, onwards to America."

"So, what would that have meant for the pattern of occupancy of the flats?" Collison asked, as Desai scribbled notes.

"It became different, certainly. He tried to provide flats for refugees, often free of charge, when they became available between lettings. He also sometimes asked people to provide short term access to their flats while they were away."

"And would there be any record of all this activity?"

"Oh yes, Jack was very meticulous. He kept a note of everything, either typed or in very neat handwriting. Even if someone only occupied a flat for a week or so, he would record it all. I think some of it might have had to do with the fact that a lot of the people he helped were technically aliens, and he wanted to keep on the right side of the authorities."

"Would there be anyone at all we might be able to talk to," Collison asked after waiting for Desai to stop writing, "who might be able to give us first-hand knowledge about life at the Isokon in the thirties?"

"Good God, no," Murfitt replied in surprise. "Why, they'd all be dead, wouldn't they? The residents weren't normally families with children, although I think there were a few among the refugees who came in."

He stopped suddenly and reached into his jacket for a pen.

"Why, I hadn't thought of that. It's just possible that one or two of them might still be around. Thank you, Superintendent, for the idea."

Collison glanced at Desai before replying.

"If you could give us whatever details of these families you have," he suggested, "and our own police enquiries happen to identify anyone who is still alive, I'd be happy to ask them if they'd like to help to you with your research."

"Done!" Murfitt cried delightedly. "Of course, your own efforts are likely to be much more successful than mine anyway, aren't they?"

"I sincerely hope so," Collison agreed drily.

"Actually, I've already said that your colleague is welcome to come round and look through the files anytime she wants," Murfitt said, looking hopefully at Priya.

"It might be easier if we just take them all away, have them photocopied, and return them," Priya said briskly.

Murfitt's disappointment was so obvious that Collison found himself smiling.

"Now then, Mr Murfitt," Collison went on. "I'm sure you'll be aware from reports in the press that a body has been found in the basement of the Isokon Building and that we are currently trying to identify him. We know that he was a young man and that he is likely to have died sometime between, say 1935 and 1945, but beyond that we're frankly struggling at present. Are you aware from your researches of any Isokon resident who might have gone missing at any time?"

"Well, there was Agatha Christie, wasn't there?" Murfitt said with a grin, "but not while she was living at the Isokon, of course. I think it had something to do with her husband running off with another woman, didn't it?"

"Really, was she there? I didn't know."

"Oh yes, Superintendent, she was probably their most famous resident of all. They had quite a few writers, actually. Nicholas Monsarrat, for example."

"Anyone else? Going missing, I mean?"

"No, I'm afraid not. In fact, I'd be very surprised if your dead body turned out to have been a resident."

"Why?"

"Well, for one thing, as I said, Jack kept such detailed records. He even kept people's forwarding addresses and stayed in touch with them after they moved away. For another, the Isokon was a very tight knit community; it was always intended to be that way, a group of like-minded individuals who could be almost like a big family to each other. It wasn't like today, when you never even meet your neighbours. They were in and out of each other's flats all the time, as well as eating and drinking together in the restaurant and bar. If anyone had simply disappeared, Jack would have known about it, and probably everybody else too."

"Unless Pritchard was given some apparently valid reason for their departure?" Priya suggested. "Somebody might have come up with a story about a resident having had to go away suddenly – a family bereavement perhaps? – and leaving a request to store their cabin trunk because they were expecting to return …?"

Murfitt shrugged.

"I suppose so, yes, but I can't think of anyone who might fit that bill."

"Damn you, Priya, I hadn't thought of that," Collison said, shaking his head, "of course, that may have been exactly how it was."

"Anything's possible, I suppose," Murfitt commented, "but I still think it's unlikely. We would describe Jack Pritchard today as the archetypal networker. Had he been alive in the internet era he would have spent his whole time on email or social media. As it was, he spent half his time writing letters to people. I can't believe he wouldn't have said something if someone had just vanished into the blue and he couldn't follow up with them."

He pushed a bulky folder across the table, glancing furtively at Priya as though hoping for a sign of approval.

"This might be a convenient starting point," he said. "I'd got as far as putting all Jack's tenancy records together. So far as I'm aware, there are the names here of everyone who ever had one of the flats right up until 1968, when a professional managing agent took over. It's all a bit of a mess, I'm afraid. I was just starting to cross-reference flat numbers and dates. It's not as easy as it sounds because some tenants changed around between different flats over time as they needed more or less space."

"That's very helpful, Mr Murfitt, thank you," Collison acknowledged.

He glanced at Priya Desai, hoping that she would favour Murfitt with a smile. Perhaps getting the message, she did.

# CHAPTER 14

"OK, everyone," Collison said next morning as the chatter in the incident room died away. "I know it's difficult keeping tabs on everything in an investigation like this when we're following so many different leads, so let's see where we are."

"Burgh House?" he prompted Metcalfe.

"We're no further ahead with the Baileys, either individually or together," the DI informed the room. "With no way of knowing who went up or downstairs when, it's going to be difficult to disprove their alibis, which are pretty vague anyway. And we know they were both legitimately in Howse's rooms from time to time, so forensic isn't going to help us much. We were hoping for either DNA or fingerprints on the handle of the truncheon, but there's nothing. Whoever used it either wore gloves or wiped it clean afterwards."

"Suggests premeditation, anyway," Collison commented, jotting down the thought in his notebook.

"Yes, guv," Metcalfe agreed. "Which argues against the passing tramp theory. I was going to come to that next, actually. No luck with house to house. We obviously haven't covered the whole area, but nobody we did manage to speak to saw or heard anything suspicious. And there's no CCTV coverage, worst luck."

Collison pondered for a moment.

"I rather think," he said thoughtfully. "That we should put the passing tramp on the back-burner, at least for the time being. There is no evidence of money or credit cards having been taken from the victim, the use of gloves suggests premeditation, and there is no reported sighting of a stranger having entered the house during the relevant period. Of course, none of this is conclusive, but I'm concerned that if we pursue this line of enquiry then it may distract us from the various other issues we have to consider."

"I agree," Metcalfe said.

"Does anyone have a different view?" Collison asked quietly, looking around the room. "If so, please don't hesitate to express it just because the DI and I are *ad idem*."

Unsurprisingly, there was no answer. First, because nobody was about to disagree with two senior officers. Second, because nobody wanted to participate in a renewed bout of house to house enquiries. Third, because nobody else apart from Karen Willis knew what *ad idem* meant.

"OK," Collison went on, "then where does that leave us on Burgh House?"

"We've had a stroke of luck on the documents front," Willis told the team. "Mr Collison asked the DI and me to check out a theory that the deceased had in fact succeeded in archiving them before his death. Happily, that does indeed seem to have been the case. They appear to have been sorted into boxes which form a sort of filing system, and we've found his master list – it's a folder, actually."

She picked up the ring binder from her desk and held it up for display.

"With assistance from DC Evans, we went through the boxes yesterday afternoon, checking their contents against the master list. It was a long job – we didn't finish until about ten at night – but we did discover that one file, and one only, seemed to be missing."

"Ah, now we're getting somewhere," Collison observed happily. "What was it?"

"According to the one line descriptions in the ring binder," Willis said with a rather strange smile, "it was a collection of four letters, each with the name 'Agatha Christie' written beside it."

As Collison grappled with this new information, Desai interjected "the DS and I heard yesterday that Agatha Christie was a resident of the Isokon," by way of explanation.

"Letters to or from Agatha Christie?" he asked.

"That's unclear, guv."

"And you're sure that's all that's missing?"

"Well, we accounted for everything else on the list. Of course, it's always possible that there may have been some other material which Howse hadn't got around to ..."

"Well, well, well," Collison said wonderingly, as he tried to prod his brain into action.

"Thoughts?" he enquired of the room in general.

"Might they have been valuable, sir?" Evans volunteered.

"Excellent point: find out. There must be specialist valuers, or auctioneers or something for things like this.

I think they're called 'ephemera' in the antiques trade. Anyone else?"

"The only other possibility is that they were taken not for their value, as such, but for something which they contained," Metcalfe ventured. "Something which somebody was prepared to kill Howse to suppress."

Collison found himself gaping again.

"Are we seriously forming a hypothesis that envisages something written in a letter over seventy years ago being so important to someone in the present day as to provide a motive for murder?" he asked.

"I know it sounds a bit far-fetched, sir," Metcalfe answered defensively.

"It's possible that the DCS may describe it less charitably," Collison commented drily, "not to mention the ACC."

"Nonetheless, sir, it is a legitimate possibility," Willis maintained.

"Yes, yes, you're right of course, both of you," Collison acknowledged wearily. "But how do we go about ruling it out? Surely we'd need to know what was in those letters, and if they have been stolen then presumably it was with the express intention of destroying them."

"That's true," Metcalfe conceded.

"As I understand it," Collison went on, "the list doesn't even specify who the letters were to or from, or the dates on which they were written. Is that right, Karen?"

She nodded silently.

"Oh dear," he said, and somehow the mildness of the

phrase conveyed perfectly his feeling of quiet despair. "We do seem to be setting ourselves an impossible task, don't we?"

"While we all think about that," Willis continued diplomatically, "perhaps I could bring everyone up to speed on the nephew of the deceased. Alan Howse came in yesterday while DI Metcalfe and I were at Burgh House and gave a formal statement. You'll see that it's been circulated overnight. It adds nothing to what he told me on the phone. He was working from home on the day of the murder – he's a self-employed IT consultant – and hadn't seen his uncle for some time. He's not aware of Peter Howse having had any enemies – though he did say that he could be unpleasant and was generally unpopular – and certainly nobody who would have had a motive to kill him."

Collison regarded the one and a half sides of Alan Howse's witness statement with the air of a schoolmaster eyeing a particularly unsatisfactory piece of homework.

"Not good enough," he said briefly. "This chap is the only living relative of the deceased, so far as we can establish. There must be *something* he knows which might help to shed some light on things. Get him back. Karen, can you see to that? And this time I'll see him together with either you or Bob."

"Right you are, guv."

"Is there anything anyone else would like to raise on Burgh House?" Collison asked, scanning the room. "No? Very well, then I'll ask Priya to bring us all up to speed on the Isokon."

The petite figure of Priyia Desai crossed the room. She stood in front of the whiteboard with some notes in her hand.

"Mr Collison and I met yesterday with a man called Tim Murfitt," she began. "He's some sort of expert on the Isokon Building, or the Lawn Road Flats as they are also known. He's a classic anorak; boring, but knows everything there is to know about this one thing."

Collison smiled sadly at the thought of what Murfitt would have made of Priya's assessment of him.

"His chief value to us, apart from his background knowledge," Desai continued, "is that he has acquired the working papers of someone called Jack Pritchard, who was the brains behind creating the Isokon in the first place and then managing it, right up until 1968, at which time it was bought by a trendy left wing magazine called The New Statesman."

Collison smiled briefly again, this time at the thought of The New Statesman being described as a magazine. Ah, the innocence of youth.

"I have now copied a complete set of the papers which matter, that is those which relate to the flats at around the time we are talking about: sometime between, say 1935 and 1955, though several different factors point to 1937 or 1938 as being when the body was most likely to have been concealed and so also, we are assuming, killed."

She stopped and turned over a page in her notes.

"My first task is to go through Pritchard's papers and

compile a list of exactly who occupied each flat, and when. This isn't as easy as it sounds, by the way. There are multiple sources for the information, much of it in Jack Pritchard's handwriting, and some tenants occupied different flats within the building at different times. I was here until about eleven last night, and I think I've almost finished."

She threw a rather tart glance at Willis and Metcalfe as if to convey that they were not the only ones on the investigation to pull late nights.

"Once I've done that, I'll pull a different list which excludes the duplications of people staying more than once, or occupying more than one flat, and then run that against all CRO records, including of course missing persons."

She paused and looked at Collison, who was observing her self-confident performance with approval.

"It's worth stating a couple of caveats," he observed to nobody in particular. "First, our – anorak did you say, Priya? – was pretty adamant that had anything untoward happened to any of the residents then Pritchard would have known about it, and thus so would Murfitt from having gone through the papers. Second, the CRO data isn't a hundred percent reliable going back that far. When the records were computerised they were taken from the old card index system at Scotland Yard, and yes I'm talking about *Old* Scotland Yard. They were a master version of the individual ones kept by different police forces around the country."

He stopped as Evans put his hand up.

"Yes?"

" 'scuse me, sir, but if there were no computers, how did you search what might have happened at different times, or in different parts of the country?"

"You took out an ad," Collison replied with a smile, "and no, that's not a joke. You put an entry in The Police Gazette asking for information. It was bought by the public, but it also went to every police station in the country, and every officer was supposed to read it; the duty sergeant used to test his PCs on it before they went out on the beat. If you saw something that struck a chord with a case you had worked on, you contacted the named investigating officer and told him what you knew."

"And did it work, guv?" asked an amazed Constable Evans.

"In fact, it worked surprisingly well," Collison informed him, "but inevitably things slipped through cracks, and continued to do so. As I'm sure we all know, the Yorkshire Ripper investigation would have proceeded very differently had computers been available to the officers on the team. But even now it's not perfect."

He saw some puzzled glances at this.

"The computer is a wonderful invention," he elucidated, "but it can't think. It processes information, but it has no intuition. So if a record has been tagged differently to another to which it actually relates, a human might make the connection regardless, whereas a computer would not. It would just look for what it had been programmed to look for and say 'no' if it wasn't there."

He stopped, and realised that Desai was still standing patiently at the whiteboard.

"I'm sorry, Priya," he said. "I think I went off at a bit of a tangent there. Did you have anything else to tell us?"

"Not about the documents, sir," she replied cautiously, "but I do have some news from forensic; two pieces of news, in fact."

"Great; tell all."

"The first is that they have managed to identify a piece of newspaper which was found in the trunk as being from 1937, which is a further indicator of us being on the right track about the date. The second is perhaps more exciting. They have managed to lift some DNA from the corpse; enough to run a full analysis against anyone we want."

"They've checked it against the national offenders' database, of course?" Metcalfe queried.

"Yes, guv, but unsurprisingly there's no match."

"Well," Collison commented with an attempt at enthusiasm, "at least we can say that none of our corpse's descendants have been convicted of any crime in the last few years."

"Do you think he is likely to have descendants, sir?" Desai, who was inclined to take things literally, enquired curiously. "After all, given that we think he was early twenties when he died, then it's quite likely that he didn't have children."

"I fear you're probably right," Collison admitted. After all, he reflected, she usually was.

"However," he went on, "there are comparisons that

can be made with other family members – nieces, nephews, that sort of thing – which can at least establish a family relationship, a common ancestor."

"That's all I have, sir," Priya told him calmly, and went back to sit down.

"Thank you, Priya. Right, Bob, action points?"

Metcalfe looked up from his own notes.

"DC Desai will put the Isokon forensic report on the system so everyone can read it. DS Willis to get the nephew back, and she and you to re-interview him, sir. I will take Evans and go through the Burgh House papers one last time just to make sure we haven't missed anything."

He stopped.

"What do you want to do about the Baileys, guv?" he asked hesitantly.

"Nothing, I think, not for the moment anyway. At some point I really should interview them myself but I'm sure everyone did a proper job first time around."

"And the second, sir," Willis interjected quietly but firmly.

He laughed.

"I beg your pardon. I was forgetting that you interviewed them twice. To be honest, though, I'm not sure how we can take things any further with them at the moment. They've given us their stories, such as they are, and the problem is that they're so vague as to be very difficult to disprove. We know that either or both could have had means, motive and opportunity, and usually that suggests some obvious lines of enquiry, but I'm not sure that it does here. The whole thing is so damn self-contained; it's too circular."

"It's funny that Agatha Christie should have reared her head," Willis said suddenly. "Funny-peculiar, I mean."

"It certainly is," Collison agreed, "but in what particular way do you have in mind, Karen?"

"Well, didn't she say that she set her murders in closed communities to make them easier to solve? Here we have a classic Golden Age situation: a man murdered in a house occupied by only a small number of people, and yet we're floundering."

The newer members of the team looked at each other uncertainly. They were not used to forays into the realms of crime fiction as part of a real life murder investigation. Those who had served under Collison before smiled indulgently.

"Well," he said, having thought about Karen's point for a moment, "I don't think even Dame Agatha, God bless her, would have come up with a case featuring a vanished letter from seventy years ago and expect Poirot or Miss Marple to solve it."

"We're going to, though, aren't we, guv?" Desai asked uncertainly.

"Oh yes, Priya," he answered, wishing that he felt as confident as he hoped he sounded, "oh yes, we'll solve it alright."

# CHAPTER 15

"Can you stay behind please, Jim?" the ACC asked DCS Morris, as yet another seemingly interminable committee meeting came to an end.

As the other committee members trooped out, he moved over to his desk, and beckoned Morris to come with him.

"I bet you had no idea just how exciting life as a DCS could be," he said with heavy irony. "How many committee meetings do you have a week?"

"Oh, one or two, sir. It's a bore, but it's all part of the job, isn't it?" Morris replied.

"I sit on eleven," the ACC said heavily, "only three of which are internal, so on all the others you have to really watch your Ps and Qs or one of the outsiders will sound off to the papers, or their MP. Fortunately, they don't all meet every week, but even so ..."

He sighed as he sat down. He looked down briefly at his diary.

"I don't have much time," he said abruptly, "and I'm sure you're busy too, but I wanted to have a quick chat about Simon Collison. How's he getting on?"

"He reported to me last night on the phone, actually, guv. The latest news is apparently that the vital clue to the murder at Burgh House may be something that Agatha Christie wrote seventy or eighty years ago."

"What?" ejaculated the ACC.

"Yes, there seems to be something of a pattern emerging," Morris said brightly. "First he takes over an investigation when Tom Allen gets kicked off it as SIO, and then he looks for answers from the world of detection fiction. It's a novel approach, no pun intended, but I'm sure it will show results."

"Sarcasm doesn't suit you, Jim," the senior man observed wearily.

Morris made no reply. The ACC sighed again.

"I know it's easy for old time coppers like you and Tom to resent how quickly some younger men are being fast-tracked right now," he said, "but like it or not, Jim, it's people like Collison, yes and that Willis girl too by the look of things, who represent the future of the Met. It's going to happen, and it needs to be seen to be successful. We all have an interest in helping that be the case."

"Yes, sir," Morris said stolidly.

"And if I can't appeal to your esprit de corps, then think about your own position, Jim. Tom's different, he might only have a few years left on the Force; he could already take an early pension if he wanted to. He knows he's never going further than DCI. But you're different. What are you, forty-eight? I'm assuming you're looking to go all the way in the Force if you can. Well, that means you and Simon Collison are likely to be working together in senior positions. It's important that you two should get on together, that you can work well together."

"I have nothing against Collison personally, sir, though I'm an old mate of Tom Allen, and that's twice in succession now that he's had a raw deal. Excuse my bluntness, but that's what it looks like from where I'm sitting as his immediate boss."

"I would probably agree with you," the ACC said mildly, "but unfortunately life isn't fair to everybody all the time, Jim. Nor is it always clear-cut; actually, you could argue that Tom had a lucky escape. You may not know this, but after he left the last case, he was using a member of the team to feed him confidential information, yes and leak it to the press too. Following a meeting with me right here in this office that officer is no longer with us, and Tom Allen could have been severely disciplined, perhaps dropped down to DI or even DS. So, you see, there are two sides to the story."

"I didn't know that, sir, no," Morris said awkwardly.

"It's not always in the best interests of the Force for things to become public knowledge," the ACC observed with a smile, "nor for individual officers, either."

"I will of course give Simon Collison all the help and advice that I can, sir," a chastened Morris proffered. "Though it's difficult because I'm not on the spot and I have no direct involvement in the investigation."

"When was the last time you visited Hampstead nick, Jim?"

"Not for some time," Morris admitted. "After all,

everyone keeps saying it's about to close."

"Ever heard of Management By Wandering About?" the ACC enquired. "No? Pity. There's a book in here somewhere which I could lend you. Why don't you drop in on Collison's enquiry one day? Take him out for a drink and a chat, perhaps?"

"If you think that would be a good idea, guv, then certainly."

"It's not really a question of what I think, is it?" the ACC replied mildly. "You're Collison's line manager, and how you choose to manage him is up to you. I'm just making a suggestion. You should mug up on all this Business School stuff, by the way. Promotion Boards are very hot on it these days."

"Yes, sir," Morris said again. This was beginning to feel like a meeting with the headmaster, and the mention of Promotion Boards was surely a thinly veiled allusion to the fact that the man sitting behind the desk with a crown and bayleaf wreath on each shoulder contributed his own comments to any review which they might study when considering the next vacant Commander's post.

"Funny thing about Allen and Collison. Don't know if you've noticed it yourself. They're like different halves of the same self, different sides of the same coin, as it were. Allen never stops talking about his copper's nose, but is actually a good, solid process-driven copper, whereas Collison is desperate to observe all the right procedure but keeps getting led astray by his intuition. He's got the sort of mind that keeps making connections that the rest of us can't see. The problem is that some of them are real but others are not."

The ACC trailed off. The atmosphere relaxed noticeably, for which Morris was grateful. He had the impression that he had just been admonished, albeit nicely and almost imperceptibly.

"Do you know about Tom Allen's daughter?" the ACC asked abruptly.

"Yes, I do. Like I said, sir, we've been mates for a long time."

"Bad business, that," the older man commented absently. "Don't know what something like that would do to me, how I'd handle it."

"It was tough, of course. You know his marriage broke up?"

"It's my business to know," the ACC nodded. "Between you and me, there was talk of a psychiatric assessment before he was allowed back to duties. It was before my time, of course, but I've read the files. My predecessor vetoed the idea, but sometimes I wonder if he really did Tom such a favour. Perhaps a period of counselling might have done him good."

"Can't really see Tom sitting through counselling though, sir, can you? Catching villains has always been the best therapy for him."

"I tend to agree with you, but keep an eye on him, won't you, as a friend as much as anything. Remember that it's often those who are most in need of help who portray the most self-confident image."

There was a quick tap on the door and the ACC said "damn", glancing back at his diary. Morris got up and they shook hands.

"Do remember, won't you, Jim," the other said by way of a parting shot, "that if these two cases remain unsolved then they don't just go on Collison's record. They go on yours and mine as well."

Alan Howse was a rather small, mousy looking man. He also seemed extremely nervous. Observing him closely, Collison tried to assess whether this was a natural consequence of a police interview, or of years spent staring at a screen, perhaps denied human contact for days on end.

"I've already been through this before, you know, with your colleague," the nephew said in a surprisingly firm and normal voice, "so I really don't see why we have to do this again."

"Bear with us, please, Mr Howse," Collison said breezily. "We really need to find out everything we can about your uncle, and so far you're the only close family member we've been able to locate."

"And the only one you're likely to, at that," Howse said, clasping his hands together on the table in front of him, and squinting at Karen Willis. It was clear that he found her a great improvement on his previous interviewer.

"Why's that?" Collison enquired.

"Well, there was just my uncle and my dad, really. Uncle Peter never had children, and I was an only child. When my parents died, I went to live with my Grandma. I was fifteen, so I was almost grown up anyway. I lived with her until she died a year or so back and then I just carried on living at her place."

"Did she leave it to you in her will?" Willis asked.

"No, she didn't own it. She was renting, but the landlord let me take over the lease. I had to sign some papers. She didn't have very much at all, actually. It was pretty much all gone. It was a bit of a shock, I can tell you. Because she'd put me through school and university I'd always assumed that she was alright for a few bob, you know? But then the solicitor told me that the money had all come from a trust that my dad had set up in his will."

"Let's come back to that," said Collison, doodling a quick family tree on his notepad. "How did your parents die?"

"In a car crash," came the reply. "Well, my dad anyway. My mum died in hospital a few days later. My dad was driving; the accident was his fault, they said."

"I see. I'm sorry."

"No need to be. I was over it a long time ago."

"OK, so let's come back to the trust then," Collison said. "Did I understand you correctly when you said you hadn't been aware of its existence until your grandmother died?"

"Yes, that's quite right. I always thought it was her money, or money that my grandpa had left her."

"Does the phrase 'accumulation and maintenance' ring

any bells?" Collison asked.

"Yeah, it does, now you come to mention it. I'm sure the solicitor used those words a few times."

"Good, so we're getting somewhere," Collison continued. "An accumulation and maintenance settlement, Mr Howse, is a trust set up in which the money is invested – that's the 'accumulation' bit – and then applied for the living expenses and education of one or more children. Now, since you seem to have been the only beneficiary of this trust, then what lawyers call 'the remainder' becomes an issue."

"I remember that word too, I think," Howse said.

"What it means," Collison explained, "is the money that is left over, which is still sitting in the trust when all its objectives have been achieved. Do you happen to know how much it is, and what happens to it?"

"According to the solicitor, it's about eighty thousand," Howse replied.

"That's quite a lot," Willis said before she could stop herself.

"Yes, it is, isn't it? Came as quite a shock, actually."

"So what happens to it?" Collison pressed him.

"Under the terms of the will, it has to remain in the trust until I'm thirty," Howse said rather bitterly. "God knows why my father did that. The solicitor says its usually twenty-one."

"But surely if you're the sole remaining beneficiary, can't the trustees just agree to wind the trust up now?"

"It's not as easy as that," Howse said, more bitterly still. "The will says that if I die before I'm thirty then whatever is left goes to Uncle Peter. That's why I remember the word 'remainder', you see. Uncle Peter was something called 'the remainder man', according to the lawyer."

"Gosh, that *is* awkward," Collison said thoughtfully. "But isn't it unusual to have the same person acting as both the remainder man and a trustee? I would have thought there might be a conflict of interest."

Alan Howse gave a sardonic laugh.

"That's what I said. I asked him to wind up the trust or step down as a trustee. I want to buy a flat, you see, and that eighty grand would do as a deposit."

"And what did he say?" Collison asked.

"Oh, he got really angry the way he does, 'did' I should say. He said that the trust was set up the way my dad had wanted it set up and that he was going to honour his wishes. What he really meant was 'get knotted', I suppose."

"And did you raise the question of conflict of interest?"

"Yeah," Howse confirmed with a grin. "That's when he *really* went ape-shit. Told me to get out and not come back. He as good as threw me down the stairs."

"When did this conversation take place?" Collison asked, as casually as he could.

"A couple of weeks before he died, I suppose. One afternoon. In his rooms at Burgh House."

"And, just to be clear about this, was that the last time you saw him?"

"Yes. I didn't feel inclined to go back after that sort of a scene."

"I can understand that," Collison acknowledged.

"How did all this make you feel?" Willis interjected suddenly.

Howse gazed at her contemplatively, though whether studying her looks or considering the question was unclear.

"Bloody livid, if you must know. There he was, my uncle, wishing me dead so he could get his hands on my money. That's the way I saw it, anyway."

There was a short silence.

"What can you remember about that last time you saw him?" Collison pressed him. "Anything you can remember may be of help to us, even though it may not seem significant. Please try."

"He was surrounded by papers," Howse responded slowly, as if visualising the scene in his memory. "Some were in folders and some were out on his desk. There were several cardboard boxes stacked against the wall. One was open on the floor, and had folders inside it."

"Good, good," urged Collison. "Anything else? Please think hard."

"There was a half drunk mug of tea on his desk. Oh, and there were a few strange things lying around. Bric-à-brac really; looked like he was running a junk shop or something. I remember a police truncheon, and maybe a gas mask. The truncheon had a label tied to it. Not sure about the gas mask and the other stuff."

He closed his eyes and fell silent. Then he opened them again.

"No, I'm sorry," he said, shaking his head, "that really is all I can remember."

"Don't worry," Collison said. "Thank you for trying."

"So, apart from yourself," he went on slowly, "can you think of anyone else who might had had any reason for wishing your uncle dead?"

"What do you mean, apart from me?" Howse demanded, flushing a little.

"Well, part of our job is to identify anyone who might have had a motive. You clearly had one, and you've just explained what it was. If your uncle died before you then the trust would come to an end and you would get the money. Exactly as will now happen, in fact."

"Well, I didn't kill him," Howse stated flatly. "I won't pretend I'm sorry he's dead, the evil old bastard, because I'm not. I even resented having made a special journey to Hampstead, somewhere I never normally come, just to see him; but I didn't kill him."

"I was going on to make it clear," Collison explained, "that our job is to identify anyone who had a motive and then eliminate them from our enquiries. That way we can gradually narrow down our search until we find whoever it was who *did* kill your uncle."

"Well, when you do," Howse replied morosely, "give me their name. I want to shake their hand and buy them a drink."

# CHAPTER 16

"Ok, everyone: updates," Metcalfe announced the next morning.

He stood by the white boards which he and Karen Willis had re-organised the previous evening. Now there were three pushed together; the one on the left for Burgh House, the one on the right for the Isokon Building, and the one in the middle for anything which seemed to overlap. He pointed to the left hand one.

"Burgh House: Mr Collison and DS Willis re-interviewed the nephew, Alan Howse, yesterday and the record of that interview has been circulated. Any questions or comments?"

"At the risk of stating the obvious, guv," Evans proffered hesitantly, "the nephew appears to have had an excellent motive for murdering the uncle, and no alibi worth talking about. He says he was at home working, but there's nobody who can corroborate that."

"That's quite right, of course," Metcalfe acknowledged.

He noticed for the first time that there was a touch of Welsh in Evans's accent, most marked when he had said 'corroborate'.

"So, are we saying then," Evans persisted, "that we are now officially treating Alan Howse as a suspect? And, if so, doesn't that have, er ... implications for the way in which we treat him?"

"Unfortunately you're right, Timothy," Collison said. "Very good point, incidentally; well done. Yes, I think any further interview of Alan Howse will have to be done under caution, and I think we all know what that means."

They did indeed. Howse would promptly ask for a lawyer to be present, and the lawyer would like as not tell him not to say anything. Duty solicitors were apt to take the robust view that anyone who was being interviewed under caution was likely to have something to hide, and would therefore do well simply to reply 'no comment' to any question.

"I think the ideal outcome for us would be to eliminate him from the enquiry as soon as possible," Collison went on. "Any ideas?"

"The most logical way to do that," said Willis, thinking out loud, "would be to find some way to validate his alibi."

"But how can we prove that he was at home on his own when he was, well at home on his own, if you see what I mean?" Evans queried. "There's nobody we can ask."

"We don't have to prove he was at home on his own, or indeed with anyone else," Willis answered with a smile. "All we have to do is show where he was not, namely Burgh House."

"And how do we do that, Karen?" Collison asked curiously. "Remember, there's no CCTV footage available from Burgh House, and we know that the door was left unsecured and unattended."

"I'm not sure, guv. Let me think about it."

"Let's *all* think about it, please," Collison said firmly. "Right now we have three suspects with clear motives. We know that we can place two of them more or less at the scene at more or less the right time. We need to find out where our third suspect was – or was not, as DS Willis says. But it's all so damn vague. We can't even use DNA evidence, as all three suspects admit to having been at the murder scene recently, and there's none on the murder weapon except the victim's."

There was a rather sad silence; Collison hoped that his own sense of growing helplessness was not contagious.

"Moving on," Metcalfe said briskly, as if reading his thoughts, and pointing to the middle board. "The missing papers. DS Willis and I are exploring ways in which these might be traced, but there's no clear answer that we can see – not yet, anyway."

"If only we could narrow it down in some way," Willis explained, "but we can't. We don't know whether the missing letters were to or from Agatha Christie, nor to and from whom. We don't even know what sort of dates we're talking about."

"Before the murder, though, surely?" Collison mused. "The first murder, I mean."

"With respect, sir, why?" came the rejoinder. "Of course it's possible that the first murder was somehow connected with the letters – covering something up, perhaps – but isn't it equally possible that it's the other way round? That it's the second murder that's connected with the letters, but covering something up which might give away the identity of the first murderer?"

"Yes, damn it, you're right," Collison admitted ruefully. "So where on earth do we start?"

"Actually, guv," Willis said awkwardly, with a sidelong glance at Metcalfe, "I was meaning to talk to you about this privately but, well, there's someone we both know who's an expert on detective fiction and I was going to ask if it would be OK to tell him enough about the case to see if he could help us on this."

"I don't see why not," Collison said ruminatively. "After all, he's already helped the police on one investigation. What do you think, Bob?"

"I'd have no objection, guv," Metcalfe replied, but there was something in his tone of voice that made Collison stare at him strangely.

"Very well, then," Collison said, "Let's go ahead on that basis. Karen, -"

At this moment Desai screamed.

Not unnaturally, everyone turned to look at her, some jumping to their feet in the process. Startled, Karen Willis knocked over what was left of her tea, grabbed a box of tissues from her desk drawer, and began mopping up operations. Had anyone been watching her, they might have noticed that her tissues were exactly the same shade of blue as her scarf, and wondered whether this was just a coincidence, and anyway, everyone was staring at Priya Desai.

She put her hands to her mouth, the picture of confusion.

"Oh, I'm so sorry," she whispered, and then broke off in embarrassment.

"You have successfully attracted our attention, Priya," Collison said with mock casualness. "Was there something you wanted to impart?"

"I'm really sorry, guv," she said again.

Everyone had resumed their seats and some were laughing. If nothing else, thought Collison, it had lightened the mood of the meeting, which had been in danger of heading into a morale vacuum.

"Tell all," he urged her.

"It's your turn anyway, Priya," Metcalfe commented, pointing to the right hand board, the Isokon one."

"Well, I completed my list of Isokon residents, and I searched against it for homicides and missing persons. Nothing came up except of course Agatha Christie, who was a missing person in 1926. We were expecting that, so at least it shows the system works."

"Agatha Christie went missing for eleven days," Collison explained quickly, since some of the team were looking baffled. "Her car was found abandoned. Some of the papers unkindly suggested that it was a publicity stunt for her new book, but in fact it now seems pretty clear that her husband had just left her for another woman and she was going through some sort of nervous episode. Go on, Priya."

"Well, then I ran a general search, which looks for any cross-referencing anywhere in the system. That takes a long time of course, and the answer only just came back."

She looked around the room.

"I really don't understand this, and maybe you're not going to believe it, but the resident of one of the flats back in the 1930s is also showing as a witness in the Burgh House murder: Professor Hugh Raffen."

Everyone stared at her incredulously.

"But that's impossible," Metcalfe pointed out, voicing all their thoughts. "That would make him, what, a hundred and fifty or something."

"Maybe he's a time traveller," someone quipped.

"No," Priya responded, tapping furiously at her keyboard, "it looks like he's a relative. There's a disambiguation notice here on Wikipedia. One Professor Hugh Raffen, presumably the one who was at the Isokon in the thirties, died in 1955. The other, presumably our one, was born in 1951. Ah yes, here we are, the first one had a son, David, who is the father of the second. Wow!"

It was obviously a day for surprises because DCS Jim Morris, security pass dangling from his jacket pocket, happened to walk into the room just as Priya said 'wow'. He looked at her enquiringly, and then at Collison.

"Good morning, sir," said the latter, clearly startled by this sudden apparition.

"Good morning, Superintendent," Morris replied, "please don't mind me; I'm having a wandering about day today."

"You've come at an interesting time, sir," Collison

observed. "We've just found out that grandfather of someone who was present at the Burgh House crime scene was a resident of the Isokon at the relevant time. That is, the scene of the other murder, the one we think probably took place sometime around 1937."

"Fine. Carry on; pretend I'm not here."

So saying, Morris rather ostentatiously went to the back of the room and sat down at an empty desk.

"Well," Collison said, his mind still reeling from unexpected events pressing upon each other, "any thoughts, anyone?"

As soon as the question was out of his mouth, he knew it was a bad idea. Nobody was going to express an opinion in front of the DCS. Sure enough, everyone sat woodenly, trying not to catch anyone else's eye. The only sound was the quiet clicking of Desai's keyboard.

"Sir?" she said queryingly, just as the silence was becoming very noticeable. "I've just run all three names through the system. There are CPO blocks on the first two names, the grandfather and the father. What's a CPO block? I've never come across one before."

"Chief Police Officer," Morris interjected from the back. "I'm no good to you, I'm afraid. It means it's only accessible to ranks of Commander and above – and even then there's usually some sort of further restriction."

"It's usually used where a file would give someone's identity away and expose them to danger," Collison explained. "Like the witness protection scheme, or an undercover operation."

"Yes," Morris concurred, "or maybe one of the spook gangs."

"Wow," Desai said again before she could stop herself.

"I'll happily speak to the ACC for you if you like, Simon," Morris said. "It's clearly relevant to your enquiry."

"Thank you, sir, that would be very helpful. To be honest, this is a totally unexpected development."

"I'm sure it is," Morris observed drily.

Evans put his hand up like a schoolboy in class, presumably overawed by the august presence of the DCS.

"Yes, Timothy?" Collison prompted him.

"If you please, sir, there was something else I meant to raise about Burgh House before we got ... ah, diverted by this new discovery."

"Certainly. Go ahead."

"Well sir, when I was working at Burgh House with Mr Metcalfe and the DS I was only carrying boxes, like, and it took them some time to go through each one, so I was standing around a fair bit and, well, I had a look round, see?"

"Yes?"

"I don't know whether this is relevant, really, but did you know that down at the back of the building is an aluminium extendable ladder? I went downstairs later and checked on it."

"And?"

"Well, there's a ground floor extension with a flat roof, which means from there the victim's back window, the bedroom one at least, is only two stories up, not three. Being aluminium, the ladder's very light. You can easily use it get up onto the flat roof and then pull it up after you and use it to reach the bedroom window. I know, because I tried it myself."

"Bob," Collison asked, "was the bedroom window locked or unlocked when the body was discovered?"

"Unlocked, guv. In fact, not just unlocked, but open as well. I noticed that as soon as I went in, and Mr Allen remarked on it later as well."

"So," Collison said, giving voice to what they were all thinking, "Jack Bailey wouldn't even have had to go up the stairs to get to the victim's room. He could have done it all from outside. Those locks are easy to undo from outside alright, though you'd have to be a real expert with some sophisticated housebreaking tools to lock it again from outside."

He gazed at Evans.

"Very well done, Timothy. It seems you spotted something which SOCO overlooked."

Evans looked suitably embarrassed.

"Where does this take us?" Collison demanded of nobody in particular.

"It makes the Professor's evidence look increasingly irrelevant, guv," Metcalfe advised. "We already know that Sue Bailey could creep up and down stairs without being heard. Now it looks like Jack Bailey might not even have needed to use the stairs at all."

"Let's ask SOCO to re-examine the bedroom area,"

Collison decided, "particularly the window area both inside and out."

"That's not going to make us very popular, guv," Metcalfe replied dubiously. "They're not going to take kindly to any suggestion that they didn't do a proper job last time."

"Is the crime scene still secured, Bob?" Morris asked from the back of the room.

"Well yes and no, sir," Metcalfe temporised uncomfortably. "Yes, it's still cordoned off, but three of us spent time there recently going through boxes of documents. We thought it would be OK as SOCO had finished."

"It's still worth a try," Morris said judiciously. "Send the request to me, Bob, and I'll approve it before it goes out. That might save a bit of time."

"Thank you, sir," Metcalfe and Collison said together.

"Very well, everyone, I think we're done here for now," Collison told the team. "DI Metcalfe will allocate action points and responsibilities as usual."

As everyone began to cluster around Metcalfe's desk, Morris walked up to Collison.

"Can I buy you a coffee somewhere, Simon?"

"With pleasure, sir."

"OK, just let me call the ACC about these CPO blocks and then we'll go."

# CHAPTER 17

Collison and Morris sat together in one of the many cafes in which Hampstead abounds, this one looking out onto the High Street beside the William IV pub. It had started drizzling again, and only a few particularly desperate smokers were braving the outside tables. They were lucky to find a couple of places by the window, and a waitress with an accent which had probably begun life somewhere in the Balkans took their order.

Collison was curious, and frankly nervous. Morris did not have a reputation for getting out among his individual teams. However, it was surely still too early in the life of the investigation for there to be bad news to be delivered. The other, too, seemed ill at ease as he awkwardly rubbed the condensation away from the window glass.

"Was there something in particular …?" Collison ventured. "We don't often see senior officers at Hampstead nick, you know."

"Management By Wandering About it's called," Morrison observed rather morosely. "Apparently you learn all about it at Business School these days. Can't say that it's my sort of thing. I prefer to leave a bloke alone to get on with it, provided he knows his job, of course."

"I'd say that was a good philosophy to have," Collison observed.

"Provided, that is," he went on rather archly, "you can trust someone to know their job. If you get a less experienced officer dumped on you against your will then I can understand that things could be a bit more complicated."

"I'm sorry if you've misinterpreted my visit," Morris replied stiffly. "It wasn't my intention to suggest that I didn't trust you. Far from it. I was hoping that it would be seen as a sign of support."

"Perhaps it's I who should apologise in that case," Collison said, "for casting aspersions when they weren't justified. I do appreciate the support, actually. This damn case seems to be getting more complex all the time. Instead of narrowing down the range of options by eliminating them one by one, each day sees to create more. Frankly, I need all the help I can get."

"Fine. Then let's start again."

He reached across the table and they shook hands.

"I thought I should come over, to get to know you as much as anything. I've worked with all my other SIOs before, but I don't think we've ever actually met. The ACC took a personal interest in your last case, so there wasn't really anything for me to do."

Their coffee arrived, but was clearly still too hot to drink.

"To be honest, Simon," Morris went on, "I was both surprised and confused when you pitched up back at Hampstead. I thought you were destined for great things in the Met. A little bird tells me that they wanted you for Commandant at the Crime Academy. What happened?"

"They did. I turned it down."

"Turned it down? But why would you do that? It's a Chief Super's post, you know, with a more or less guaranteed leg-up to Commander when you leave."

"I know, I know," Collison said wretchedly, "and that was a big part of it – my decision, I mean – but I couldn't really explain it to the ACC. I'm afraid he's rather disappointed in me."

"Explain it to me, then," Morris suggested, picking up his coffee and blowing on it experimentally.

"Well, what you said is absolutely true, of course. I'd have gone from Inspector to Commander in about eight years, which feels way too quick. I was afraid that it was just a stratagem to jump me ahead of other officers, and quite an obvious one at that. I don't really want any sort of special treatment; I just want to get ahead on my merits."

"That's a very good attitude to have," Morris said approvingly and, it must be admitted, in some surprise, "but you may be being a bit hard on yourself, you know. Why, I can't think of anyone else in the Met who would be more suitable for that Crime Academy job. Look at your qualifications ..."

"Perhaps, perhaps," Collison fretted, "but how would it look? How would you feel if I was suddenly the same rank as you, but with years less experience? How would Tom Allen feel, and others like him?"

"I see your point," Morris agreed cautiously, "but if the powers that be – because this will have been a collective decision, not just the ACC – if they have decided to groom you to be Commissioner one day, then has it struck you that you may be playing a rather dangerous game? They won't like having their plans thwarted. Look at all the publicity you got after your last case. You can't tell me there wasn't a purpose to all that; I know how these things work. The Yard's PR boys have obviously been told to build you up. Do you really want to swim against the tide?"

"Well, there's something else as well, actually," Collison admitted. "You see the way to the top, at least the way the ACC seems to envisage it for me, is a series of desk jobs. This Crime Academy things is a perfect example. I'd spend about three years there, gaining no experience at all as a Chief Superintendent, and then suddenly I'd be a Commander and further away from the front line than ever. I want to do *real* policing. I want to take on complex investigations and solve them. I want to make a difference. Above all, I don't want to get bored. God, can you imagine sitting in committee meetings all day long?"

"Yes, I can," Morris said with feeling. "I just found out the other day that the ACC sits on eleven, and only two of them are internal. I'm already beginning to wonder whether I want to go beyond DCS, for exactly the same reasons you've just been talking about."

There was a growing sense of companionship as they sipped their drinks.

"Well, you're a brave man," he conceded. "Brave to take on homicide as SIO with so little investigating experience. A lot of scope to fall flat on your face, you know."

"I was rather hoping that wouldn't happen," said Collison sardonically.

Morris laughed.

"I hope so too," he said. "I really did mean what I said about support, you know. Anytime you want a quiet chat, someone to bounce some ideas off, I'm only at the end of the phone."

"Thank you, I appreciate that."

"Brave to defy the ACC as well. I must say, if I were you I'd be a bit worried about that. He's obviously decided to fast-track you all the way to the top, and he's building you a profile accordingly. I don't think that envisaged you hanging around at a nick that's a political embarrassment because it's slated for closure getting your hands dirty. Not to mention being SIO on a case which just may prove not possible to solve."

"I think you're right about the profile," Collison concurred, trying not to think about Morris's last sentence. "He wants me to put up a paper of some kind. Apparently the Commissioner takes that sort of thing very seriously."

"Do it," Morris urged him at once. "What harm can it do? Just the opposite, in fact. Anything that keeps the ACC happy must be worth doing. Have you thought what you might write about?"

"As a matter of fact, I have," Collison mused, "but let's see what you think. You see, a few years back the Met apparently commissioned a report from one of the big consultancy firms on their organisational structure, but ended up not very happy with the results. I thought that if I could look at the same situation but come to a different view, then maybe everyone would end up happy. The ACC would get a paper to put on my CV, the Met would get an alternative view …"

"Sounds good," Morris commented. "But how would you do all the background research? There must be a huge amount of reading that has to go into something like that."

"Yes, there is. But I have a friend who teaches at Business School, and he tells me that every year they have MBA students desperate for a research project to do, so I thought I might rope one or two in to help."

"You seem to have thought of everything," the DCS said drily.

"Perhaps you should do an MBA yourself?" he suggested mischievously. "Think how it would look on the CV."

Collison laughed.

"I don't have the time, the money or the inclination," he replied.

"Well, as to the first two you might find the Met would provide … but I see your point. It's not exactly running around chasing villains, is it?"

"Exactly."

Morris drained his coffee and looked across the table.

"I'm glad we've talked," he said. "I like you, Simon, though to be honest I wasn't expecting to."

"Ah," Collison said sadly. "You've probably been talking to Tom Allen. He didn't take kindly to being replaced by someone who was junior to him not so long ago. The first time, I mean, but then I suppose he probably doesn't feel too differently about it this time either."

"Probably not," Morris acknowledged.

"The rotten thing is," Collison went on, "that it's all so unnecessary. I like Tom. I admire and respect him, in fact. He's a hugely experienced and successful officer. It's just that whenever we get together I seem to rub him up the wrong way."

"I've known Tom a long time," Morris said non-committally.

He gazed out of the window for a while and then suddenly spoke.

"Do you know about his daughter?"

"I know that he had a daughter who died. I don't know any details."

"He prefers it that way, but there's no reason you shouldn't know. His daughter disappeared from the garden when she was six. Just vanished one day. She was never found; no body, nothing. Of course everyone assumed pretty quickly that she was dead – six year olds don't just go missing – but with no body ever being found, Tom's had to live with it all these years. No 'closure' as they say now."

"Oh, my God," said Collison. "I had no idea."

"Marriage broke up," Morris went on. "Tom's wife blamed herself for not keeping a closer eye on the garden, but you know what these opportunist paedophiles are like. She went to pieces, and Tom started drinking heavily. They broke up within about six months."

"Was there never any clue as to what happened?"

"Not immediately. Dog handlers claimed they could follow the girl's scent through the side gate into the road, and someone thought they'd seen a small white van parked there, but that was it. It was a quiet road on a quiet day, and the whole abduction probably only took about a minute or so. Later, though, now that was a different story."

"What happened?"

"About a year later a paedo got picked up in Birmingham. He'd been caught trying to nick a child from outside her house. The mother was quick witted enough to take a photo of him, and jot down the number of his van – and yes, it was a small white van. So he was picked up at home, quite peaceably, sitting down having tea with his mum as though nothing had happened. Michael Ryde, his name was. Almost at once they linked his DNA to another little girl, who'd been abducted from a playground a mile or two away some months previously. She'd been raped and then released, but badly battered around the head, which inflicted serious brain damage. She hasn't spoken a word since the attack, but there was no denying the DNA evidence of course, so he went down."

"And you think he was responsible ...?"

"It turned out he'd been staying in Tom's area a month or so either side of his kid going missing. So, yeah, most of us put two and two together given the white van and the similar MO. But he never coughed to it, no matter how hard anyone tried to break him"

"Poor Tom," Collison observed soberly. "He's a detective but he's had to deal with the knowledge that we couldn't catch the killer of his own child."

"You said it," Morris concurred. "And it's been eating away at him from inside ever since. There's the hard shell, which is getting more brittle all the time, but inside there's nothing much left, I'm afraid. Just a soft, gooey mess. The ACC's noticed it too, to be honest. I think he's hoping that Tom will take retirement before anything really bad happens."

"I don't know Tom as well as you do," Collison proffered, "but I would have thought that the best thing for him would be to carry on working."

"Exactly what I said to the ACC," growled Morris, "but he took him off the case anyway."

He looked at Collison thoughtfully.

"After the event, I think it was probably the best decision for everybody," he commented, "though I didn't at the time. I wasn't convinced the two cases were connected. I'm still not, to be fair, but from what you blokes have dug out so far I think there's at least a very strange coincidence, and I don't like coincidences; they disturb me."

Suddenly a miniature but very loud police siren began to sound.

"Talk of the devil," Morris said as he pulled out his

mobile phone. "That's the ACC. I've given him his own ring tone. Hello sir? ... I see ... yes, I see ... well, he's here with me now as a matter of fact Hang on, I'll pass you across."

"Simon," came the ACC's voice, "I've followed up on a couple of CPO blocks for you, at Jim's request. Can you and your DI come and see me at four?"

"Yes, sir."

"Good. Oh, and Simon, no need to tell anyone else about this for the time being, OK?"

# CHAPTER 18

Bob Metcalfe found the idea of a meeting with the ACC a daunting prospect. He resolved to take notes and say as little as possible. The first objective was to prove abortive and short-lived.

The ACC was not alone. At the round meeting table in his office was already sitting a middle-aged man with strikingly blond hair wearing a smartly tailored blue pinstripe suit with a double-breasted jacket. The cut showed off a powerful upper body, though now inevitably turning slightly to flab. A former rugby player, Metcalfe guessed.

"Ah, Simon, Bob, come in," the ACC greeted them.

Metcalfe found it slightly odd to be addressed as Bob by a man he was pretty certain he had never met before, but presumably this was an attempt by the great man to put a humble DI at his ease.

"Allow me to introduce Commander Philip Newby of Special Branch," the ACC went on.

Metcalfe did a quick calculation in his head. By his reckoning the three other men in the room were senior to him by two, four and six ranks respectively. Both the CPOs gave him a firm handshake and a shrewd glance. He said "sir" twice, sat down and pulled out his notebook in what he hoped was a calm and efficient manner. Instantly the ACC frowned and shook his head. Bad move, Bob, Metcalfe thought.

"Please don't write anything down, Inspector," Newby said. "This is just an exploratory meeting to discuss whether the Branch may be able to assist you with your investigations, in so far as may be consistent with not compromising national security, that is."

"Speaking of which," the ACC broke in, pushing two forms across the table, "perhaps you'd each be kind enough to sign one of these?"

"I'm sure you've heard of signing the Official Secrets Act?" Newby asked jovially. "All wrong, of course. You sign one of these Confidentiality Declarations acknowledging that you are subject to the Official Secrets legislation. I've brought the MoD version, which is usually known as Form 134. We haven't got around to doing a special one for the Met, I'm afraid. Not much call for it. All branch types sign on appointment, and we don't usually need to share anything with outsiders."

Collison paused with his pen poised.

"Just so I'm clear, sir," he asked Newby, "does signing this mean I'm not allowed to share Special Branch information with the rest of my team?"

"It certainly does," he replied as the ACC nodded in the background. "Just you and your DI. If any information is passed over then you'll have to be sure that you've got a process set up that doesn't allow anyone else to see it. I'd suggest that you let us set that up with IT so you can both view stuff online. Just make sure that you don't print off hard copy, and that nobody's looking over your shoulder."

"That's going to be awkward," Collison commented as he signed and pushed the form back across the table.

"Nevertheless, that's the way it's got to be, Simon," the ACC responded. "We're even excluding Jim Morris on a 'need to know' basis."

"Now then," Newby said as he put the two signed forms tidily to one side. "What do you want to know about the Raffens?"

"Well, I can't really answer that question, sir. All we know so far is that Hugh Raffen senior, the one we're calling the grandfather, seems to have been around at the time and place of one murder, while his grandson seems to have been around at the time and place of another murder, which seems to suggest some connection. But it's still early days and we don't know what that connection might be. Our instinct was to trawl through the system for anything we could find, but of course we ran into your computer blocks straightaway."

"Yes, as you would," Newby acknowledged.

He gazed levelly at Collison for a moment. Then he continued.

"I can appreciate your dilemma, of course, but I can't just divulge loads of sensitive information in the hope that some small part of it might prove relevant. Particularly since I understand from the ACC that neither grandfather nor grandson is officially a suspect for either murder. Unless I can go back to my committee with something more specific, they'll just dismiss this as a fishing expedition."

"Yes, I do see that," Collison admitted.

"Tell you what," Newby offered. "Why don't you tell me everything you know, all the background to these two murders, and I'll tell you if we have anything that might have a bearing?"

"Gladly, sir."

Newby listened intently while Collison explained the background to the two linked enquiries, occasionally grunting and jotting something down.

"So what it amounts to is this, then?" he asked when the summary was over. "Grandson Raffen was at the scene of the second murder when it was committed. Grandfather Raffen may have been present at the scene of the first murder when it was committed, but we don't really know. That's not much of a connection really, is it? More of a coincidence, I'd say."

"The connection, sir," Collison urged upon him, "is that the second murder victim was working on an exhibition based on the scene of the first murder at about the time when it was committed. *And* a folder of letters relating to another Isokon resident at the time of the first murder seems to have gone missing from the second victim's room, suggesting that something they contained might have been sufficient motive for murder."

"But you do have two serious suspects for the second

murder, plus a third if you can crack his alibi, plus the possibility of a passing stranger," Newby reminded him.

"That's true, but I still think there's a connection, sir," Collison maintained.

Suddenly Newby's face cracked into a smile.

"Don't worry, Simon, I'm just having a bit of fun pointing out how ludicrous this could sound if someone wanted to make mischief for you. In fact, what you've got here is a classic sort of intelligence situation. We're often really sure we've rumbled someone, but equally sure that we'd never be able to prove it in court."

He laid down his pen and sat back in his chair, unbuttoning his jacket.

"I know you've both just signed those damn forms," he said conversationally, "but I want to make it absolutely clear that what I'm about to tell you goes way beyond 'sensitive'. Do we understand each other?"

They both nodded.

"Back in the thirties, and after the War too, there were some damn strange things going on at the Isokon. Without putting too fine a point on it, the place was a positive nest of communist agents. Funnily enough, some of them didn't know that other residents were active agents too, particularly after the War because some of them worked for the Russians while others worked for the East Germans. Naturally these people should have been pursued and picked up, but for various reasons that wasn't done. Why not, you might wonder?"

He leaned forward and started to answer his own question.

"It was a very strange time in the period before the War, particularly in the sort of academic and literary circles that frequented the Isokon. Most of them were socialists, but that didn't really stand out as so were a lot of people in those days, and nobody thought that just because you were a socialist you were automatically suspect from a security point of view. That's how a lot of Isokon residents ended up working in Government departments, and translating confidential documents."

"No," Collison breathed.

"Well, a lot of them had come across from Germany as opponents of the Nazis, you see, and that sort of lent them a false *bona fides*. There was that period of the Nazi-Soviet pact, when a few of them were actually rounded up and shipped off, but ironically as potentially pro-Nazi German aliens. And Jack Pritchard must have given himself writer's cramp corresponding with everyone and anyone he knew who had any influence at all, pleading for them to be taken into responsible jobs – after all, most of them were highly educated. And after Hitler attacked Russia his task become easier and easier. Some of the people he helped even ended up working on code-breaking. There were very few native German speakers around, let alone those who had the sort of mind to understand cryptography."

"Do you think Pritchard knew, that he was in on it?" Collison asked curiously.

"I think not," Newby said judiciously, "though naturally the question has been asked. I think he was just a genuinely nice man who was trying to help people. I think he had a great affinity with them, or with what they seemed to be on the surface, anyway. He was pretty left wing himself, and he hated the Nazis for what they'd done to Gropius and that lot, and he was a humanitarian, so he had a natural feeling for people who were anti-Nazi, Socialist, and refugees."

"Concentrating on the thirties, which is the period you're concerned with, and on Grandfather Raffen, we now know – we've suspected since the sixties but have only been relatively sure recently – that he was actively involved in recruiting Soviet spies from amongst his students and other young people, and that a lot of this activity took place in his flat at the Isokon."

Collison and Metcalfe exchanged glances.

"And nothing of this was suspected at the time?" Collison enquired.

"No, even though he didn't exactly go out of his way to hide his political sympathies. He used to entertain people from the Soviet Embassy at the Isokon Bar. It turns out some of the other Soviet agents at the Isokon were livid; they thought it was compromising their own positions, which of course it would have done had anybody been concerned enough to do anything about it."

"So Grandfather Raffen was a Soviet agent, but never suspected of being one?"

"Not until much later, no. There was a lot of naiveté,

I'm afraid. It was thought that if you were British then that came first, and your political sympathies a long way second. So being a socialist wasn't seen as a security risk, not in itself anyway. Don't forget a lot of Brits were out in Spain at the time, fighting in the Civil War for the International Brigade. And the other thing was that if someone was a senior establishment figure, which Raffen undoubtedly was, then they were pretty much beyond suspicion of anything. It was only a few years after you think this first murder took place that he was given a peerage, which of course were hereditary in those days, which explains why Grandson Raffen is the Honourable Hugh. As soon as Daddy pops his clogs then he'll be the next Baron Raffen of Grantchester."

"And Daddy is …?" Metcalfe asked, intrigued.

"If you look him up," Newby replied, "you'll see that he's held a number of senior non-executive directorships, and that before that he was working at the Foreign Office."

"And when he was working for the Foreign Office," Collison asked, feeling that he was groping in the dark, "did he have access to any sensitive information?"

"You might say that," Newby concurred. "You see for a while he occupied a post which until recently the Government refused to admit existed."

"You mean -?"

"I mean that for a few years he was head of the Security Intelligence Service, more commonly known as MI6."

"Jeez!" said Metcalfe involuntarily.

"The reason that he only held the post for a few years,"

Newby went on, ignoring the ejaculation, "was that doubts did finally start to emerge surrounding him. A large number of our agents in Eastern Europe started to get picked up. Finally, a Soviet defector gave us various things, a codename overheard here, a piece of paper seen there, which started to point fingers. And most of those fingers seemed to point to David Raffen. By coincidence, at about the same time something came out of the woodwork about his father's activities. Suddenly a lot of very important people started to get very scared for their own careers."

"You confronted him?" Collison asked.

"Not me personally, no, it was before my time. A lot of it's not even documented. It's part of the collective memory which is passed down from one Head of Branch to another whenever there's a handover."

"So you know what happened, then?"

"I do. Raffen was taken off to a safe house and kept there for several weeks while his story was broken down and put together again time after time. At the end of the day, it was one of those intelligence situations I mentioned, where you're sure you're right but it wouldn't hold up in front of a jury. So finally, a deal was struck."

"What sort of deal?" Collison asked.

"Well, he could protest his own innocence all he liked, but he couldn't deny what his father had done; our source was too compelling; a senior KGB defector who'd seen Hugh Raffen's name *en clair* in a file in the archives, and details of his handlers at the Soviet Embassy. David Raffen is a very vain man. It was put to him that if this information was made public then his father would probably be stripped of his peerage posthumously, which would mean that the present Lord Raffen would have to go back to being plain Mr Raffen. He didn't like that idea. Plus, he knew that whatever his own guilt or innocence, you couldn't have a head of MI6 with a traitor for a father. He agreed to go quietly. In return everyone agreed to keep quiet about his father's activities. I think that as much as anything we were desperate to hide the truth from the Americans, who already thought that our security services leaked like a sieve."

"Just to be clear, sir," Collison queried, his head reeling, "is there anything at all of which you are aware, which would link the grandfather to a dead body at the Isokon."

"No," said Newby, the disappointment evident in his voice, "there isn't. But all my instincts tell me that if a place was a hot-bed of communist agents at a certain time, and a body turns up which seems to have been murdered at the same place at the same time, then it's ten to one that the murder and the espionage activities are related."

"Let's not jump to conclusions, now," the ACC cautioned. "It's important that Simon and his team should investigate all possible angles."

"Agreed, of course," Newby replied. "But if you come across anything specific for Special Branch to investigate, Simon, please just let me know."

"I will of course," Collison acknowledged, "But might I just ask you a question?"

"By all means."

"If this is all so sensitive – and I see that it is – then why are you sharing it so readily with us? As you say yourself, there is no obvious relevance or connection. Aren't you putting at risk your cosy little arrangement with David Raffen? I suppose what I mean is: if it wasn't in the public interest for the facts to come out back then, why should that be any different now?"

Newby grinned delightedly at the ACC.

"I see now that everything you said about Simon is true, sir. I hope you'll make Special Branch part of his career path."

"Um," the ACC said non-committally.

Newby turned back to Simon.

"It may just be possible," he said dreamily, "that David Raffen might be looking to publish his memoirs. I don't know, I really couldn't say. One hears rumours, snippets of information ..."

"But surely he wouldn't dare?" Collison wondered. "What about his father?"

"Times change, and we change with them. Perhaps – who knows? – perhaps he has taken advice and discovered that a hereditary peerage cannot be as quickly or as neatly eliminated as might have been suggested to him at the time ... Suppose one were to 'fess up' as the Americans say, about Hugh Raffen's little recruitment drive, but explain it away as a harmless left wing eccentricity on the part of an elderly academic? Suppose he were to go on to claim that he had been hounded from office for the sins of his father, if sins they be, and sins of which in any event he was entirely ignorant?"

"And do we think that's what he's about to do?"

"Yes, I'm afraid we do," Newby said. "That's why I've been so open with you, Simon. You see, there are quite a few of we practitioners of the dark arts who don't like that idea one little bit."

He leaned across the table again.

"Getting some fuzzy-minded modern schoolkids to believe that recruiting young men into the socialist cause is a relatively harmless occupation is one thing. Explaining away a murder is quite another. If we can link Hugh Raffen to this case, Simon, no publisher will touch that manuscript. If you can do that for us, then I think I can safely say that it wouldn't harm your career prospects one little bit, nor yours of course, Bob."

He looked, as is for confirmation, at the ACC, who nodded thoughtfully but significantly.

# CHAPTER 19

Peter Collins was reading as Karen Willis came into the living room, and looked up as she entered. Every time he saw her these days he was struck by the enormity of what he was in the process of losing. Every glimpse heightened the sense of unreality of living with the woman he loved, but living with her in name only, under the same roof but in separate rooms. Sadly, he reflected that she had also changed the way she dressed, abandoning the skirt suits he loved in favour of trousers; it was almost as though her wardrobe had decided upon a spontaneous and independent divorce. Not that they were married, of course. He wondered for a moment if it might have made a difference if they were.

"Am I disturbing you?" she enquired, feeling her chest tighten at the sight of his forlorn expression.

"No, of course not," he reassured her quietly, "what can I do for you?"

"Well," she said, perching on the arm of the sofa, "Collison thought you might be able to help with something concerning the case, but I wasn't sure whether to ask. I didn't know if you'd want to, you know, ... in the circumstances."

"Ask away, old thing," he said as lightly as he could manage. "Always happy to oblige the old Parker bird."

She frowned. Whenever he lapsed into his Wimsey persona these days she was unable to tell whether it was just normal behaviour, or as close to normal behaviour as Peter could approach, or the beginning of a relapse into the traumatic state in which he had suffered so recently. Seeing her concern, he smiled.

"Don't worry," he said, "I'm still here."

"Well," she said again, "it's not much really, but I thought it might be right up your street. You see, it concerns Agatha Christie."

They both glanced involuntarily at the serried rows of crime fiction on the shelves around the room.

"Ah, yes," he affirmed, "Lady Mallowan".

"Her proper title before she became Dame Agatha," he explained as she raised her eyebrows. "Her second husband was Sir Max Mallowan, the archaeologist. But I'm going off at a tangent as usual. Do go on."

"It's like this," she said, and gave him a full briefing on the situation, after which he remained silent for a while, considering what he had just been told.

"I see," he said at length. "Well, I must say you've landed yourself a tough assignment this time, Harriet. You've got to find some letters which have been stolen, but whoever took them has presumably destroyed them by now so you'd need to find copies, not the originals."

"Correct."

"But you don't know for sure when they were written, although you suspect sometime around 1937, and you believe Agatha Christie was a party to them, but you don't know which one: the sender or the recipient."

"That's about the size of it, yes," she acknowledged. "Shouldn't be too difficult a feat for your elephantine brain, should it?"

"Or 'the little grey cells' as I suppose we should be saying, since we find ourselves in Christie country."

"Yes, I suppose so," she said, but sounded distracted.

He gazed at her soberly.

"There's something you want to tell me," he observed shrewdly.

"Yes," she said, but then stumbled over the words. She stopped and tried again.

"Oh, it's ridiculous to be embarrassed, or even to be having this conversation," she said with quiet desperation. "I just wanted you to know that I'm going to be away tonight; I'm staying at Bob's."

"You don't need my permission, you know," he replied, "it's not as if we're sleeping together any more. But thank you for telling me."

"I just didn't want you to worry when I didn't come home," she explained.

"Very thoughtful," he responded with a smile. "As I said, thank you for telling me. I can ask Bunter to bolt the door with a clear conscience."

"Yes," she said giving his hand a sudden squeeze, "you can."

"As for this little puzzle of yours, Harriet," Peter

informed her, "I will indeed put my little grey cells to work. But I warn you: it may just prove impossible – even for me."

"Well," Collison observed as he and Metcalfe walked down the hill from Hampstead underground station, "I'm not sure whether I'm less confused or more by all these new revelations. I thought the ACC was going to find all this 1937 stuff a bit hard to take, instead of which I find myself being positively urged to pursue it."

"With a specific objective in mind don't forget, guv," Metcalfe warned. "The Commander made it very clear that the spooks have their own agenda, and they're expecting us to deliver."

"Oh, I don't think that matters all that much, does it? It's all useful background certainly, but we'll go wherever the investigation takes us. If that involves fingering Special Branch's suspect that's fine, but equally if it doesn't then that's fine too."

Metcalfe stopped walking so abruptly that a lady with a dog of a certain type blundered into him, wrapping him helplessly in her dog's lead, and shrilly labelling him a silly man while he disentangled himself.

"Are you really that naïve?" he asked bluntly once he had done so. "I thought it was made pretty clear that our careers are on the line here. Either we find the proof that Special Branch are looking for, or we're in big trouble."

Collison smiled and gestured to him to keep walking.

"Perhaps I am being a bit naïve," he admitted, "but the

important thing is that it's *us* trying to find the evidence, and all I'm saying is that if it isn't there then it isn't there, and that's all there is to it. There'd be no disgrace in leaving a murder from between the wars unsolved. As a cold case, it doesn't get much colder than that."

Now, as they crossed Gayton Road, it was Metcalfe's turn to smile.

"Why is it I feel you're trying to convince yourself rather than me?" he enquired.

Collison had the grace to laugh.

"OK, touché. I'm just a bit nervous that we're being pushed so hard in one particular direction. It's important that we keep all avenues open."

"You must admit though, guv, it's a pretty long coincidence. It would be bloody weird in the light of everything we know if there didn't turn out to be some connection between the two cases."

"I would happily admit that," Collison acknowledged, "but let's not forget first that we have three suspects for the Burgh House murder who have no connection with the Isokon at all, and second that it's entirely possible that there is a connection between the two but that it turns out to have nothing to do with the Raffen clan."

"I hadn't thought of that," Metcalfe replied, "another possible connection, I mean. That would make life very awkward. Frankly, I wouldn't know where to start."

"No more would I," Collison admitted cheerfully as they approached the police station, "so let's just hope I'm wrong."

As they walked up the steps in companionable silence Collison paused and looked back up Rosslyn Hill. It was one of those rare afternoons of burnished sunshine when to be in Hampstead was to experience not London but somewhere else entirely.

"Einem Zauberland," he mused appreciatively.

"I'm sorry, guv?"

"Sorry, something from 'Dichterliebe'. It goes on to talk about 'goldnen Abendlicht' – golden evening sunshine. Not quite evening yet, I know, but I always think of Hampstead as a wonderland."

Metcalfe stood beside him and also gazed back up the hill.

"You know," he said as if feeling forced to respond with a cultural reference of his own, "I'm reading a Ngaio Marsh book at the moment."

"Karen recommended it," he said a trifle defensively as Collison looked at him questioningly.

"I'm sorry," Collison said at once, "I didn't mean to look surprised. I just didn't clock you for a natural Ngaoi Marsh fan, that's all."

"Well, like I said, Karen recommended it. Anyway, there's a moment when the detective says that simple cases, like one drunk hitting another one on the head with a brick and running off, are often quite difficult to solve whereas fancy, elaborate ones are usually pretty simple because it's only a question of finding the one thing the murderer has overlooked."

"Quite true in principle, I suppose."

"Well, in that case we're unlucky, aren't we? We've got a very complicated case ranging across a huge time span, and yet it's not at all easy to solve. In fact, right now it's looking ruddy impossible."

Collison thought about this for a moment as an ambulance went screaming past towards the Royal Free Hospital.

"I wonder," he replied as the siren died away. "Is it really so complicated? Murderer bashes victim on head and buggers off without being seen. Isn't that really what it comes down to? Perhaps we should treat everything else as just noise. We know what, where and how. We have a reasonable idea about when. So all we need to find out is who and why. That's true of the Isokon case as well."

He took a last lingering look at Hampstead and then turned to go into the station.

"We must think about this," he said vaguely as he crossed the threshold.

Karen Willis was waiting for them in the Incident Room. Watching she and Metcalfe glance at each other, Collison felt more sure than ever that his wife Caroline's feminine instincts were justified. Surely they were more than just friends and colleagues?

"Christie, guv," Evans said to Metcalfe as he went to his desk.

"What?"

"Christie. Timothy Evans. I looked it up."

"Ah."

As Evans wandered back to his own place, smiling, Collison came across and sat down in front of Metcalfe.

"He seems like a smart lad," he commented.

"Evans, guv? Yes, I think he's got the makings of a decent copper. He seems genuinely eager to learn."

"What have got him working on?"

"The nephew's whereabouts on the day of the murder. I doubt we'll get anywhere since it seems he was on his own, but you never know. One of his neighbours might remember having seen him go out for milk or something, so then we can cross him off the list off the list for good and all."

Collison nodded in approval.

"I was just wondering about the Baileys," he said. "After all, they are two of our three possible suspects – four, if we believe that the Honourable Hugh might be involved somehow. It's a bizarre situation, but we don't really seem to know very much about them. Every time we interview them the wife gets hysterical, and the husband just says he didn't do it and effectively dares us to prove it. And of course we can't because we don't know what we don't know, if you see what I mean."

"You mean, we don't know what questions to ask because we don't know enough about what happened?"

"Yes, exactly. It's like tipping a jigsaw puzzle out of its box but not knowing which piece to begin with. So every time we interview them we just keep going back over the same ground but not getting any different answers. I suppose this ladder scenario might give us a new angle, though."

Collison slumped back in the chair and gazed ruminatively at the ceiling.

"It could be a good excuse to re-interview him, guv," Metcalfe suggested. "Though it doesn't alter the fact that they are each other's alibis and they've had ample chance to get their stories straight together."

"So, we could just end up going round in the same circles?"

Metcalfe nodded wryly.

"But that's not to say that we shouldn't try," he added.

"I rather think," Collison said, coming to a decision, "that we should re-interview them both again separately. Let's ask them about anything we can think of, regardless of its relevance to the investigation, and then suddenly throw in the ladder and see what happens. At least we might get some reaction."

"And what about Professor Raffen?" Metcalfe enquired.

"What indeed?" Collison echoed. "The problem with him is that we still don't know for sure whether there is a connection between the two killings, other than a purely coincidental one, nor even what form it might take."

"So, once again, we don't know what questions to ask," Metcalfe ventured.

"My thoughts exactly, Bob. No, my instinct is to hold off on him at least until we can do some research on those missing papers. For one thing, as soon as we pull him in for interview he'll know, or guess, that we're looking for an angle. Whereas as long as we hold off he'll have no idea that we are even linking the two enquiries. Let's talk about it at the briefing in the morning. I'll be in my office for a bit if you want me."

He got up from his chair to move towards the door.

"Excuse me, guv," Willis said.

As he turned and looked at her she seemed subtly different somehow. Something to do with her make-up perhaps? He was sure that his wife would have put her finger on it straightaway.

"Yes, Karen?"

"I just had a call from Peter, guv. He says he's made some progress on the Agatha Christie angle. Wonders if you could pop round for a chat this evening. Maybe about six?"

"I'd be delighted," Collison said warmly. "I haven't seen Peter since his recovery."

A strange expression flitted across her face.

"He *has* recovered, hasn't he?" he asked hurriedly. "I mean, he hasn't had a relapse or anything like that?"

"No," she said with a little shake of her head, "don't worry, he's fine. I think he's found a friend of a friend who's doing some research on Christie, and he's invited you round this evening to let you know what he's found out."

"Wow, that's quick work."

"Yes, well, I'll tell him that's OK then, shall I?"

"Absolutely. I look forward to seeing you both at six."

"I won't be there actually, guv," she said awkwardly. "I'm going out, so it'll just be Peter."

He gazed at her curiously, noticing that she did not meet his eyes.

"Oh, OK, fine," he replied as casually as he could manage.

Once more he found himself wishing that Caroline was there.

# CHAPTER 20

Simon Collison glanced around as he approached the door of the Victorian house in which Peter Collins shared a flat with Karen Willis. The quiet street by Christchurch was elegantly tranquil, and exuded the delicate fragrance of discreet wealth. It could have been a world away from the everyday hubbub of Central London, rather than just three or four minute's stroll from Hampstead High Street.

He paused for a moment with his finger on the entry phone, recalling his last visit, which had been in very different circumstances. Then they had been locked in a dispiriting search for a multiple murderer, and Peter had been very ill, very ill indeed, so ill and sunk in upon himself in fact that all had wondered if he might ever recover. All save Karen, that is. She had passionately refused to admit the possibility of any other outcome, and had insisted that unconventional therapy be applied, so unorthodox that the medical profession had washed their hands of any responsibility for what might ensue. Back then, things had looked very black, he reflected. Hell, they *had* been very black.

He shook his head as he brought himself back to the present, and pressed the button. Peter answered and buzzed him up. Collison walked up the first flight of stairs and found Collins waiting for him on the landing outside the door to his own flat.

"Simon," he said with a faint smile, as if any display of emotion was in itself a little tiring, "how nice to see you again."

"Ditto," Collison replied warmly, shaking him firmly by the hand. "So glad to see you recovered. You had us worried, you know."

"Ah yes," Collins commented rather distantly, as though they were discussing a mythical third party rather than himself.

He held up a bottle of something white and Italian and raised his eyebrows enquiringly.

"Is that a Gavi?" Collison asked. "Yes, please."

Peter Collins poured them each a drink. He handed one to his visitor, and they both sat down in facing armchairs.

"Yes," Collins said with another of those fey smiles as he placed his glass carefully but languidly on the coffee table, "I believe I was, ah, 'not myself' the last time we met. How very embarrassing. At least, it would be if I had the slightest recollection of it, which I'm afraid I don't."

"Do you not?" Collison asked, intrigued. "How fascinating."

"Well, I can remember little flashes of what may or may not have been reality," the other replied. "Sitting here in this room, lying in bed, but nothing was connected somehow. It was a bit like when I had a really bad fever once. You get the strangest feelings. I can remember at one stage feeling that someone had just left the room, but having no memory of them being there before they left, that sort of thing."

"Well," Collison said determinedly, "we're all damn glad to see you recovered anyway."

"Thank you," Collins said rather vacantly.

There was a pause, as though they were both searching for the right thing to say next. Then Collins reached out and took up a pad on which he had clearly been jotting down notes, as it was covered with his spidery handwriting which most people, including frequently himself, found largely illegible.

"I understand you're anxious to trace some old correspondence of Agatha Christie," he said by way of preamble.

"Exactly. We believe that some papers have gone missing from the murder scene at Burgh House, and we strongly suspect that they were letters either to or from Agatha Christie dating from the period when she was a resident at the Lawn Road flats: the Isokon, that is. We're hoping that they can somehow be identified, or even reconstructed."

"That's all, is it?" Collins asked in amusement. "Do you have any idea how many letters Christie wrote and received in a single year? Several thousand, certainly. And even if it were possible, which I'm sure it isn't, to bring them all together, how would you know which ones were missing, since – by definition – they wouldn't be there?"

"I know, I know," Collison concurred lamely. "We may be setting ourselves an impossible task, but isn't it just possible that one of the letters that can be found might refer to one which can't?"

"It's possible, of course," Collins agreed, "though it would presumably mean reading all the damn letters and cross-referencing them. But even then, how will you know what the letter actually said even if you know that it should exist, but it doesn't?"

"The same, I suppose," Collison muttered doggedly. "Look at the context of the other letters and try to piece together what is missing from what's there."

"Makes sense," Collins agreed. "I'm sorry, Simon, I'm just playing devil's advocate to clarify my own thinking as much as anything. A Socratic dialogue, as it were."

Collison gave a thin smile. He was beginning to hope that he wasn't wasting his time. Was Peter really back to his old self? A full recovery seemed like a lot to expect in such a relatively short space of time.

"Well, let me tell you where I've got to," Collins said, gazing intently at his notes and clearly trying to decipher them.

"I won't give you all the boring details of the many calls I've made, mostly without success. I'll just cut to the chase, as it were."

"Fine by me," Collison encouraged him.

"The bottom line is that the official archive of Agatha Christie's papers is held at the University of Exeter. Gaining access to it is only possible with the consent of the estate, which is managed by a company controlled by her descendants, but I'm assuming that won't prove a problem if the police make a formal request."

"That's good, Peter. Many thanks indeed. Do you have any contact details?"

"I do indeed."

Collins passed across a piece of paper with handwriting on it, hesitated, took it back and then, leaning over the coffee table, laboriously copied out the name and telephone number again in block capitals.

"I have a friend at Exeter University, by the way," Collins went on as he finally passed the details across to Collison. "He's in the psychology department, so nothing to do with any of this, but I asked him to make some enquiries and the archivist was quite forthcoming. It's not necessarily good news though, I'm afraid."

"How so?"

"Well, apparently most of the papers are from the 1950s onwards. There's not much from the 1930s. She was travelling frequently with her husband, as you know, and a lot of stuff probably went missing between relocations."

"Oh," said Collison gloomily, "I thought this all sounded a bit too good to be true."

"Well, you never know," Collins said encouragingly. "At least now we know where to look."

He crossed the room, picked up the bottle and refilled their glasses.

"I've been thinking about this very carefully," he continued as he sat down again. "Logically, each of the missing letters must be to or from Agatha Christie. If they were *to* her then by definition they won't be in the archive at Exeter, because we're talking about original documents and there can't be more than one of each in existence. So our only hope would be as you suggest, that there may be some reference to them in other documents which are in the archive, and we might be able to surmise something from the context."

"That's true," Collison concurred, looking puzzled, "but why are you drawing a distinction? Surely the same would hold true for any letter *from* her, wouldn't it?"

Collins took a sip at his wine and shook his head thoughtfully.

"Not necessarily," he replied mysteriously.

He ran his finger round the rim of his glass, and looked at Collison hesitantly.

"I don't want to raise false hopes," he explained, "but my research has shown that Christie was dealing with so much correspondence during her time at the Isokon that she employed a full time secretary there. And back in those days secretaries took carbon copies, yes and usually filed them away too."

"Peter!" Collison almost shouted. "But that's marvellous!"

"Well, it may or may not be," Collins said cautiously. "Logically those carbons must have existed, but there's no guarantee that they still exist today."

"Well, it's something anyway," Collison averred firmly.

"And something is more than I had when I came into the flat, so thank you for that – and for the wine, by the way, it's delicious."

"If you like," Collins offered, "I could go down to Exeter for you. I've done a lot of research and I know my way around archives."

Collison shook his head.

"It's a nice idea," he said regretfully, "not to mention a very generous offer, but it really needs to be a serving officer, I'm afraid."

"Anyway," he went on quickly, seeing the evident disappointment in the other's face, "I'm sure you've got a lot to occupy yourself with right here."

"To tell the truth," came the reply, "I'd welcome a chance to get away for a bit. I don't know if Karen's told you or not, but we're splitting up."

"Oh, I'm so sorry, Peter," Collison responded instinctively. "No, she hadn't told me but I suspected something wasn't right. She's been a little strange really, distant somehow."

Collins nodded sadly.

"It's her and Bob Metcalfe, of course," he said, "but then if you knew something was wrong then you probably suspected that anyway, didn't you?"

"I did," Collison admitted, "although to be fair it was more Caroline than me. She said something the next morning after that time we all got together for dinner – do you remember?"

"As early as that, eh? My goodness, female intuition is a powerful thing, isn't it?"

"I'm so sorry," Collison repeated. "it must be really dreadful for you, Peter; awkward as well, what with all of you knowing each other."

"Actually, it's not," Collins said with a wry grimace, "or not in the way you mean, anyway. The real problem is that we can all see everyone else's point of view, and we all like each other. Or at least I like Bob, and I think he likes me."

"I'm sure he does," Collison assured him quickly.

"I can see exactly why a woman would prefer a man like him to one like me, someone who inhabits the real world rather than a runaway escape space like I tend to do. But equally, I think he recognises that there are times when a woman wants to feel like a lady, or to do something really special."

"And what about Karen?" Collison asked cautiously.

Collins shrugged helplessly.

"I think she's just in love with two men at the same time, as simple as that. But I think that for her it's different with Bob; that's what she says, anyway. With him she just feels some sort of helpless and very strong attraction without really knowing why. I assume it's the same with him."

Collison remained silent. There were times when someone just needed an audience as an excuse to talk to themselves, and he sensed that this was one of them. Sure enough, after a reflective pause, the other man went on.

"I've always known that this would happen someday. I

mean, I've always known that a man like me couldn't hope to keep a fantastic woman like Karen for ever. To be honest, I'm not sure what she ever saw in me in the first place. Perhaps she felt sorry for me, I don't know. God knows what I'm going to do without her."

This time the pause was longer. Collison sensed the barely contained pain in the facing armchair and felt wretched for his friend who was in such depths of despair. Wretched, yes, and helpless too, largely because he knew deep down that Peter was right. Karen had been his whole life, in much more than the rather shallow sense in which that phrase was often employed, and he struggled to imagine Peter living without her.

"Oh dear," Peter said suddenly, "this will never do. I'm getting quite maudlin. I'm sorry, Simon, to have inflicted that upon you."

Collison felt his insides twist again. Peter was of an age and upbringing that regarded showing any sign of emotion as both weak and selfish. It was yet another indication of how completely out of sorts he was with modern everyday life.

"Karen tells me that you're writing a paper," Collins said brightly, changing the subject very obviously.

"Thinking of writing a paper would be more like it," Collison clarified. "It's the ACC's ideally, actually. He seems to think it's something every senior officer should have on his CV."

"Then it's rather nice that he's shepherding you in the

right direction, isn't it?"

"I suppose so," Collison said dubiously. "but you know, sometimes I suspect his motives. He's a wily old bird."

"Really? Why, what do you think he might be up to?"

"Well, it may just be me being paranoid, but he's been pressing me very hard to apply for the job of Principal of the Crime Academy, and it occurs to me that putting up a paper would position me very firmly on the academic side of things, and thus an obvious candidate – in some people's eyes anyway – to head the Academy."

"But can't you just say no?" Collins enquired.

"I have," Collison answered shortly, "but at the end of the day he could always just post me somewhere. I'm actually very fortunate even to have been asked. Most officers don't get much choice in the matter, although they can always request certain postings, of course."

Collins nodded slowly in understanding.

"Have you considered," he asked slowly, clearly thinking out loud, "putting up a paper on something that would not necessarily be relevant to the Crime Academy's curriculum? That way you could do what the ACC wants, but not play into any secret plans he may have re the Academy ...?"

Collison gave a quiet little "ha".

"That's exactly what I've already thought of myself," he beamed. "Great minds think alike, eh? Yes, I think I'm going to focus on something organisational."

"Sounds good," nodded Collins. "Wasn't there some report a while back, an external one by some management consultants, which proved very embarrassing because it didn't come up with the conclusions the Home Office had expected?"

"You know about that?"

Why was he surprised? Peter Collins seemed to know everything about everything.

"It was in the papers," Collins said mildly.

Yes, thought Collison, but probably on the inside pages of a supplement to one of the weightier Sundays.

"Well spotted, in that case," he said, "and yes, as it happens I think I may take that as my starting point. My instinct is that the Met would be very happy for someone to shoot holes in it. As it is, every so often some MP or other who's in search of a bit of instant media coverage can jump up and down and demand to know why the police commissioned a very expensive report and have then done nothing about it."

"That shouldn't be too difficult," Collins observed. "All you have to do is cast doubt on it, or even just come up with some alternative suggestions. With a nebulous subject like organisational structure it's impossible to show that any one approach is right or wrong; it's all so subjective. Let me know if you'd like a hand with it, even if it's only just reading a draft and making some suggestions."

"Thank you, Peter, I'll take you up on that," Collison said. "Or, at least, I will when I have time to think about it, rather than about a pressing engagement with Dame Agatha Christie."

# CHAPTER 21

Bob Metcalfe and Karen Willis were sitting rather self-consciously at a coffee shop on Hampstead High Street, savouring their first experience as an openly-admitted couple. One of those awkward silences had descended, when each knows that the other expects them to say something, but is unsure what to say without risking striking the wrong note.

"Don't think that because I'm quiet, I'm unhappy or anything," Willis suddenly blurted out. "Last night was lovely, really."

Suddenly Metcalfe could relax.

"I'm so glad you said that," he replied, reaching across the table to squeeze her hand. "It was exactly what I was thinking myself."

She smiled a rather thin smile, and squeezed back.

"Damn!" Metcalfe exclaimed angrily, "why does this have to be so difficult?"

"Things are bound to feel a bit strange to begin with, I suppose," Willis responded, "but I'm really going to have to lean on you, Bob. Peter was the only really serious relationship I've ever had, so I've never been through anything like this before. To tell the truth, I'm feeling rather lost."

"Well you're one ahead of me, then," Metcalfe said ruefully. "I had what I thought might be a serious relationship, but in my heart of hearts I always knew it wasn't meant to be a long term thing, and then ... and then I met you."

"And did you know straightaway?"

"Yes of course, although to start with I wondered if it might be some sort of stupid crush or something. I couldn't handle how I wasn't able to stop thinking about you."

"Ah, that's sweet," she said gently.

"Maybe, but I can tell you I've never been so confused in my life. Like I said, I couldn't stop thinking about you, so I had to ask myself if you were the person I was supposed to spend my life with, but, if so, then why were you so happy with Peter? And then of course I met him, and in spite of my feelings for you I found that I really liked him, and I understood what you saw in him ..."

He tailed off uncertainly. Her expression hardened, and he cursed himself for his clumsiness.

"Let's just take each day as it comes, Bob, OK?"

"And talking of the day," she went on, glancing at her watch, "we'd better be going or we'll be late for the morning meeting. Damn these places. Why do they have to serve everything too hot to drink?"

"What are we going to tell anyone at the nick?" she asked as they walked down the hill together.

"There's a protocol about these things," Metcalfe answered. "I've looked it up. As we're acting on the same investigation, we have to tell the SIO. After that we have to register as a couple, but only when we believe it's a settled long-term relationship, and it looks like we have quite a lot of discretion on that."

"So there's no need for the team to know?"

"God no, and I'd rather keep it that way if you don't mind."

"Agreed," she said with feeling.

"You OK with Collison knowing?" he asked, as they waited to cross Downshire Hill.

"Yes, no problem," she replied. "Anyway, I think Peter was going to tell him last night."

"Morning, everyone," Collison called out shortly afterwards, waiting for the hum of conversation in the Incident Room to die away.

"Since last we met," he went on, "DI Metcalfe and I have met with Special Branch and the ACC in connection with the restricted access to information on the Raffen family. The good news is that some information was passed onto us which may help to narrow our search for the missing papers. The bad news is that I'm afraid we can't share with you what we were told."

A murmur ran around the room.

"Yes, I know, I'm sorry but that's just the way it is. Special Branch are very sensitive about certain matters, and they are only prepared to provide any information at all on a very selective basis, and even then only after asking the DI and myself to sign the Official Secrets Act."

Another murmur, this time tinged with a note of excitement.

"I know that all sounds very John Le Carré," Collison acknowledged with a smile. "All I can promise is that we'll keep you as fully briefed as we can without compromising security. Bob?"

"Thank you, sir. OK, first up we have the question of accounting for Alan Howse's whereabouts on the day of the murder so we can eliminate him from our enquiries. Any progress with that?"

"None so far, sir," Evans piped up. "We've drawn a blank with all his neighbours, but if I could have another day or so, I'd like to look into the chance of him having shown up on CCTV anywhere near his flat."

Metcalfe looked at Collison, who nodded.

"OK, Timothy, go ahead," Metcalfe confirmed.

"Now," he continued, consulting his notes, "there are the Baileys. Any further action there, guv?"

Collison appeared to be wrestling with his thoughts, but then came to a decision.

"I think it's right that you should all know," he said slowly and deliberately, "that, without revealing any state secrets, there are certain circumstances in which Professor Raffen could be classified as a suspect in the Burgh House murder."

This time the excitement was palpable.

"Let's not get carried away, OK?" Collison pleaded, holding up his hands. "I'm just telling you this for the sake of completeness. In order for him to be a serious suspect we would need to establish a particular connection between the two killings and as yet we are unclear whether any connection at all exists, let alone what it might be."

Everyone watched as Metcalfe solemnly added 'Professor Raffen' to the names of Alan Howse, Jack Bailey and Sue Bailey on the whiteboard.

"So," Collison said, "as far as Burgh House is concerned we are really no further ahead except that we now have an additional suspect. Hopefully we will shortly be able to rule the nephew out altogether, but in the meantime I propose to interview all four again myself with DS Willis and DC Desai sitting in."

"And the papers, guv?" Metcalfe prompted, ticking off the penultimate item on his list.

"We have a lead from a very valued source," Collison announced, with a smile to Karen, "who has established that the Agatha Christie archive is held at Exeter University. We are making urgent arrangements with the Christie family for DI Metcalfe to travel down there and access it. We now know that when she was at the Isokon she had a full time secretary, so we are hopeful that we might find some carbon copies of her outgoing correspondence at the time."

"Can I go too, guv?" Desai asked.

"Afraid not, Priya," Collison replied apologetically. "You're on the wrong side of the Chinese wall, so DI Metcalfe won't be able to share with you what he's looking for or, more importantly, why. It has to be him and nobody else."

"Tell you what," Metcalfe said quickly, noticing Desai's crestfallen countenance, "there's still the question of any original Agatha Christie correspondence turning up on the ephemera market. Timothy was originally going to deal with that but now he seems to be knee-deep in the nephew. Why don't you take over that line of enquiry, Priya?"

"OK, guv," she responded with a marked lack of enthusiasm.

"Good," Metcalfe said, crossing off the last item on his list. "Everyone else continue with house to house, please. We still have a lot of properties where we haven't been able to raise anyone. DS Willis has the list. OK, that's everything."

There was a collective groan which he chose to ignore as he walked over to Collison.

"Excuse me, guv," he said, "but before I go to Exeter, could we have a quiet word?"

In a different police building, DCS Morris was at that very moment having a quiet word with Tom Allen.

"I have to be honest with you, Tom," he was saying. "I think I misjudged Simon Collison. I didn't really know the bloke before – I'd only met him once, I think – so I was really just going on what I'd heard about him from other people, but now that I've spent some time with him, I think he's alright."

"So he's been working his public school charm on you, has he?" Allen asked with a sardonic smile.

"Nothing like that, Tom," Morris replied irritably. "It's just that I reckon you've got a bit of chip on your shoulder about him. It wasn't his fault that he relieved you on that last case, you know. He was acting under orders from the ACC."

"It's got nothing to do with that," Allen said, bridling. "It's a question of what sort of copper he is at the end of the day. Do you really want someone taking charge of murder investigations who's got very little practical experience?"

"I don't think that's fair. He worked under you for a while, didn't he? Yes, and you got on fine with him then, too. I've read your notes on his file from when you were his guvnor."

"That's when he was a DI," Allen pointed out, "and pretty young to be a DI too, if you ask me. Now suddenly in the blink of an eye he's jumped to DS. He was a fair DI, I'll give him that; he was through and methodical which is exactly what you want in a number two. Always knew where everyone was and what they were doing, kept the paperwork neat and tidy. Just like Bob Metcalfe does now."

"Is that what this is really about, Tom?" Morris asked gently. "Collison being leapfrogged ahead of you? That was inevitable sooner or later, you know. He's clearly cut out to be a CPO. You're not, and you wouldn't want to be. I'm not sure any longer that I want to be either, to be honest."

"It's not about that," Allen replied stubbornly, "though since you mention it I do think he's been promoted too far too quickly. Now you say the ACC is looking for an opportunity to bump him up to DCS. Bloody hell, what's the world coming to?"

He shook his head.

"Actually, I think the wheels may have fallen off that idea," Morris commented.

"What do you mean?"

"Nothing. I'm sorry I said anything. I'm not supposed to know."

"Know what?"

"Forget it, Tom," Morris said awkwardly. "You'll find out soon enough."

Allen stared at him and then shook his head again, though this time in bemusement rather than exasperation.

"What this is about, Jim," he said, "is about enquiries being run by officers without the necessary experience to do the job properly. You know that he'd never been an SIO before when he took over on that last case?"

"We all have to fly solo for the first time sooner or later, Tom. It's just that with him it was a bit sooner than with us, that's all."

Allen looked unconvinced.

"And I'm sure that he had a chance to learn a great deal by observing you in action."

"I don't think so," Allen retorted. "If he had, then he wouldn't be poncing about with all those la-di-da ways of his."

"You can't blame someone for their upbringing, Tom. He went to public school, you and I went to the local comprehensive. He went to University, and a bloody good one too, and we didn't. It's just the way things are. Personally, I think he's OK."

"As a bloke?"

"Definitely. I've been spending time at Hampstead nick, you know, listening to what people say, and watching how the case is going. Everyone's a bit suspicious of him at first, but once they've seen him in action, they like him. He's straight with people; they like that. He doesn't throw tantrums when things go wrong; they like that. He gets everyone involved, asks their opinions; they like that too. Yes, and they like the fact that he's bloody intelligent as well."

"And as a copper?"

"Yes, and as a copper too I reckon."

"What are you basing that opinion on? His last case? He got lucky on that you know. He made a lot of mistakes, and came up with some crazy ideas."

"One of which turned out to be correct," Morris reminded him, "and I think you'd agree that's it's not one which would have occurred to either of us."

"He still made mistakes," Allen maintained.

"For God's sake, Tom, we all make mistakes. We're human beings. It's not like you see on the telly when the clues just pop up and they follow them, you know that. Jesus, look at the Yorkshire Ripper case; that was a complete Horlicks from beginning to end. Look at the Jeremy Bamber case; the SIO – an old style copper like you, incidentally, not a Simon Collison whizz-kid – decided up front the girl had killed herself, and refused to change his mind even when new evidence came forward. We all make mistakes, Tom. That's why so much detective fiction is so unrealistic. In real life we often stumble and blunder our way to a solution without any clear idea of which path to follow."

Allen looked at him suspiciously.

"Do your read detective fiction?"

"It's nothing to be ashamed of, Tom. The way you say it sounds like you're asking me if I go around nicking women's underwear from washing lines."

"Do they have washing lines anymore?" Allen asked sourly.

"Probably not."

There was a pause. An uncomfortable one on the part of Morris, and an unrepentant one on the part of Allen.

Morris sighed.

"Look, Tom, I've said what I wanted to say. I was hoping I could mollify you about Collison. I hope I haven't been wasting my breath."

Allen stared at him in amazement.

"What did you just say?"

Morris thought for a moment and then shifted uneasily as he realised what Allen was getting at.

"I said I was hoping I could mollify you. It means making someone feel better about something."

"Jesus, Jim," Allen exclaimed in disgust, "when did you ever use words like 'mollify'? You're starting to speak like him, you know that? You bought yourself a dictionary, or something?"

Before he could stop himself, Morris glanced self-consciously at the top left hand drawer of his desk.

# CHAPTER 22

Bob Metcalfe's visit to the University of Exeter was only half a day old before he was phoning his SIO excitedly.

"I think we've hit the jackpot, guv," he reported. "Peter's hunch was a good one. There are some of those carbon copies filed away. They're very fragile and faded, but they're clear enough with a special viewer like they've got here in the library. You can scan and print them with it as well, which is what I've done. I'm planning to get the train back this evening, by the way, so I should be back at the nick in the morning."

"Fine, Bob, just do long as you're happy there's nothing else there you might be missing."

"I'm pretty sure of that, guv. The archivist here couldn't remember anything relating to Professor Raffen at all, so I reckon we've done well to find what we have. There's very little from the 1930s, actually, and I've been through it all twice. Most of it is from much later: the 50s and 60s mostly."

"Well, put me out of my suspense, Bob. What have you found?"

"There's some boring everyday stuff which I don't think has much to do with the case, but I'm bringing it anyway. The jackpot is a letter which she wrote to a friend of her husband who works at the Home Office. She says that a young man called Alexander Hamilton came to have tea with her, and was very concerned that Professor Raffen had been trying to recruit him 'to spy for a foreign power', in her words."

"Wow! Does it say anything about him that might help us to trace him?" Collison asked.

"Only that he was a student at Oxford."

"OK," Collison said making a note, "I'll get someone started on that. Does the letter say anything else?"

"It says that Christie confronted Raffen with the allegation, without naming Hamilton, but that he guessed where the information had come from."

"Crikey! That was a bit foolhardy wasn't it? Not to mention rather stupid. Surely, it would just put him on his guard."

"Yeah, she does say 'perhaps foolishly' as if she's realised it wasn't a very good idea."

"Well, she was right about that. Does she mention his reaction?"

"Yes, she says he got very upset, guessed that she was referring to Hamilton, and said that he'd been trying to recruit him into the British security services, and couldn't understand how he had got completely the wrong end of the stick."

"I see!"

"Yeah, she closes the letter by saying that from his manner she 'wasn't convinced by his explanation' and that's why she's writing to lay it before someone who can investigate it properly."

"I wonder why our chum from Special Branch didn't mention any of this?" Collison asked thoughtfully.

"Dunno, guv, but doubtless you'll enjoy asking him."

"You said there was other stuff too?"

"Yes, but only one that's interesting. It's from Christie to Raffen a week or so later, and it sounds like it's in answer to a letter from him. If so, that letter's not here. It's good stuff though. It says she was very surprised to hear from Raffen that Hamilton should have decided to fight in Spain, and should have gone off without telling her anything about it. It says she's checked with his mother too, so maybe she and the mum were friends."

"Good Lord," Collison marvelled. "An unexplained disappearance, a sinister professor, agents of a foreign power ... it all sounds like something straight out of John Buchan. Can it really be true, Bob?"

"Well, the letters are real enough," Metcalfe replied, "and lucky we are to have them; the security at this place is diabolical. The archivist said they've had two break-ins lately. The first time some cash that was lying around got nicked. The second time nothing seemed to have been taken, but after the first one they'd taken the precaution of putting locks on the filing cabinets. Nothing that would deter a professional, mind you, but presumably it was just some local kids looking for easy pickings."

"Well thank God nothing happened to them, Bob. Now,

just get back here with those letters, and remember that only you and I have clearance to see them. In the meantime, I'll call the ACC and report what we've found."

Having passed Alexander Hamilton's details to Karen Willis, who was running the team in Metcalfe's absence, Collison returned to the privacy of his office to call the ACC, who listened intently to his report.

"I wonder why Newby didn't tell us about this?" he asked,

"My thoughts exactly, sir. Perhaps we could ask him."

"Hm."

There was a pause for reflection.

"No," the ACC said, obviously coming to a conclusion. "Tell you what, just send him copies of the letters and tell him you'd be very grateful for any light he can cast upon them. Copy me."

"Yes, sir."

"Well done, by the way, Simon. This suggests strongly that the two murders are linked, doesn't it? After all, if the originals of those letters were in Howse's office, and our present day Hugh Raffen got to know about them, then stealing them and silencing Howse to protect the family reputation, not to mention his title, could be a powerful motive for murder."

"It certainly looks that way, sir. After all, Raffen could hardly have known that there might have been carbon copies floating around."

"Quite. So how do you want to proceed?"

"I've been thinking about that. We now have four official

suspects: Raffen, the Baileys and the nephew."

"The nephew's a suspect in name only, really, isn't he?"

"Nonetheless, we have to treat him as one until we can verify his whereabouts on the day in question."

"Of course," acknowledged the ACC, "I'm just trying to think through the practicalities. As for the Baileys, as long as they alibi each other and you can't break their stories, then I don't see how we move ahead, unless one of them suddenly comes forward and confesses, which hardly seems likely."

"Whereas Raffen appears to have had motive, means and opportunity," Collison pointed out, "and to have no alibi apart from the time he was in the Flask."

"The Flask?"

"The local pub, sir. In Flask Walk, which got its name when Hampstead was a spa, and people used to bring flasks to fill with the local water from the springs."

"Never mind the general knowledge," the ACC replied gruffly. "What are you going to do?"

"So far as Burgh House is concerned, sir, I'm proposing to re-interview at least the three most obvious suspects under caution. I'll test the Baileys' stories all over again and see if they make any mistakes. I'll explain to Raffen that in the light of new evidence we have to treat him as a suspect until we can eliminate him. Hopefully that will reassure him a bit. Then I'll hit him with everything we know and see if he cracks."

There was another silence at the Scotland Yard end of the line.

"Suppose he doesn't?" the ACC asked at length. "It seems to me that we have to find some way of proving that he actually knew about those letters, or our motive goes out of the window. If I can see that, then surely he will as well? He's an intelligent man, after all."

"I'm open to better suggestions, sir," Collison said drily.

The ACC chuckled.

"I don't have any, Simon. I only wish I did. You press on and we'll see what happens. By the way, do keep Jim Morris informed, won't you? So far as you can, of course."

Collison put the phone down and stared blankly out of the window for a moment, watching an ambulance muscle its way through the traffic with its blues and twos towards the Royal Free Hospital a short distance down the hill towards Belsize Park. He wondered for the umpteenth time why he was so obsessed with being allowed to run homicide investigations; they had a knack of making him feel helpless, an impostor. He had a recurring dream in which he was an actor walking on stage in front of a live audience but knowing full well that he knows none of the lines in the play and can only improvise; doubtless Peter Collins or one of his psychologist friends would spot the obvious explanation. Recently it had been getting worse; now it was an opera, not a play, and the conductor was raising his baton at him expectantly as the orchestra launched into an aria to which he knew neither the music nor the words.

He sighed and, for something to do as much as anything,

went back down to the Incident Room, where Karen Willis was just finishing a phone call.

"How are we getting on?" he enquired.

"Pretty well, guv, I think. That was Oxford University I was talking to just now. They have a name and a date which seem to fit. He was at Balliol, but never finished his degree. He left at the end of his second year, which means the summer of 1937. That's why they took a few minutes to find him; there's no record of him having graduated. They're going to make some more enquiries about what happened, and come back to me."

"It might be worth asking them if they can cross-reference Professor Raffen and see if Hamilton took any of his courses," Collison suggested.

"Yes, I thought of that actually, but they said straightaway that it wouldn't be possible. Apparently all lectures at Oxford are open; anyone can go. Which means both that people who aren't even studying that subject can attend, and that students currently on the course might not."

"Damn, I knew that," Collison admitted, rubbing his forehead. "Why did I forget? Maybe I'm tired."

Willis smiled sympathetically, but it was a tight little smile, devoid of that sudden flash of warmth which usually came into her eyes.

"I've been meaning to have a word, by the way," he said suddenly. "Why don't you come up to my office when you've got a minute?"

He stood up as she closed the office door behind her a

few minutes later, and motioned her to a chair.

"Bob spoke to me before he left," he said abruptly, "so I know about you and him. Officially, I mean. Actually Peter told me the night before, and I'd already guessed anyway."

"You'd guessed?" she echoed, raising her eyebrows. "Oh dear, was it really that obvious? I thought we were hiding it rather well."

"You were," he acknowledged, "and no, it wasn't at all obvious. Caroline guessed, to be honest. That evening when we all had dinner together."

"Feminine intuition ..." she observed.

"Yes, very much so. She's quite remarkable like that. She's rarely wrong about people. I think in that respect she's much wiser than me. She has a sort of instinct for it."

He rolled a pencil around in his fingers, wondering how to frame what he wanted to say. Dammit, he wasn't even sure what it was he wanted to say.

"I'm not very good at this, am I?" he mused out loud.

She laughed suddenly and, reaching across the desk, briefly touched the back of his hand.

"You're a very nice man," she said sincerely. "Let me make this as easy as possible for you. You're worried about me and you want to ask me if I'm OK."

"Yes," he said simply. "Are you?"

"No," she said, exhaling sharply, "to tell the truth, I'm not. I thought once Bob and I were able to get together properly, openly that is, everything would be OK, but it's not. I just feel desperately guilty."

"Couldn't that just be the natural pain of ending a relationship?" he asked.

"I suppose so, yes," she nodded uncertainly. "The problem is that Peter was the only really serious relationship I've ever had, so I really just don't know. I have nothing to compare it against."

"And I'm really not the best person to be advising you," Collison admitted. "I've only ever had one really serious relationship too, and I can't even begin to imagine what it would feel like for it to be over, particularly if –"

"Yes," she agreed.

"I was going to say ..." he went on, floundering.

"You were going to say 'particularly if it was me who'd brought it to an end', and you'd be quite right," she said quietly.

"I'm sorry," he said abjectly, "that was really thoughtless of me."

"No it wasn't," she countered calmly, "it was honest and natural and sincere, and those are exactly the qualities I admire and respect in you, so please don't start apologising for them."

"It's nice of you to say so," he relied awkwardly, "but like I said, I'm really not very good at this."

"I was expecting to be unhappy, you see," she explained, ignoring his response. "I knew there'd be something like a grieving period, a sorrow for the ending of a relationship. But I didn't expect to feel like this: this remorse, this guilt. And, yes, this sense that maybe I've done the wrong thing."

"Oh," he said. "That would be ... awkward."

"And then I start thinking that I'm being unfair to Bob. I really do have very strong feelings for him you know."

"It sounds like you're between a rock and a hard place," Collison observed sympathetically. "You have strong feelings for both men, and because of that you feel you're being unfair to either or both of them no matter what you do."

She nodded dismally. She was clearly on the verge of tears.

"I'm really not the right person for you to be discussing this with," he repeated. "Isn't there a woman you can talk to – your mother maybe?"

"I never knew my real mother. I was adopted. The lady who brought me up is a wonderful lady and I love her dearly, but she wouldn't know where to start with something like this. It would simply be beyond her ken."

"I didn't know you were adopted," Collison interjected.

"No reason why you should. I don't think it's in my file or anything. So was Bob, actually. I often wonder whether that was part of the attraction. A common bond, as it were."

As he cast around for something to say, Collison suddenly had what he thought might be a very good idea.

"I say! Would you like to talk to Caroline? Like I said, she has a real instinct for this sort of thing. I'm sure she'd be happy to meet up for a coffee or something."

"I wouldn't want to be a bother. I'm sure she's got a hundred and one things to do."

"It wouldn't be a bother," he assured her. "I'm sure she'd be only too happy to help in any way she could."

"Look," he said decisively. "It's Friday today. Why don't I give you her phone number and you can arrange to meet up over the week-end? Or this evening if you like, while Bob's traveling back from Exeter."

"All right," she said with a poor attempt at a smile.

As she left the room, Collison reached for the phone to call his wife, an awkward feeling growing within him that he was passing the buck in a particularly shameless fashion.

# CHAPTER 23

"I do think you passed the buck there, you know," his wife remarked as she slipped back into the house that Sunday afternoon. "Aren't pastoral problems supposed to be part of your job description?"

"I know, I know," he admittedly wretchedly. "I really hated asking you, darling, but she seemed so unhappy – no not unhappy, more desperate somehow – and I just had no idea what to say for the best."

"Don't worry, silly, I'm teasing you," Caroline said, as she sat down opposite him and kicked off her shoes. "And I can understand your concern. She *is* unhappy."

"Were you able to help her, do you think?"

She curled her legs up under her on the sofa and grimaced.

"No, not really, I'm afraid. I'm not sure anyone can, except perhaps by listening, which is what I did."

"She told me that she was worried she might have made the wrong decision," Collison proffered after a pause.

"Yes, she is," Caroline mused, "but I think that's a symptom, as it were. The cause of all this distress is that she finds herself in a very unusual situation."

"How so? People split up all the time, don't they? And

surely it's always very unpleasant for at least one of the couple?"

"Yes," she agreed, "but usually what happens is that meeting the new person acts as a catalyst to make you realise that your existing relationship isn't giving you what you want, and so you move on. With regrets, certainly, and probably with some guilt if you're the person who's making the break, but deep down you know that you're doing the right thing, and that everyone involved will be better off in the long term once all the pain and upset subsides."

"And this isn't like that?"

"No, it's not like that at all. Imagine a happily married person, someone like you or me, having to be around someone every day for whom we felt an enormous attraction. Nothing we could explain or rationalise, but something overwhelming and all-consuming. Imagine going to bed with your partner but finding yourself thinking about the other person at the same time. Or being with that other person but knowing that you're still in love with your partner. That's what she's been going through."

"Good God! Poor kid, but ..."

"What?" she prompted as he hesitated.

"Well, doesn't that sound more like infatuation than love? And, if so, doesn't that go away after a while?"

"Yes, that's what she thought," Caroline replied grimly. "So she kept it all bottled up inside her, and believed that if she ignored it long enough it would disappear and everything would be back to normal."

"But it didn't?"

"Obviously not."

"Oh dear," Collison said helplessly. "So all the way through that last case ...?"

"She was suffering, yes."

"As you spotted when we had dinner together," he said admiringly, "the first time you ever met them altogether."

"It wasn't that difficult, really," she protested. "There was a sort of electricity that crackled around her. Did you really not notice? I thought policemen were supposed to be observant?"

"Observant, yes. Psychic, no," he countered.

"But hadn't you noticed that her appearance has completely changed recently?" Caroline asked incredulously. "Surely that must have registered with you, Simon? Please tell me it has."

"Well yes, of course," he said defensively, "but I wasn't sure what it was."

His wife gave him the sort of glance that conveyed the word "men" in a sad and contemptuous manner without actually saying so.

"I mean," he went on uncertainly, "I thought she'd lost weight or something."

"She certainly has lost weight," she affirmed, "which is hardly surprising given how unhappy she's been. But it's much more than that. With Peter they inhabited a distinct little world together which was somehow detached from real life. How many people go to concerts or art exhibitions all the time? Or vintage dances like the one we saw them going to – do you remember? Or take the trouble to dress elegantly all the time? Well, they did. And she enjoyed it too, just as much as he did. And in leaving Peter she feels she's lost that world."

"Did she tell you all this?" he asked.

"Not in these exact words, but it's pretty much as I've described it. She *did* say that she's put away all the clothes she used to wear with Peter, that she feels like she's gone to live in a different country now, where people dress differently. For example, she used to wear stockings when she lived with him – stockings, not tights – whereas now she hardly ever even wears a skirt. And she's hardly wearing any make-up, or at least she wasn't when I met her just now. It's as if she really has gone to a different country, a rather alien one where she's trying to fit in. Oh really, darling, surely you must have noticed some of this?"

"We're not encouraged to try to discover if female colleagues are wearing stockings or not," he said lightly. "There are things called disciplinary hearings, you know. They can rather set one's career back."

She laughed and beckoned him over to sit beside her.

"You're really not very observant, you know, Superintendent," she said, as she laid her head on his shoulder and, taking his hand, placed it on her belly.

He let it rest there idly, but then looked at her sharply as she suddenly started laughing.

Collison had still not come to terms with the fact that he was shortly to become a father when he finally managed to speak to Commander Newby.

"Simon," Newby greeted him, "I'm very sorry I didn't get back to you after you called on Friday. We had a bit of a flap on here about something or other. I see you sent something over on Friday evening for me to look at. Was that what you wanted to speak to me about?"

"Yes, sir. I'm about to go into our morning briefing meeting and I need to know if this is something I can tell the troops about, or whether it comes under the heading of classified material."

"Of course, I do understand. Well, it's all a bit of a mystery, I'm afraid. I've had a team here all weekend digging into the files and I have to say that we've been unable to find the original."

"Is that significant, do you think?"

"Almost certainly not," Newby said breezily. "I manged to speak to one of the ladies who used to run the archives here – she's rather frail now and rather like something out of John le Carré – and apparently one of the cellars where a lot of files were kept during the war was flooded when a bomb burst a neighbouring water main, and a lot of stuff was lost."

"I'm surprised that national security files weren't moved somewhere for safe keeping," Collison observed.

"They were," Newby said with a laugh. "The cellar. Everyone was thinking about the chance of a direct hit by a bomb, and the possibility of flooding was overlooked. Not a very good day for the Service, I'm afraid."

"Well, that explains one thing at least," Collison replied. "I was wondering why you didn't tell us about this approach from Agatha Christie when you briefed us – so was the ACC, actually."

"I didn't tell you because I didn't know," Newby said curtly.

"Yes, so I understand, sir," Collison acknowledged calmly, "but the question remains: is this something I can tell my team about, or do Bob and I have to keep it to ourselves?"

There was a pause for reflection.

"I don't see any reason why you shouldn't tell them about it," Newby said finally, "or why you shouldn't put it on file. But don't go anywhere near David Raffen. We want to interview him again ourselves with this letter in our hands; we're going to try to do that today, actually."

"How about Hugh Raffen, sir? I'm due to re-interview him along with the other possible suspects for the Burgh House murder."

Again there was a pause.

"Go ahead," Newby said judiciously, "but you might want to hang fire for a day or two. We'll obviously share with you anything we can from our interview with the father – anything that may be relevant to your enquiry, that is."

"Such as whether the father told the son anything about the grandfather's activities, you mean?" Collison asked quickly.

"Absolutely. I would think that's pretty fundamental for you, isn't it? Unless you can prove that Hugh Raffen junior knew about what his namesake was up to then you've got no motive, have you?"

"No," Collison admitted, "that's the way it looks. In fact, it's even more tricky than that. First we have to show that he knew about whatever letters it was that were stolen – and that's tricky in itself, since we have no idea what they were."

"Hm," Newby agreed, "rather you than me, Simon. Well, best of luck with it. Let's stay in touch."

So it was that when Collison addressed the morning briefing meeting he was able to disclose the full contents of the letters Metcalfe had found. There was an instant buzz of interest.

"All right, settle down," he said. "Yes, these are exciting finds but they don't actually establish anything, although they may point the way. We know that Grandfather Raffen may have been up to no good, and that a young man called Alexander Hamilton may have gone missing in mysterious circumstances. Karen, where are we on that, please?"

"We have a preliminary identification by Oxford University, guv. There was a student of that name at Balliol College-"

"Peter Wimsey's alma mater, wasn't it?" Collison observed without thinking. By the time he had realised that a reference to Lord Peter might be both awkward and painful to Willis at the moment, it was too late to bite his tongue.

"Yes, it was indeed," she concurred with a little smile that might have meant anything. "As I say, we have a preliminary ID on this chap who seems to have dropped out without trace in the summer of 1937. In order to save time, I've gone ahead and run him through some heir-hunting software and we've identified various family members, though nothing closer than a great-niece. She lives in London and she's coming in this afternoon. Apart from what she might be able to tell us, I'd like to take a mouth swab from her. We have enough DNA recovered from the Isokon victim to put it beyond doubt that it's Hamilton, assuming there's a match."

"So surely this puts Raffen, our Raffen that is, squarely in the frame, doesn't it, guv?" Desai asked.

"Yes and no," Collison said slowly. "It seems to me that we have to show two things. First, that Hugh Raffen junior knew that his grandfather had been trying to recruit potential traitors back in the thirties. Two, that he knew Howse had unearthed evidence of those activities. Even then, it's only circumstantial. We really need something specific, such as being able to show that Raffen stole the original of the letter which DI Metcalfe found down in Exeter."

"On that," Metcalfe proffered, "it seems reasonable to assume that if Raffen did steal the letter, then he took it with him when he left the building at lunchtime. It doesn't seem likely that he'd leave it at Burgh House knowing that a murder enquiry was about to kick off there."

"Agreed," Collison nodded. "His instinct would have been to dispose of it as soon as possible and, by the same argument, before returning to Burgh House after lunch."

"Which points to the Flask," Metcalfe went on. "Where we've drawn a bit of a blank, I'm afraid. Their rubbish was collected the day following the murder, worst luck, so that particular trail goes cold. We've had people there interviewing the staff. They recognised him from his photo as a regular lunchtime customer, though nobody can remember whether he was there that particular day."

"Excuse me, guv," Evans cut in, "but I did some of those interviews. One thing that may be of interest is that they confirmed they had steak and kidney pie on the menu that day."

"Don't they have it every day?" Willis asked.

"Apparently not, no," Evans said in his gentle Welsh lilt. "It's a regular dish, because it's very popular, but the menu does change daily."

"So we can't prove that Raffen was there that day," Collison summed up, "but equally we can't prove that he wasn't."

"Also, sir, they did remember Raffen as regularly doing the crossword at lunchtime and drinking a glass of red wine – a large one if that's of any interest."

"OK," Collison said wearily, "let's assume, since we've got no better idea, that Raffen kills Howse sometime before 1245, steals the letters, whatever they may have been, goes and has lunch cool as you like at the Flask, and while he's there he disposes of the letters. Then he returns to Burgh House around two."

"We can't be sure about the 1245 bit," Willis pointed out. "He was seen returning at two, but nobody actually saw him leave. Forensic reckons Howse probably died sometime after twelve, so there's still a big window."

"True," Collison conceded, "and it's all conjecture anyway."

Silence fell on the room. The initial excitement generated by news of Metcalfe's discovery had died away, and the atmosphere now felt distinctly flat as the realisation sank in of how far from a solution they still were.

"Let's meet the Hamilton relative this afternoon," Collison said. "Then I still can't think of a better way of progressing than re-interviewing all four of our official suspects. Unless of course we can eliminate young Howse yet, Bob?"

"Timothy?" Metcalfe queried in turn.

"Nothing yet, guv, I'm afraid. You know what London's like. Nobody seems to speak to their neighbours, or even know who they are."

"Well, keep trying," Metcalfe said curtly. "We need to eliminate him. We've got to find something that places him well away from the murder scene at about midday. Anything will do."

He looked down his list of responsibilities.

"Priya," he said, "there's not much point you continuing to work on the Isokon case as there's stuff we can't talk to you about, and anyway, it looks like we've identified our victim there. Why don't you carry on with the ephemera point you picked up from Timothy? It sounds like he's still got a lot on his plate."

"Is that still relevant, guv?" she queried. "If Raffen threw the letters away at the Flask, and their rubbish was collected the next day ..."

"It's an avenue we need to pursue, Priya," Collison said firmly, "if only to show that we've done so. After all, there's always the chance that someone other than Raffen stole them – a passing tramp, as it were – or that someone saw him throw them away at the Flask and retrieved them for some reason: curiosity perhaps. I agree that both possibilities are highly remote but we need to pursue them just the same. I can't imagine that original signed letters from Agatha Christie come on the market very often, so it shouldn't be that difficult."

# CHAPTER 24

That same afternoon, at about the time that David Raffen was answering a ring on his doorbell with a strong sense of foreboding, Collison and Willis were welcoming Clare Wilson to Hampstead police station. Once seated in an interview room with a cup of tea, Willis opened her notebook and smiled across the table.

"Just so we can get our bearings, so to speak, can you explain for the record how you're related to Alexander Hamilton?" she asked.

"My grandfather was his brother, so I think that would make me his great-niece, wouldn't it?"

"Yes, I think it would," Collison agreed. "But are there any other relatives, at all?"

"Oh yes, a few," she replied. "My father died of cancer about five years ago, and my mother emigrated to Australia after she got over it – she has a sister out there. But they never knew brother Alex anyway – none of us did."

"Why do you call him 'brother Alex', by the way?" Collison enquired curiously.

"Oh, that's what Grandpa used to call him," Clare Wilson explained. "Actually I think it was a sort of private joke. Alex was apparently a bit of a socialist back then, so 'brother' was sort of like 'comrade. I think trade union people call each other 'brother', don't they?"

"Yes, I think they do," Collison concurred. "Now, Mrs Wilson, what can you tell us about brother Alex?"

"Only what I remember from Grandpa. Apparently Alex ran off to fight in the Spanish civil war but never came back. He was killed out there somewhere, but nobody ever knew where, or when or how. It was dreadful for the parents. They only had two children and one of them had gone, and they had no way of visiting his grave or anything like that. His mother, in particular, never got over it."

"Hm," Collison said thoughtfully. "Did your grandfather remember anything about the exact circumstances of Alex going to Spain? Whom did he tell, for example? Your grandfather? His parents?"

"No, that was the awful thing," she said sadly. "He just went. He sent his father a telegram saying he was off to Spain and would write to let everybody know that he was alright, but of course he never did. Grandpa was terribly upset at the thought that Alex should have just disappeared like that without talking to him first; they were very close, I think."

"Did it never puzzle people that he simply vanished without trace?" Willis asked.

"Yes, of course it did. Grandpa tried to find out what had happened when the fighters disbanded and came back, and then later my Dad actually did a lot of research, going through casualty lists at the International Brigade archives and that sort of thing. Of course if you've read 'Homage to Catalonia' then you'll know that a lot of them got imprisoned, tortured or even bumped off by their own side if they happened to be the wrong sort of communist in the wrong place at the wrong time, and I think everyone assumed that something like that must have happened, even though it was a horrible thing to think about."

She stopped and took a sip of tea.

"Both sides killed a lot of prisoners, too," she added. "So one way or another his death could quite well have gone unrecorded. But one thing we did think was odd was that when Grandpa tracked down a lot of members of the British Battalion – I think he even spoke to Orwell – nobody could remember brother Alex at all."

Willis and Collison exchanged glances.

"We think it's possible, Mrs Wilson – I can't put it any higher than that at the moment – that brother Alex never actually went to Spain at all," Collison said carefully.

"Why? What do you think happened to him?"

"Well, we're hoping you can help us there, which we'll talk about in a minute, but we have a theory that he may have been murdered right here in Hampstead, back in 1937, in which case somebody else sent that telegram in the hope of throwing the family off the scent."

"Does this have anything to do with that body that was found at that old block of flats?" she asked eagerly. "The one that was in the papers and on the telly?"

"Yes, it does," Collison nodded. "I'm the Senior Investigating Officer on that case, and Karen here is on the team too. And, as I said, the hypothesis we're testing right now is that the body was that of Alexander Hamilton."

Willis produced a plastic tube with what looked like a small toothbrush inside it.

"I'm sure you've heard of DNA," she said. "Well, our forensic people managed to retrieve some from our victim and we were hoping that you could give us some of yours for comparison."

"Yes, of course," Clare Wilson agreed at once. "Only too happy to help. How do we do it?"

"It's very easy, and it won't hurt a bit," Willis assured her. "I just need to take a quick swab of some saliva. If you could just open your mouth while I come round to your side of the table ..."

And so it was done. Willis put the swab back carefully inside the tube, sealed it, and wrote carefully on the label.

"There!" she said. "Thank you so much. I'll get this off to the lab straightaway."

"When will you know?" the great-niece enquired.

"Probably in a day or two," Willis answered. "It depends how busy they are."

"Will you let me know?" the other woman asked plaintively. "I mean, is that allowed?"

"Of course we'll let you know, Mrs Wilson," Collison assured her. "It's the least we can do after you've been so helpful. But if the result is positive then I'd be very grateful if you'd keep the news to yourself until it's announced publicly, because of course our enquiries will be ongoing."

While Willis went away to despatch the sample to the laboratory Collison saw Mrs Wilson off the premises, thanked her again and went back to his office.

He was feeling more optimistic about the case (and he felt increasingly that it was safe to think about it as one case rather than two). Provided the DNA sample turned out to be a positive match then they had identified the Isokon victim, and that alone would be more than had at one time seemed likely. More than this, however, they had at least one of the links they needed to point to the identity of the Burgh House killer. Whether they could yet come up with a prosecution case which would stand up in court remained to be seen.

He was not a man who was tolerant of loose ends, though, and he remained uneasy about the multitude of possible suspects. The Baileys, Raffen and young Howse made four, even if one ignored the Passing Tramp theory, and four was too many. Surely there must be some way of eliminating at least some of them? He pulled the files towards him with a sigh and prepared to go through them once more with a pen and notebook beside him. However, before he had been immersed for more than about twenty minutes or so, the phone rang. Answering it, he found himself speaking to Philip Newby.

"Simon, thought I'd bring you up to date. We've just re-interviewed David Raffen. Didn't take very long."

"You mean he coughed to his father having killed someone?" Collison asked incredulously.

"No, on the contrary, he stonewalled us. Said he'd never seen the letter before, nor did he have any knowledge of the contents."

"How did that compare to what he told you chaps earlier, when he was being held somewhere?" Collison queried.

"I wasn't involved myself of course; it was before my time. But I've read all the files and I also managed to speak to someone who was involved. He's a bit gaga now, but what he told me squares with what's in the files. Raffen always admitted to his father having been involved with recruiting double agents, although he always claimed he had no knowledge of it himself."

"Actually," he corrected himself, "it would be fairer to say that he's always admitted there is strong evidence of what his father did, although he's never given up hope that it may turn out to have been false."

"Is that likely?" Collison asked, intrigued.

"Not really. The argument would be either that the defector made it up to curry favour with us, or that he wasn't a genuine defector at all and it was a false trail deliberately planted by the Russkies to discredit our Head of Service and sow mistrust between us and the Americans. It's not impossible, of course, but it's most unlikely. Our chaps who did his debriefing were very thorough. We were given the names of his father's contacts at the Soviet embassy back in the thirties, for example, and they all seem to check out. There were other details too, thing I can't go into, which were corroborated by reports from agents in the field."

"I see," said Collison. "So where does that leave us?"

"It leaves us, the Branch, no further forward," Newby replied mournfully. "Rather worse, if anything. David Raffen told us that he's intending to apply for permission to publish his memoirs, and that he's planning to run this whole theory about his father having been wrongly accused."

"Oh."

"Oh, indeed," Newby said heavily. "As for us, the Met, meaning you, then it doesn't help you one bloody bit either, does it?"

"Not really, sir. Ideally we needed Lord Raffen to confirm that he knew his father had been involved in some way in the disappearance of our victim and, crucially, that he had passed this knowledge on to his son. After all, if Hugh Raffen junior didn't know that Hugh Raffen senior had been a naughty boy, then he couldn't had had any motive for abstracting the Christie papers and killing Howse in the process."

"I suppose," Newby proffered hopefully, "that it might be sufficient if he just knew that Grandpa had been up to something naughty in general? Particularly if Daddy had told him that the party line was that he'd been wrongly accused, and these papers might just blow that idea out of the water."

"Perhaps," Collison agreed unenthusiastically. "But it's all a bit tenuous, isn't it, sir? All we can do is ask him the question, and if he just looks innocent and says 'no' then that's an end to it in my view."

"I see your point," the Commander acknowledged.

"Did you by any chance ask Lord Raffen if he'd said anything to his son about all this?" Collison asked diffidently.

"Yes, we did, and he said no he hadn't because it was all classified and anyway he didn't want to get Hugh involved," Newby said curtly. "Sorry, Simon, I'm afraid we haven't been much help to you."

"Not to worry, sir," Collison said, though he felt strangely empty inside. "I suppose it was too much to hope."

"What will you do now?" Newby asked sympathetically.

"I'll take advice from DCS Morris of course," Collison replied. "I'm reporting to him more or less every day. But my view remains the same: that all we can do is re-interview our official suspects, pick over their stories, and see where we go from there. My nightmare is that we end up with the sort of problem you mentioned coming across in intelligence affairs, where you know instinctively that someone is guilty, but can't come up with enough hard evidence to convince a jury. I don't want to have to recommend closing down the investigation with the case still unsolved."

"It happens," Newby said wryly. "Happened to me a couple of times, actually. There was a gangland killing where we knew damn well who'd done it, but everybody was too scared to talk."

"No DNA evidence, then?"

"No body," came the grim rejoinder. "It went into the Royal Docks somewhere, we reckoned. We tried diving for it, of course, but it was useless. You're talking about an area of water the size of Central London. I did wonder if it might come to light when they built the City Airport ..."

"Is it likely, I wonder," Collison mused, "that Lord Raffen would actually be given permission to publish his memoirs? I thought there was a rule that intelligence service employees weren't allowed to. Remember the 'Spycatcher' case?"

"Ten or fifteen years ago I'd have agreed with you like a shot," Newby replied gloomily. "Secret used to mean secret, and that was that. But in these Freedom of Information days, who knows? Even if the Home Secretary says no, you'd probably find that Raffen could appeal under the Human Rights Act, or whatever other bit of nonsense they've come up with recently. And of course there's the internet now. He could simply arrange for someone to put the relevant extracts on a website somewhere – one of these anonymous ones on a server in Outer Mongolia – and then swear blind that someone must have nicked it and put it up without his permission."

"Difficult," Collison said feelingly. "Do you know, I think on the whole I prefer to be in charge of an apparently insoluble double murder. At least I don't have the Home Secretary breathing down my neck."

"Well, don't forget what I said in the ACC's office, Simon. I was serious, you know. You're exactly the sort of bloke we're looking for. What's all this I hear about heading the Academy or writing a paper, for God's sake? Come and work with us. As a matter of fact, we've got a Chief Superintendent's post coming up in a few months when someone moves on. I'd happily put you up for it, if you like. It would be a good leg up for you, and you could carry on doing proper investigative work rather than sitting on committees and going on courses."

"That's very kind of you, sir," Collison said diplomatically. "I will think about it, but right now I have a murderer to catch."

There was a silence at the other end of the line.

"We do make a difference, you know, Simon," Newby said seriously. "The work we do, I mean. That matters to some people. I think you're one of those people."

"Thank you again, sir," Collison replied in some embarrassment. "I do appreciate the offer, and I will think about it. I promise."

# CHAPTER 25

"So there it is," Collison observed as he, Metcalfe, Willis and Desai sat in his office the next morning. "This all feels like a bit like that Anthony Berkeley book where different detectives can take the same facts and make equally compelling cases against different people. We have four suspects, all of whom had motive, means and opportunity, none of whom we've been able to eliminate."

"We do have a clear favourite now though, guv," Metcalfe replied, "and we've been able to establish a connection between the two killings. That's progress, isn't?"

"Ye-es," Collison drawled uncertainly, "but let's not allow ourselves to get carried away. Strictly speaking, we've got what looks like it could be a connection, but the fact that we have three other suspects, none of whom have any connection with the Isokon, shows that, despite everything, this could still all be a massive coincidence."

"Plus," Desai contributed rather viciously, "right now we can't even prove what we suspect about Raffen, and it looks like we're not going to be able to unless he puts his hand up for the murder of Howse, which doesn't seem very likely, does it? So, like the guvnor says, let's not get carried away."

Metcalfe looked rather startled. Even after all the time

they had spent working together on a previous case he still had not come quite to terms with Desai's directness.

Collison winced theatrically.

"Yes, thank you, Priya, for keeping us all grounded in reality," he said ruefully. "You're quite right, of course."

He looked down at the four names he had written on his pad, names which he had started at repeatedly over the last few days, hoping against hope that some random thought or association would suggest itself.

"Hugh Raffen: we think he's our man but right now we can't prove it, and as soon as we start asking him about it we put him on his guard."

He stopped and looked at the others.

"There's something else which we haven't considered before because we didn't know Raffen was a suspect," Willis interjected.

"Go on," Collison said.

Her hair was scragged back in a plain band in a way he had never seen before. He wondered if it was that which was making her look drawn.

"Well, if Raffen is our man, then that means we can't rely on anything he told us, and it was his statement we were using to try to establish a timeline within Burgh House. If that's no good, then it's possible that several people may have gone upstairs, or equally that none did."

Collison nodded in acknowledgement. None of this was getting any easier.

"Sue Bailey; we know she was having an affair with

Howse, and was probably in love with him. We all know what Congreve said about a woman spurned."

"Except he didn't, actually," Willis said before she could stop herself.

"Sorry, guv," she went on apologetically, "it's just that ..."

She had been about to say that it was one of Peter's favourites, but paused, feeling awkward and wretched at the same time.

"It's just that a lot of people get it wrong," she substituted. "It's actually 'Heaven has no rage like love to hatred turned, nor hell a fury like a woman scorned'."

"Nothing like a heroic couplet, is there?" Collison said appreciatively. "Very well, I stand corrected; a woman scorned."

"And at the end of the day," Desai ventured, "What has she actually told us? Virtually nothing. Every time we start questioning her she just dissolves in tears and we have to end the interview without making any progress at all."

"Suggestions?" Collison enquired.

"Time to take off the kid gloves," Desai replied enthusiastically. "Put her under pressure. Lay it on the line that she's a suspect in a murder enquiry and that she'd better start to talk."

"I must confess that I'm inclined to agree with you," Collison said. "She could just be a natural hysteric who can't handle life's ups and downs, but there again she could be a murderer who's hiding behind a fit of the vapours and relying on our gentlemanly instincts."

He glanced at Metcalfe and Willis, who both nodded.

"Jack Bailey: the jealous husband, another great motive. We're told that the affair was over, really over, but the only person who could confirm that would be Howse, and he's dead. And even if it was over, Bailey could still have been motivated by revenge."

"Neither of the Baileys can account satisfactorily for their movements on the day of the murder," Desai commented, "and their alibis are each other. Either could be lying to protect the other. But again, unless one of them suddenly confesses, it's difficult to see how we can shake their stories."

"True, but we must try," Collison replied. "Let's take them through every little aspect of their stories again and try to find a crack somewhere. Priya, I think we'll turn you loose on the wife."

Desai gave an eager smile.

"Alan Howse: the trust fund kid who was upset because his wicked uncle wouldn't give him what he wanted. Oh, if only we could find some way of eliminating him. Bob, surely we can find something, somewhere? Why are we still wasting time with this bloke?"

"Well, it's up to you, guv, whether you still want to classify him as a suspect. It's true we can't place him as being at home, but we can't place him at the scene either. I've had a couple of bodies checking the CCTV footage from Hampstead tube station that morning between 10am and 2pm; there's no sign of him."

"He might have taken a bus," Willis suggested.

"He might, but there's no direct route. Also, there are no entries on his Oyster Card, but that's not conclusive because he hardly ever uses it. Maybe he buys a travel card instead."

"One more try," Collison decided, "just like the Baileys. If we can't make any progress that way, then we have to focus all our efforts on Raffen and just hope we get lucky."

Willis's mobile buzzed discreetly.

"Sorry, guv," she said, looking down at it, "I'm waiting for a text from the lab. Ah yes, here we are. No surprises. Our victim at the Isokon was a close relative of Clare Wilson."

"Alexander Hamilton it is, then," Collison said reflectively. "Thank you, Dame Agatha."

As things turned out, Priya Desai was to have little opportunity to display her hardnosed interview technique. Susan Bailey arrived with an accompanying solicitor, a rather sour-faced middle-aged woman, who regarded both Desai and Metcalfe with a pinched expression and marked suspicion.

"Is my client a suspect?" she asked straightaway.

"She's being treated as a suspect until we are able to eliminate her from our enquiries," Metcalfe replied carefully. "We would like to interview her with that end in mind: to eliminate her from our enquiries."

"Will the interview be under caution?"

"Of course. It has to be; you know that."

"Then you should know that I have already advised my client not to answer any questions."

"And why is that?"

"My client is entirely innocent of any crime, and it is not appropriate for her to be questioned under caution on suspicion of murder."

"You can't possibly know that," Desai interjected immediately before Metcalfe could give her a restraining glance.

"Know what?"

"That your client is innocent."

"I do," maintained the solicitor stoutly.

"Then you clearly have evidence that we do not," Metcalfe cut in smoothly. "In which case things can proceed very simply. You share with us the evidence of your client's innocence and we can eliminate her from our enquiries. That way everyone gets what they want."

"Don't be silly. Of course I have no evidence to share with you."

"Just to clear about this," Metcalfe said pedantically, "are you saying that you have evidence which you are choosing to withhold from us, or that you don't have any evidence?"

He knew this was a pointless exercise, but no more pointless than the woman's obvious hostility, and it was fun to wind her up.

"I'm not withholding anything," the woman said at once.

"Which presumably means that you have no evidence of your client's innocence," Metcalfe continued, "which means that your original statement was incorrect. You can't possibly *know* that your client is innocent."

The solicitor was by this stage going rather red in the cheeks. Metcalfe could almost feel her barely suppressed anger.

"Do you have any questions for my client or not?" she hissed.

"Whether we do or not seems irrelevant, doesn't it, since you've advised your client not to answer them?" Metcalfe asked.

Turning to Susan Bailey, he addressed her directly.

"Mrs Bailey, please believe me: we desperately want to eliminate you from this enquiry, but we can't do that without your help. If someone won't answer our questions, then we have to assume that they have something to hide, and proceed on that basis. Please will you reconsider your position? We only want to ask you about what you can remember about the morning in question."

Susan Bailey, who seemed as always on the brink of tears, looked plaintively at her lawyer, who very firmly and ostentatiously shook her head.

"Then this interview is terminated," Metcalfe said regretfully, turning off the tape recorder.

"Really," he said in exasperation after the two women had left the interview room. "I do wish we had the power to arrest obstructive solicitors. Why do they have to treat us as if we're the enemy all the time? I suppose it's because they really do believe that their clients are innocent."

Priya laughed.

"Don't be so naïve, guv," she told him. "It's not because

they believe they're innocent, it's because they know they're guilty. So anything they say is more likely to incriminate them than exonerate them."

"Tell you what though," she said with an arch smile, "you're starting to sound awfully like Mr Collison."

Metcalfe flushed. The same thought had occurred to him during the interview, and he had realised that he found the idea quite agreeable.

"How about you?" he asked, fighting back as best he could. "You just said 'exonerate'."

Collison and Willis had more luck with Susan Bailey's husband. Though he too appeared with a solicitor, the latter was content to sit quietly at his client's side and make notes.

"I'm sure you'll appreciate, Mr Bailey," Collison said after turning on the tape recording and administering the caution, "that we're anxious to eliminate you from this investigation – and your wife for that matter. So we're anxious to hear anything you might be able to tell us about that morning when Peter Howse was killed."

"I went on the desk when we opened at 9.30, like I said before," Bailey said wearily, "and I stayed on it for about an hour, but I couldn't say precisely. I went down to see if Sue could take over. She didn't mind if it was quiet, see, because she used to read a book on the desk. I'm not much of a reader, me."

"But she didn't take over?"

"Nah, she was busy with stuff downstairs, ironing mostly."

"And you didn't go back on the desk yourself?"

"Nah. Suppose I should have done, but nobody had come in, not a dicky bird, and Howse said it was OK to leave the desk unattended from time to time."

"From time to time, yes," Collison pressed him, "but surely not half the day? If you came off the desk at 10.30 and nobody took over from you at any time, then that means the building was unsecured for about four hours – until Howse's body was discovered, in fact."

"Yeah, well, I wasn't feeling like it, was I? I was still pissed with Howse for what he'd done to my missus. To tell the truth, I was almost hoping that someone would come in and nick something. Then maybe he'd get into trouble and get the heave-ho."

"You might have got the heave-ho yourself," Willis pointed out.

"It was his responsibility to make sure the desk was manned, not mine," Bailey maintained stubbornly. "He was supposed to arrange a roster of volunteers to do it."

"But he didn't?" she asked.

"Nah. Couldn't be bothered, could he?"

"What happened after you came off the desk?" Collison asked.

"Sat with me wife for a bit, then got on with fixing a window I'd been meaning to do for a while. I thought it would only take an hour or so, but the cord was broken so I had to take it apart. It's one of those old sash windows with weights inside."

"But even if that took you two hours," Collison pointed out, "that only takes us up to 12.30. What did you do then?"

"Had a bit of dinner with Sue. We had words. She ran off into the bedroom. I watched the racing for a bit on the telly."

"Where was it coming from?" Willis asked at once.

"Cheltenham, I think. First race was at 12.30."

"And then what?"

"Waited for Sue to come back but she never did. Watched the racing until a bit after two. The rest you know about. The Professor come running downstairs and all hell broke loose."

"While you were fixing the window," Collison queried, "were you inside the building or outside?"

"Both, but mostly outside."

"And could you see your wife from there?"

"Yeah, through the window."

"While you were outside, did you have any occasion to use the ladder?"

"Nah, it was a ground floor window."

"And you didn't see Peter Howse at all that morning, whether upstairs or anywhere else?"

"Nah."

"So when was the last time you saw him?"

"The day before. I found a box of old junk in the attic and took it down to him to see if he wanted any of it for the exhibition. A gas mask, a truncheon, a steel helmet, some old webbing, that sort of thing, like you see in junk shops. I wanted to know whether I should keep it or throw it away."

"What did he say?"

"He just said something like 'just put it down, will you?'. Never even looked round, did he? Just sat there at his desk with his back to me. So I put the box down and left. Glad to get out of the room, to be honest. I couldn't stand being near him."

Karen had been studying a plan of the building intently.

"While your wife was out of the room, you can't vouch for her whereabouts, can you?" she demanded suddenly.

"Yeah, she was in the bedroom. I told you."

"But you didn't actually go into the bedroom, did you? So you can't say for sure that she stayed there."

"Well, there's nowhere else to go, is there? There's no other door."

"No, but there is a window," Willis pointed out, jabbing her finger at the plan.

Collison sat up in sudden interest, noticing inconsequentially that her nail varnish was chipped.

"Yeah, so?"

"The window gives onto the back yard area. She could easily have climbed out of the window, used the ladder to climb upstairs, and then returned the same way, replacing the ladder behind her."

"Nah," Bailey relied, shaking his head. "For one thing, I'd have seen her, wouldn't I? And for another, that ladder would be way too heavy for a woman to lift."

"You said you were watching the TV," Willis pressed him, "and from what I remember from the layout of the room, you'd have been sitting near the door to the bedroom. I don't think you'd be able to see the flat roof from there, or only a bit of it anyway. And the ladder's aluminium. One of my colleagues said it's very light. I bet if I tried to lift it, I could. And I'm a woman – just like your wife."

Bailey gave a sudden twisted smile.

"You're a woman all right," he said, "but nothing like my wife, more's the pity."

Collison tried not to laugh and almost succeeded.

"I don't think we can ask Mr Bailey to speculate on what his wife may or may not have been doing," he said once he had swallowed his chuckle, "but we do need to establish exactly what he could see and what he couldn't. Mr Bailey, I'm going to ask DS Willis to visit your flat again later today with a colleague. I hope you'll have no objection to that?"

"None at all, Superintendent," the solicitor chipped in, finding his voice at last. "My client is eager to co-operate."

"Good," Collison replied. "In that case, interview terminated."

"And Karen," he said, after they had handed the solicitor his copy of the tape and seen them both back to the front door, "make sure you try that ladder, won't you?"

# CHAPTER 26

The next morning the phone on Collison's desk was ringing as he entered the office. He ran a couple of steps to it and snatched it up.

"Collison," he said.

"Simon? Philip Newby. There's been a development I wanted to make you aware of as quickly as possible. David Raffen topped himself overnight."

"Dear God," Collison said automatically. "But why? I thought you said that he stonewalled you. That must mean that he thought you couldn't prove anything. So why kill himself?"

"Suicide's hardly a rational act, you know," Newby observed drily. "He seemed pretty depressed when we interviewed him. Maybe he realised we were closing in, or you were closing in, or even both."

"Are we sure it was suicide?" Collison asked cautiously.

"What's the matter, Simon," Newby asked in jocular fashion, "are you looking for yet another murder to link to your investigation?"

"No, don't worry," he went on before Collison could reply. "It's suicide all right; overdose of sleeping pills. He left a note. That's why I'm calling, actually. Quite a lot of it is relevant to your case – maybe to both of them. You can't see it all, I'm afraid. There's quite a bit which bears on Service matters, and while they're old, they're still very sensitive. So we'll have to 'redact' quite a bit of it, as the Americans say. But there will be plenty left for you."

"Can you give me any clue what it's about, sir?"

"It's basically a confession on behalf of his father. Hugh Raffen senior panicked when Agatha Christie approached him and he realised that he was in danger of being exposed by young Hamilton. He went to his Russian handler, a chap from the embassy called Andrei Vassilyov, who incidentally went on to become very senior within the KGB. Vassilyov had Raffen invite Hamilton back to his flat, where Vassilyov and one of his thugs was waiting. They strangled the lad in front of Raffen – made him watch, apparently; presumably as some sort of punishment for having screwed things up. Then they left the body in his flat until very early the next morning, when they came back with a cabin trunk and took him away. They told Raffen they'd done a deal with the builders who were working in the basement to ignore the trunk when they bricked the wall up. The foreman was a communist from Scotland, or so they said."

"Dear God," Collison said again.

"Yes, grim business, eh? You could almost feel sorry for Raffen, being forced to watch the youngster being strangled – can't have been pleasant – and then having to sit with the body for hours. Our Raffen, David Raffen that is, says in the note that his father told him about it just before he died.

Said it had been on his conscience ever since, and that not a day went by but he didn't think about it. Old Hugh Raffen apparently claimed that he nearly turned down the peerage when it was offered, but ended up accepting it because he thought it might look odd to refuse."

"So we know that Vassilyov killed Hamilton, and that Hugh Raffen senior was an accessory," Collison said slowly, "but I'm not sure that takes us any further with the Burgh House case. Unless we can show that Hugh Raffen junior knew what his grandfather had done, then we can't show that he had any motive for stealing the Christie papers."

Newby chuckled softly.

"Oh, but you can, Simon," he said triumphantly. "The note goes on to say that he told his son Hugh all about it when he heard from him a few weeks ago that Peter Howse was planning an exhibition on the Isokon building and its residents. Wanted to warn him to be on his guard for anything which might link Raffen to Agatha Christie; apparently he knew all about her approach to his father."

"Wow!" Collison exclaimed, feeling a sudden need to sit down. "Talk about things falling into place ..."

"Well, I'm glad things have worked out for you, Simon," Newby said kindly. "You and your chaps have worked very hard on what's a very difficult case, and you're due a break."

"Thank you, sir," Collison replied. "Incidentally, just out of curiosity, did David Raffen mention the letter to the Service which we found in the archive? Or having removed it from the files and destroyed it?"

"Didn't mention it, no. I suppose it's quite possible that he did never hear about it. He would have been a very junior bod at the time, and a lot of stuff really did get destroyed or otherwise lost during the war."

"Yes, I suppose so," Collison said reflectively.

"Well, I'd better go," Newby said. "We're pretty busy at this end. There are a few people we've suspected for a long time, and this note gives us some new material to put to them. If nothing else, it's a perfect excuse to re-interview them. Good show, Simon, once again. Let's talk when we both have more time."

"Just before you go, sir, may I assume it's OK to pass this information on to the team, and to Jim Morris?"

"All except that last bit, yes. I'll try to get your redacted version biked round to you later today. Bye."

As he came out of his office, Collison blundered into Metcalfe and Willis, who were standing close together by one of the windows holding hands. Because of the official 'about to be closed' status of the police station, only he and Allen had offices there, so the corridor was deserted for most of the time, and the pair had obviously seized the opportunity for some quiet time away from the open plan floor below. He smiled at them and was about to pass without comment, but Willis pulled away from Metcalfe and spoke to him.

"I do hope you'll thank your wife very much for giving up her time like that," she said, with something like her old smile. "I did feel very embarrassed being such a nuisance."

"You weren't a nuisance at all," he assured her, "and certainly she didn't think so."

"Well, it was very sweet of her anyway," Willis insisted. "She was wonderful. She even had a big hankie ready in her bag for when I started crying all over her. Come to think of it, I suppose it was one of yours, wasn't it?"

"I suppose so," he admitted.

"By the way," he said as Metcalfe joined them, suddenly realising that he hadn't told anyone yet, "it seems we're going to have a baby. Caroline found out the other day."

"Oh, that's wonderful!" she enthused. "Bob, did you hear that?"

"I certainly did," Metcalfe said, wringing Collison's hand, "congratulations, guv."

"And I've got some good news about the case," Collison went on. "It looks like we're getting much closer to Raffen."

"Really? What have you found out?" Metcalfe asked.

"Not me: Special Branch. But let me tell everyone at once. Come on, let's go downstairs."

They entered the room together and the team fell silent expectantly as he stood at the front and imparted his news, exactly as Newby had told it to him. As he did so, he looked round the room and noticed that Priya Desai's desk was unoccupied.

"So are we going to feel Raffen's collar, sir?" came a forthright request from Evans.

"We're going to interview him under caution, just as

we're doing with the other suspects, if that's what you mean, Timothy," Collison answered with mock severity.

"But surely this takes us a lot further, guv," Metcalfe asserted. "We can now fix him with motive, means and opportunity."

"So can we with the others," Collison reminded him. "Well, the Baileys anyway. We still haven't found any corroboration for where Alan Howse was at the time."

"But Raffen is the only suspect who makes any sense in terms of a connection with the Hamilton case," Willis pointed out. "If he didn't kill Howse then all we're left with is a massive coincidence."

"Beyond massive, sir," Evans volunteered.

"Oh, but massive coincidences do occur," Collison observed mildly.

He sat on the table at the front of the room, feeling rather like a schoolmaster.

"Can anyone other than DS Willis tell me who Margery Allingham was?" he asked.

An awkward silence fell. People looked at each other but said nothing.

"All right, Karen, tell them," he adjured her as it became clear that nobody was going to answer.

"She was a crime writer from the Golden Age," she replied. "One of the 'Queens of Crime'. She created the detective Albert Campion."

"She did indeed," he agreed, "but before she created Campion she wrote another book, her first real grown-up detective novel. It was called 'The White Cottage Mystery' and tells of a farmer who is shot dead at his home called White Cottage, which was generally reckoned to be a real life property called White House Farm in a little place in Essex called Tolleshunt D'Arcy, where she lived."

He looked around the room again, but it was clear that none of this meant anything to the assembled police officers.

"Over fifty years later," he went on, "a real life farmer and his entire family were shot dead at White House Farm. You may remember the case; it featured a rather unpleasant young man called Jeremy Bamber."

"And that's why," he said as he slipped off the table and stood up, "that despite the overwhelming attractiveness of this apparent coincidence, we should try very hard to remember that it is just that: a coincidence."

He thought this a particularly telling remark on which to leave the room, but his attempt to exit stage right was thwarted by Priya Desai, who scuttled in looking so excited she could hardly speak.

"I'm sorry, sir," she said breathlessly. "Sorry I missed the briefing, but when I tell you why, I think you'll be pleased."

"Then you'd better tell us all," he replied, turning back into the room.

"It's the letters!" she exclaimed, pulling out of her bag some sheets of paper, each carefully encased in a clear plastic wallet. "Or, at least, some of them."

A palpable hiss of excitement ran through the team. Collison stared at the proffered letters as Desai held them out to him and took them, as if in a daze.

"But where on earth did you get them?" he asked, bemused.

"It was your idea actually, guv," she answered, grinning widely. "Do you remember your idea about ephemera, about the letters having value in themselves just because they were original letters signed by Agatha Christie? Well, I was making a list of dealers to go and check out, and I discovered that one of them was right here in Hampstead, in the antiques market just up the road, so it seemed to make sense to start with him. And as soon as I asked him about Agatha Christie he said straightaway that someone had brought them in a week or so back."

"Who?" Collison, Metcalfe and Willis all asked together.

"An old woman. Looked a bit like a tramp, he said. But she left a name and address. I checked it out on our system, but there was nothing, so before I went out to see her – that's where I've just been – I mentioned it to the desk sergeant downstairs, and he recognised her at once. Apparently she's a real local character."

"A Hampstead eccentric?" hazarded Collison.

"Something like that, guv. She's a klepto, and a nutter with it. Can't keep her hands off anything, but always has some weird story about how she got it. She stole a moped a while back from outside a house in Willow Road. Months later the woman who owned it saw Maggie – that's her name – riding down Rosslyn Hill on it and ran in here to get help. When she was brought in she swore blind she'd been having a secret affair with Prince Charles, and he'd given it to her as a present."

"So, what's her story this time?" Collison asked.

"She said they were family heirlooms, handed down by her mother, who was a great friend of Agatha Christie. Said she'd given her the plots of quite a few of her books."

Collison groaned.

"So she's not going to make much of a witness, then?" Metcalfe asked sarcastically.

"Hang on, guv, there's more," Priya said smugly. "I kept on at her and eventually she said she'd got them from some bloke in a pub. It wasn't easy because she kept just going silent and staring at me and then muttering to herself. I asked if it was the Flask and after a bit she said yes. Then she pretended to go to sleep and I ... well, I woke her up."

Seeing Collison frown, she pressed on quickly.

"I said we knew they were stolen and she said they weren't, that the bloke didn't want them and she just picked them up when he threw them in the bin at the pub."

"Then where's the other one, the one we really want?" Collison demanded.

"Well, she mentioned that he tore one up and stuffed the pieces in his pocket. Then he went off to the Gents. When he came back, he just folded the others in half and chucked them in the bin. So I reckon he probably ripped it up very small and then flushed it down the loo."

"And did she give you a description?"

"Not really. Said he was 'not old, not young', but I asked

if he was doing a crossword puzzle and drinking red wine, and she said yes."

"You didn't show her a photo of Raffen, did you?" Collison asked anxiously.

"Of course not," Desai said, looking hurt. "I didn't want to screw up an ID parade."

"Sorry, Priya," Collison apologised, "Well done. Very bloody well done indeed."

He turned the plastic wallets over in his hands as a hum of conversation began to grow. Metcalfe and Willis came and stood beside him, looking at them too.

"What are they?" Willis asked curiously.

"This one's to Jack Pritchard, asking if he can have some work done while she's away traveling with her husband," Collison replied. "It sounds like they've taken two adjoining flats and want to have them knocked into one. She says here that they'll pay for them to be divided again when they move out."

He placed it on the table and looked at the next one.

"This one's to Jack Pritchard as well," he announced. "Maybe they all came from his own files or something. 'Miss Christie regrets that she is unable to accept Mr Pritchard's kind invitation to cocktails owing to a prior engagement.' Handwritten, I see."

He stood holding the letter and staring into the distance.

"Miss Christie regrets," he murmured thoughtfully. "Oh dear, how very ironic."

"How do you mean, guv?" asked Metcalfe.

"Well, don't you see? If she hadn't bearded Raffen about what Hamilton had told her, then almost certainly none of this would ever have happened. By letting him know that he was in danger of being discovered she caused Hamilton's death, and quite possibly another one many decades later. A good job she never found out the truth, I suppose."

They fell silent, thinking this through.

"You're right," Metcalfe agreed soberly.

"Miss Christie regrets," Willis said slowly, as though rolling the words around her mouth and tasting them. "It could almost be the title of a book, couldn't it?"

# CHAPTER 27

"Lord Raffen", Collison said formally, "may I first express my commiseration on the death of your father. It's very good of you to come and see us at what must be a very difficult time for you."

Raffen smiled thinly.

"I think you're only the second or third person to call me that, and it still sounds a bit strange I must say. But thank you for your condolences. It's all been a bit of a shock, as I'm sure you can imagine."

"I can indeed," Collison replied, "and I'm sorry to have to intrude on your grief, but we are trying very hard to resolve this sad business at Burgh House. The only way we can do that is to eliminate people from our enquiries, and the only way we can do that is to re-interview all the people who had, or may have had access to the scene of the crime at the relevant time."

"I understand," Raffen nodded, "and I'm very happy to help in any way I can."

"Good," Collison said, and gestured to Willis to turn on the tape recorder.

"Before we begin, Lord Raffen, I should explain that we

are proposing to interview you under caution, just as we have with various other people. I'm happy to explain the procedural requirements for this if you wish, but suffice it to say that unless and until we can eliminate you from our enquiries then we are obliged to treat you formally as a suspect. After all, it was you who discovered the body."

"I quite understand," Raffen said. "Please carry on, Superintendent."

Having administered the caution and stated the date and time for the tape, Collison drew a deep breath and went on.

"It's also my duty to inform you that, since you are being interviewed under caution as a possible suspect, then you are entitled to have a solicitor present."

Raffen considered this for a moment.

"I don't want one at the moment," he said finally, "but I reserve the right to call for one should I wish."

"Of course," Collison acknowledged. "You have that right anyway at any time."

He glanced down at the folder in front of him, which contained the redacted suicide letter and Raffen's original statement.

"I'd like to take you back to the morning of the murder," he said. "You told DS Willis here and DCI Allen that you didn't go into Mr Howse's rooms at all that morning. Can I ask you formally for the tape whether that was so?"

"Yes, that's what I said, and yes it's true. I didn't go into Howse's rooms until after I got back from lunch, which is when I discovered that he'd been killed."

"Good," Collison said and then, quite unnecessarily, "make a note of that please, Sergeant."

"And you also told them," he continued, "that you thought you heard footsteps on the stairs three times that morning, and that shortly after one of these occasions, the third in fact, you heard what sounded like an argument coming from the victim's rooms. Again, I'd like you to confirm that for me formally under caution because we've been basing our investigation on what you told us that day, so if it's not true it could have serious implications."

"I'm happy to confirm my original statement," Raffen said calmly. "All of it. You may remember, for example, that it was I who told you about Howse having had an affair with Susan Bailey, thus giving both her and her husband a clear motive for killing that odious man. May I ask if they too are being treated as suspects?"

"I'm not at liberty to divulge details of our investigation," Collison replied formally, "but I've already told you that other people have also been interviewed under caution. We are in the position of having to treat various individuals as suspects unless and until they can provide us with information which enables us to eliminate them. Some have been anxious to co-operate with us in doing that; others less so."

"I see. I'm sorry. I am anxious to co-operate, as I said."

"Good. Incidentally, why did you just describe Peter Howse as an odious man?"

"Because he was. He was deeply unpleasant. Nobody

liked him so far as I could see – apart from Susan Bailey, of course."

"Nothing specific then? Nothing he did to you?"

"No, nothing specific. Just a general impression."

"Are you aware," Collison asked, changing tack completely, "that shortly after Peter Howse's murder, the body of another murder victim was discovered at the Lawn Road flats, commonly known as the Isokon Building?"

"Yes, of course, I read about it in the papers. But wasn't it from a long time ago?"

"Yes, we believe the young man in question was killed in or about 1937."

"I see."

"Are you aware, Lord Raffen, that in 1937 your grandfather, the first Lord Raffen, was a resident at the Isokon?"

"I believe he was, yes."

"A bit of a coincidence, wouldn't you say?"

"How do you mean?"

"I mean that within a few days two bodies turn up, one of whom we believe to have been murdered at the building where your grandfather lived, and the other of whom was murdered at a building where you worked just a few feet away."

"Correlation is not causation, Superintendent. A coincidence, certainly, I would admit."

"But add into the mix," Collison proffered conversationally, "that the second murder victim was curating an exhibition about the site of the first murder at the time of the first murder, and surely it becomes a very striking coincidence indeed?"

"Extreme coincidences do happen," Raffen replied urbanely in the manner of a university tutorial. "Jung wrote a book about it."

"I'm well aware of Jung's theory of synchronicity," Collison answered, "and it's why I'm striving to keep a completely open mind about what does seem to be a most unlikely combination of circumstances."

"A concatenation of events," murmured Raffen, and then there was silence.

"I'm giving you every chance, Lord Raffen," Collison said after the silence had lasted some time, "to volunteer anything you may know which might bear on these events in any way. Is there anything at all you'd like to tell me?"

"No, I don't think so. I've already made a full statement."

"Very well. Then let me tell you some more about what *we* know, in the hope that it may ... jog your memory, shall we say."

"By all means, Superintendent."

"Then let me take you back to 1937. We have evidence from at least two sources that your grandfather was actively involved in recruiting intelligence agents for the Soviet Union."

"For the *British* secret service, I think you'll find," Raffen said with smile, "one of whom, incidentally, was my father."

"That's what everyone thought at the time, yes. But the reality was different. Oh, they'd work for MI6 or MI5 right enough, but their real loyalty would be to the Russians, to whom they'd start passing sensitive information as soon as they were senior enough to have access to it."

"If you say so," Raffen replied. "Personally, I don't believe a word of it."

"Oh, there's no need to take my word for it, Lord Raffen. Various high level defectors came across from behind the Iron Curtain in the decades which followed. Some of them knew all about your grandfather's activities. Perhaps understandably, your own father came under suspicion. That's why he was 'eased out' of his position as head of MI6."

"Even if that's true – and incidentally, wouldn't all this be highly classified, in which case how would you know about it? – what does it have to do with me?"

"As to the first point, evidence has come to light during this investigation which may well put these matters into the public domain, as lawyers say. As to your second point, bear with me while I continue the story."

Raffen said nothing, and Collison went on.

"Probably your grandfather had been up to his tricks for some time by 1937. Certainly the Spanish civil war must have been quite a recruiting boon for him; democracy under attack by fascists, and all that sort of stuff, and communists from all over Europe rallying to fight them. It must have seemed to many people that politics was polarising into a straight choice between fascism and communism."

"But in 1937 something went wrong – seriously wrong. Your grandfather was suborning, if that's the right word, a young man from Balliol College Oxford called Alexander Hamilton. From what we know he had communist sympathies all right, but he was fundamentally a patriot. So, when the suggestion came that he should sign up as a double agent, he was deeply shocked. Uncertain of whom to turn to, he confided in an old friend of his mother who by another coincidence was living at the Isokon at the same time. I refer to the detective writer, Agatha Christie."

"Appropriate enough," Raffen commented sardonically. "This sounds like a work of fiction."

"Foolishly," Collison said, ignoring the interruption, "Agatha Christie confronted your grandfather with Hamilton's allegations. He assured her that Hamilton had got the wrong end of the stick and that his approach had been solely on behalf of the home side, as it were. Panicked, and knowing that the great detective writer was unlikely to let this particular puzzle rest, he invited Hamilton to his flat, where he was murdered by your grandfather's Soviet handler, a man called Vassilyov. Afterwards he told Agatha Christie that Hamilton had run away to fight in Spain, which he knew to be a lie. Hamilton was dead; in fact, your grandfather had personally witnessed his murder. Vassilyov and his cronies arranged for the body to be bricked up in the basement of the Isokon that night, where it remained until it was discovered recently by accident."

"A fascinating story," Raffen commented, "though perhaps 'fantastic' might be a better word. And pure supposition on your part."

"Not so," Collison replied calmly, shaking his head. "You see, less foolishly, Agatha Christie also reported her suspicions to a friend who worked for MI6. We have the carbon copy of her letter, though the original seems to have gone missing. Certainly it was never acted upon, which meant that your grandfather was able to continue his activities undisturbed. If there had been any suspicions that he was a traitor he'd surely never have been awarded a peerage."

"But the murder of Hamilton, that's supposition, surely? How can you possibly know who killed him?"

"Again, we have evidence, though I'm not at liberty to divulge at this stage what it is. Let's just say that we're confident that the story I've just told you is in fact a true account of what happened."

Raffen looked around the bare room, appearing to gather his thoughts. The counter on the tape machine ticked on inexorably as though recording the very measure of humanity.

"Very well," he acknowledged conversationally, "let's assume you're right. I don't have any evidence either way but you say you have, so let's just accept that you're right for the sake of argument. Even if my grandfather was a traitor and a murderer, what connection does that have to Peter Howse's murder at Burgh House many decades later?"

"A pretty direct one, I think," Collison responded. "Let me state a hypothesis which I think seems to fit the available facts."

"By all means."

"Let's suppose that your grandfather was not naturally a violent man, or even a bad one, just misguided and rather naïve. Isn't it likely that he would have been horrified by the events of that night, traumatised even?"

"Assuming that he was involved in the murder, yes."

"Granted. But if we make that assumption, and as I say we have evidence to back up our version of events, let's also assume that he would have been tormented by the memory for the rest of his life. Many people in that situation feel an overpowering need to confess. Now we know that he never confessed to the authorities, not even on his deathbed, but perhaps somewhere along the way he told your father all about it."

"Well, if he did, then he never told me about it," Raffen said imperturbably.

There was a pause, deliberate on Collison's part.

"You're quite sure about that, are you?" he demanded finally, staring hard at the Professor.

"Quite sure, yes. I think I would have remembered being told that my grandfather was a murderer."

"Very well, let's leave that for the moment, but allow me to make that assumption for the time being, because my hypothesis doesn't work without it."

"Under protest, then."

"Agreed, thank you. Purely as a working assumption, let me posit that grandfather confesses to father, and that father in turn tells son."

As Raffen opened his mouth, Collison held up his hand.

"Don't worry, Lord Raffen, I'm very clear about what you're saying. Your position is that the first conversation may or may not have taken place, but if it did then you have no personal knowledge of it yourself, and that the second conversation definitely never took place. Is that correct?"

Raffen nodded and then, glancing at the tape recorder, said very firmly "yes, quite correct."

"But humour me a little more. Let me extend my hypothesis. If you did know about your grandfather's activities then when Peter Howse said he was planning to put together an exhibition covering the residents of the Isokon at the time in question, you'd have been pretty concerned, wouldn't you? Particularly if you knew about Agatha Christie's approach to him. Since she was by far the most famous resident the Isokon ever had, he'd be sure to focus on her as much as he could. Suppose that some of her papers might come to light? Something which might rake up lots of old stuff which had been thought to be safely dead and buried – or shall we say, safely dead and bricked up?"

"It's your hypothesis," Raffen said in a very detached fashion. "I've already said what I think about it."

"It's a good working hypothesis nonetheless," Collison said calmly. "You see, we think the motive for the murder of Peter Howse was the theft and destruction of some letters from Agatha Christie. Letters which Howse had already catalogued, and therefore presumably also already read. So he had to be murdered at the same time, because it was the only way to silence him."

Again Collison let a silence build.

"I'm asking you once more, Lord Raffen. Is there anything at all you want to tell me?"

"Only that so far as I am aware the hypothesis you're putting forward is complete fantasy."

"Very well. Do you remember that after the murder we took the fingerprints of everyone who worked at Burgh House in order to eliminate them from any found at the crime scene?"

"Yes," Raffen replied warily.

Very deliberately, Collison took the Christie letters in their plastic wallets and laid them on the table.

"For the tape," he said, "I am now showing Lord Raffen a number of letters from Agatha Christie. Lord Raffen, could you explain how these letters come to have your fingerprints on them, and would you care to comment on a statement made by a witness who saw you throw them away into a bin at the Flask public house in Hampstead at lunchtime on the day of the murder?"

Raffen paled visibly and swallowed hard.

"I think I'll have that solicitor now," he said.

"Interview suspended at 1611," Collison intoned, looking at the clock, "in order for Lord Raffen to speak to a solicitor."

He switched off the machine, removed one of the tapes, initialled it, and pushed it gravely across the table.

# CHAPTER 28

"So what's happening now?" Metcalfe asked as he and Willis sat over mugs of something which purported to be tea.

"Raffen's with a brief, then we're hoping to re-interview him," she replied.

"How long is that likely to take?"

She shrugged.

"Who knows? That's why I can't leave the nick."

"But from what you say, the guvnor's got him bang to rights, hasn't he?"

"He was great!" she enthused. "He got Raffen to flat out state that he didn't know about Hamilton's murder, or the Agatha Christie connection, all of which we know from his dad's suicide note to be untrue. All of that's on tape and under caution, which makes it admissible in court. I really don't see how he's going to wriggle out of it. You should have seen his face when Collison produced the letters! He'd been pretty cocky up until then – I assume because he didn't think we had any hard evidence – but he went white as a sheet."

"So I wonder what he'll do now?" Metcalfe mused.

"Stay shtum, surely. Isn't that what his brief will be advising him?"

"I'm not so sure," Metcalfe replied thoughtfully. "I'm sure that's what he would have advised had he been in the interview from the beginning, but things are different now, aren't they? Raffen's put a lot of things out there which we can show to be wrong. No, somehow I think that he's got to come up with *something*. Unless he just confesses, of course, which is not impossible."

"He won't cough," Willis said determinedly. "He's not the type. He's got an ego the size of London. He thinks he's smarter than we are. I don't think he could handle having to admit to everyone, himself included, that he underestimated us."

"Then he'll have to come up with something, won't he?" Metcalfe reasoned. "I can't wait to see what it is. Maybe he'll say he was still in shock from the death of his father and didn't understand the questions properly."

"Oh, come on, Bob," Willis said in amusement. "Surely no jury's going to believe that?"

"You'd be surprised what a jury will believe," he said seriously. "One of my first collars when I was in uniform was a petty villain I found loitering outside a house. He ran off when I challenged him, and hid up a tree. It was a quiet night so I was able to whistle up a couple of squad cars and one of them found him, with housebreaking tools dropped underneath. He told the jury that the tools weren't his, and that he'd just climbed the tree to rescue a cat, which had then come down of its own accord and run off."

"And the jury acquitted?"

"Yes, and looked at me pretty accusingly too. They obviously thought we'd tried to fit him up."

She shook her head in disbelief.

"Karen," he said suddenly, "are you OK?"

She sighed and stiffened in her seat.

"I'm sorry," he offered quickly, "that was a stupid thing to say. Of course you're not OK, you're very unhappy about breaking up with Peter. I know that."

"Oh, Bob-"

"No, listen, let me finish. I just wanted to say that if you think you've made a mistake you mustn't pretend for my sake, do you understand? I can't bear to see you unhappy, nor to think that it's me who's made you unhappy."

Just as she was saying "oh, Bob," again a uniformed PC approached.

"Sorry, Sarge, message from Mr Collison. Your suspect's ready to go again."

"Damn!" she said quietly, and then "sorry, Bob we'll have to talk about this later" and, brushing the back of her hand quickly and furiously across her eyes, she gathered up her bag and folder and headed back to the interview room.

Raffen was looking distinctly nervous as he was ushered into the room and sat down. With him was a well-groomed man in a blue pinstripe suit. Definitely a cut or two above the usual solicitors who ventured into North London nicks, Willis thought; presumably he had been summoned by Raffen from some smart firm in the West End which dealt with his family affairs.

"My client would like to clarify certain aspects of the answers which he gave in interview earlier," the blue pinstripes said after the formalities had been observed and the tape was running.

"Clarify?" Collison queried innocently. "I don't think we need anything clarified do we, Sergeant?"

"No, sir," she replied. "I think Lord Raffen's replies were all very clear. I have a note of them here if the solicitor would like them."

"Thank you but that won't be necessary," said the latter with a tight little smile. "I have listened to the tape. Perhaps I didn't express myself properly. Rather than clarify his answers, my client wishes to make certain amendments."

"Amendments?" Collison echoed. "You mean that he wishes to change some of his answers?"

"Precisely."

"So what you're saying is that in his previous interview your client, despite being on tape and under caution, and despite being urged on various occasions to tell the truth in order to eliminate himself from our enquiries, did not in fact tell the truth?"

"Not the full truth, certainly," the solicitor conceded. "My client wishes to make it clear for the record that he is still in shock from the recent unexpected death of his father, and that this may have affected his understanding of the full implications of what passed during the previous interview. However, he is anxious to assist the police with their enquiries in every way possible and it is in that spirit that he now offers a fuller version of events. He doesn't have to, as you well know. He could simply choose to remain silent."

"That would be something on which you would need to advise your client, of course," Collison replied smoothly. "Given what you have just said I assume you have taken the view that it would be unwise to allow your client's previous statements to remain on the record without ... 'amendment' is how you put it, I think."

The solicitor chose to ignore this sally.

"Can I suggest, Superintendent, that you put your various questions to my client again?"

"Very well. Lord Raffen, let's start with your grandfather. Were you aware that under the cloak of recruiting agents for the British security services he was in fact also recruiting potential double agents for the Soviet Union?"

"Yes, I was."

"When and how did you become aware of this information?"

"From my father, some years ago."

"You're quite sure of that, are you? The timing, I mean? It wasn't more recently, perhaps just a few weeks ago?"

"No, I remember distinctly. It was on my twenty-first birthday."

"Were you also aware that he had been instrumental in the murder of Alexander Hamilton?"

"Yes, my father told me about it all at the same time."

"Did the name Vassilyov mean anything to you?"

"I had forgotten it until you mentioned it earlier, but I

believe that was the name of the killer, yes. I think he was an intelligence agent based at the Soviet embassy in London."

"And were you aware of an approach made by Agatha Christie to your grandfather based on information which she had received from Alexander Hamilton?"

"Yes, of course. That was the whole point, the whole reason for the murder. My grandfather was frantic that he was about to be discovered. He could have been hanged as a traitor. My father told me that he, my grandfather that is, told Agatha Christie that Hamilton had been mistaken, and this seemed to satisfy her."

"And later he told her that Hamilton had run away to fight in Spain?"

"I believe so, yes."

Collison glanced at Willis.

"I want to be very clear about one thing, Lord Raffen, so at the risk of labouring the point, let me ask you one more time. Are you quite certain that your father told you about all these matters many years ago, on your twenty-first birthday, rather than, say, a week or two before Peter Howse's death?"

"Yes, of course. It's not the sort of thing one's likely to forget."

"Very well, then let's move on. Earlier I showed you some letters from Agatha Christie, original letters signed by her. These letters have your fingerprints on them and you were observed by a witness to throw them into a rubbish bin at the Flask public house at lunchtime on the day of the murder. Is it true that you had them at that time, and disposed of them in this fashion?"

Raffen swallowed hard.

"It is, yes."

"Then, Lord Raffen, I invite you to tell me how you came by them."

"I ... took them."

"From Peter Howse's room?"

Raffen nodded.

"For the tape please, Lord Raffen."

"Yes," he rasped.

"On the day of the murder?"

"That morning, yes."

"So when you told us earlier under caution that you didn't go into the victim's room on the morning of the murder, that wasn't true?"

"No."

Collison now deliberately let a silence grow in the room. The tape machine hummed almost inaudibly. Collison and Willis gazed levelly at Raffen, who refused to meet their eyes. The solicitor appeared to have turned into a waxwork, pen poised on notebook. Seemingly from far away came the sound of an ambulance siren.

"He came to my room," Raffen blurted out at last. "The day before. He was bragging about having found something which would destroy my family's reputation. He was laughing about it. Oh yes, he thought it was all a great joke. He really was a vile and disgusting man."

Collison and Willis sat impassively.

"Of course, I knew what it must be," Raffen went on after a pause. "I had been afraid of something like this happening ever since I heard about his plans for an Isokon exhibition. I even tried to talk him out of it. Said nobody today would be very interested, all that sort of thing. But it didn't work."

"I could hardly speak I was so agitated. But I tried to ask him what it was all about, said 'what on earth are you talking about?', and so on. He just laughed that nasty sneering laugh of his and said I'd find out soon enough, because he was going to tell the newspapers and make a big story out of it. But he couldn't resist a little Parthian shot just as he was going out of the room. He distinctly said something like 'who'd ever have thought that Agatha Christie could have been sitting on top of a real life mystery all the time' or some such stuff."

"Of course, then I knew. I rang my father straightaway and he said I absolutely had to get whatever it was Howse had found from Agatha Christie. I lay awake all night thinking about it and decided that the thing to do was to offer Howse money for whatever letters he had found. He was always hard up, so I thought there was a good chance he'd say 'yes' as long as the amount we offered was big enough. I hung about in my room all morning plucking up courage and then just before lunch I went into his room to have it out with him."

The silence which grew again was more eloquent than anyone asking 'and what happened then?'.

"I didn't kill him," Raffen said at length. "I know what it must look like, and I'm sorry I lied before, but I didn't kill him. He was already dead. He was slumped forward over the desk and it looked as though somebody had bashed the back of his head in. It made me feel sick, but I noticed there was a box open with a folder marked 'Agatha Christie' on top, so I snatched out everything that was in it – only a few pages – and ran back to my own room as quietly as I could. I sat down for a minute to collect my thoughts; I was shaking. I glanced at the papers and knew I'd found what I'd needed to. It suddenly occurred to me that as soon as his death was discovered there would be a great brouhaha and the police would seal the building, so I had to get the letters out of there straightaway and never bring them back. So I decided to go to the Flask for lunch as usual, dispose of them there, and then come back and pretend to discover his body all over again, if nobody else had done so."

"When you say you'd found what you needed to," Collison interjected for the first time since Raffen had launched into his story, "can you just confirm for the record what it was?"

"It was a letter to my grandfather from Agatha Christie," Raffen stated. "It expressed surprise that Hamilton should have left for Spain without speaking to anyone, not even his parents; it made it pretty clear she didn't believe him about that. It also referred expressly to Hamilton's accusations against him. It was a very dangerous document, because we knew by then that the Isokon was due for refurbishment and so there was a chance that Hamilton's body might be found and identified."

"So it would be clear that your grandfather had lied about Hamilton going to Spain?"

"Exactly, yes."

"What did you do with this letter?"

"I would have preferred to take it home with me and burn it, but I was scared that everyone at Burgh House might be searched that afternoon, so I tore it up and flushed it down the loo in the Gents."

"And why didn't you do the same with the other letters as well?"

"Because I knew how difficult it can be to flush ordinary writing paper down the toilet. Even though I tore the other one up as small as I could, it still took three or four goes to get rid of it all. I reasoned the others weren't incriminating in any way and so could safely simply be chucked away. I didn't reckon on someone seeing me do it."

"So, let me summarise what you are now saying," Collison said briskly. "You admit that you knew about your grandfather's activities, including his role in the murder of Alexander Hamilton. You admit that you knew about the Christie intervention. You admit that you and your father knew that Hamilton's body was bricked up in the basement of the Isokon, yet neither of you did anything over the years to bring this to light. You admit that you knew Howse had found some incriminating material, and that you stole this from his room and destroyed it."

"Yes."

"And you say that you didn't murder Peter Howse. You say that he was dead already when you entered his room, having been killed by some other person."

"Yes."

"Then there's just one last point which I don't understand, Lord Raffen."

"And what's that?"

"Well, on your own evidence, Howse had found and read the Christie letter, so how did you expect to resolve the matter simply by acquiring the letter itself? You said yourself that Howse was short of money. Surely even at best he might keep coming back to blackmail you again and again whenever he needed more money, and at worst he might take your money but go to the press anyway out of spite. How did you know that he hadn't taken a copy of the letter, for example?"

"I'm not sure what you're suggesting, Superintendent," the blue pinstripes said suavely.

"I would have thought it was pretty clear what I'm suggesting," Collinson replied. "I'm suggesting that the story your client has just outlined, the plan he says he hatched with his father to keep the family reputation intact, simply doesn't make sense. It wasn't enough to get hold of the letter, and never could be. Howse had to silenced permanently."

The solicitor shut his pad with a decided snap.

"In that case, I'm advising my client not to answer any further questions," he announced.

"Very well," Collison said equably. "Interview terminated."

As the solicitor's copy of the tape was being handed over, Collison drew him aside.

"I think we should discuss your client being granted police bail," he murmured, "against delivery of his passport."

# CHAPTER 29

The next morning, Willis looked in on Collison.

"Morning, guv," she said. "I just wanted to say very well done for yesterday. It seems like we've got Raffen bang to rights."

"Yes and no," he replied. "He did actually come up with a story, didn't he? And while you and I may find it implausible being the cynical police officers that we are, you never know – a jury might just swallow it."

"Yes, that's what Bob said."

"Well, there you are then," laughed Collison "that's at least two of us who have reservations. Mine are very small ones though, I have to say. It will look very bad that he lied under caution and then changed his story. And he still hasn't explained how he was intending to keep Howse quiet except by murdering him."

"So you're going to charge him, then?" she asked excitedly.

"I think so, yes. In my view we've got enough. But I'd like to speak to DCS Morris first. Out of courtesy, but also because I'd value a second opinion."

"Remember we've got Alan Howse coming in to be

re-interviewed this afternoon, guv. Would you like me to cancel that?"

"No, not at all, we need to see him. If I was Raffen's defence brief I'd start pointing the finger at all the other suspects, so we need to be able to show that he has an alibi. At the very least, we need to be able to show that we've gone absolutely all the way in our efforts to find out."

"OK, he's due in at two."

"That will do very nicely," Collison observed, glancing at his watch. "I want read the whole file right through one last time. That'll take a few hours, then I can phone the DCS at lunchtime before I see Howse."

"By the way," Willis informed him. "I didn't want you to think that I'd forgotten about that ladder business. As I was with you in interviews, I asked Priya Desai to go round and try it for size. She just confirmed to me this morning that she was able to lift the ladder onto the flat roof, and also that she could do so at a point which was out of the view of anyone sitting where Bailey claimed he was."

"So she could have gone up the side of the building unobserved and in through the window," Collison reflected. "Come to think of it, so could he. Well, I suppose it hardly matters now, but ask Priya to put a note on the file, will you?"

As Willis left the room, he drew the bulky folder towards him, settled a pen and a pad at his elbow, and began to read through the witness statements.

A couple of hours later he was on the phone as anticipated

to DCS Morris, who listened intently to what he had to say.

"So you think you've got your man?" he asked.

"Yes, sir, I think the discrepancy in the statements is pretty conclusive, don't you?"

"Yes, I agree. Ideally you need a confession to be certain, though. You know what juries are like; they can take a lot of convincing these days. But what you have already is pretty compelling."

"Of course there are still other suspects whom we've not been able to eliminate ..." Collison proffered.

"But you haven't caught them out in a lie, have you? Not like you have with him."

"So you're happy for me to go ahead and charge him, sir?"

"Absolutely, and well done. Oh, Simon, before I forget, there's some information that might be of interest to you. That Crime Academy position ..."

"Yes?"

"Well, I reckon you can forget about it. Don't know if that will make you happy or sad, but there it is."

"You mean they've offered it to someone else?" Collison asked.

"No, I mean the Crime Academy is being closed down, or most of it anyway. The present Commandant will be the last."

"But that's impossible!" gasped Collison. "Where will the Met train its detectives if not at the Academy?"

"On the job," came the terse response. "The Commissioner's under pressure from the Home Office to cut costs and get more bodies on the street to increase clear-up rates. This move does both. Apparently the idea is for each Detective Sergeant to have four trainee DCs under his wing and sort of teach them the ropes as they go along; a bit like an electrician or a plumber."

"Sorry, sir, but are you sure this information is kosher?"

"It's on the square," came the rather cryptic response.

"I see. Well, thank you for letting me know."

"You're welcome, Simon. Bye now."

Collison's head was still reeling from this new development when he sat down with Willis to re-interview Alan Howse that afternoon. He switched on the tape, explained the need for the caution, and administered it.

"Now then, Mr Howse, as I've just explained, we are trying very hard to eliminate you formally from this investigation but we have not yet been able to do so as we haven't been able to establish your whereabouts on the day of the crime, well, the morning anyway because we're pretty sure your uncle was dead by one o'clock."

Howse nodded his understanding.

"Now, we've examined footage from the CCTV cameras at Hampstead tube station, and that's all fine. We're happy that you didn't arrive at the station that morning, which is of course consistent with your having been working from your home in Hackney, as you say. We've tried to go further. I'm afraid we've taken the liberty of having a look at your Oyster card account, and that wasn't used at all that day, so that's fine too."

Howse nodded again.

"By the way, Mr Howse," Collison said conversationally, "we've noticed that you hardly ever seem to use your Oyster card. How on earth do you get around London? Surely you have customers to visit, and that sort of thing."

Howse indicated a large canvas bag by his feet.

"I have one of those folding bikes. It's great. Saves me money and keeps me fit at the same time. If I have a really long journey to do then I can take it with me on the tube, but usually I just cycle."

"That's wonderful," Collison said, "but I'm afraid it doesn't make our job any easier. It would be so convenient if we could just establish some sort of firm alibi for you. Are you sure that you can't think of anyone, anyone at all, who might have seen you in or around your flat that morning?"

"No, I'm afraid not. I slept quite late and then I just got out of bed and started working. I didn't even need to go out to the shops for milk, or anything like that."

"Oh dear," Collison commiserated, "what a shame. You see, in that case I'm going to charge you with the murder of Peter Howse."

Willis, taken completely aback, could only gape in consternation. Had he gone mad?

As if echoing her thoughts, Alan Howse went a very strange colour and croaked "have you gone mad?"

"Not at all, Mr Howse. Now, I know you're already under caution, but just so there's no possible misunderstanding, I'm going to caution you again before you tell me whether there's anything you want to say in answer to the charge."

He did so.

"Now then, Mr Howse, is there anything you want to say?"

"You're mad," Howse persisted. "I was nowhere near Burgh House that day. You said so yourself."

"No, I said we hadn't been able to establish that you were at Burgh House, or anywhere else for that matter. Until very recently, that is. Just an hour or two ago in fact, when I re-read the whole file and noticed something I should have spotted earlier."

Willis, who was still in a state of shock, realised that she had dropped her pen, and picked it up to resume taking notes.

"In an earlier interview," said Collison, turning to a page in the file which he had marked with a yellow sticky indicator, "you described the scene in your uncle's room the last time you saw him. You mentioned that there were papers everywhere for an exhibition he was preparing, and various other items including an old policeman's truncheon with a label on it."

"Yes, that's right."

"A truncheon which was then used as the murder weapon, actually," Collison informed him. "We never released that information to the press. Which is a shame – a shame for you, that is."

He paused and stared at Howse. A look of intense concern was starting to gather across the latter's face.

"You see, the truncheon wasn't there when you claim last to have visited your uncle. It only came to light the day before his murder. Cataloguing and labelling it must have been one of the last things he did. So, you can't have read about it in the press because we kept its existence secret – it was the murder weapon after all – and the only time you could have seen it, particularly with a label on it, was when you visited your uncle that morning and used it to kill him with. No wonder it stuck in your memory ..."

At this point Howse slumped down over the table, his body racked by a series of convulsive sobs.

"I didn't mean to kill him," he managed to say. "That evil, miserable, chiselling bastard! Yes, I was there, but I didn't mean to do it."

He subsided in a racking weeping fit. The two detectives let the tape run and sat still, saying nothing. Gradually the weeping stopped, and Howse sat back upright in his chair, turning his tear-stained face towards them.

Collison was about to say "why don't you tell us what happened?" but there was no need.

"I went back that morning," Howse said, controlling himself with a visible effort, "to have one last attempt at persuading him to let me have the money – *my* money. The place was deserted. There was nobody on the reception desk, which I thought was a bit odd. It was a nuisance, actually, because I'd wanted to leave my bike at the desk as I usually do, but I was afraid it would get stolen, so I had to take it up with me. I ended up leaving it in the bend in the stairs up to

Uncle Peter's room."

"And what happened?"

"Nothing happened," Howse said bitterly, "well, nothing good anyway. As soon as I started talking he said that if I'd come to talk about what we'd already discussed then I'd had a wasted journey. He had no intention of letting me have the money, and no intention of resigning as a trustee. Then he just blanked me. Turned away very ostentatiously and got on with his work, completely ignoring me."

"And then what?"

"It just happened. Suddenly I was there with the truncheon in my hand and he'd fallen forwards over his papers with blood coming out of his head. It all felt totally unreal. I knew what I'd done but I didn't remember actually doing it. I was just conscious of this feeling of intense, unspeakable rage, but it had gone very suddenly and now there was just, like, total disbelief at what had happened."

"Did you check to see if he was dead? Whether there was anything you might be able to do to help him? Phone for an ambulance, for example?"

"No, I didn't. I suppose that sounds bad, doesn't it? But somehow I just sort of knew that he was dead."

"So, what *did* you do?"

"I just wanted to get away from there before anyone saw me. I realised that my fingerprints must be on the truncheon, so I wiped it on Uncle Peter's overcoat which was thrown across one of the chairs. Then I slipped out of the room as quietly as I could, shutting the door behind me, went downstairs, picking up my bike as I went, and then pedalled away like hell, hoping nobody had spotted me."

"What did you do next? You must have been in a bit of a state, weren't you?"

"I didn't know what I was doing or where I was. I remember later realising that I should get rid of all the clothes I was wearing, so I took them all off, put them in a bin bag and left it in a bin area a few roads away. I did it in the middle of the night, and I don't think anyone saw me."

He looked hopelessly at them both. Collison sighed.

"So, just to summarise," he said, "you admit that you killed Peter Howse in his room that morning, you admit that it was a deliberate act not an accident, and you say that you didn't mean to do it. That you did it in a sudden fit of rage."

"I suppose so."

"Well, is that correct or is it not?"

"Yes," Howse said quietly, "that's quite correct."

Collison reached out towards the tape machine.

"Interview terminated at 1521," he announced. "DS Willis and I are now going to escort Mr Howse to the desk sergeant, who will enter him formally into custody."

# CHAPTER 30

"So what will happen to him?" Caroline Collison asked the next morning.

"With a good defence brief he might get away with manslaughter on grounds of diminished responsibility," her husband replied judiciously, "but somehow I doubt it."

"But you said that the uncle was a horrible man and that the nephew killed him in a fit of rage," she protested.

"Both true, but that's a very slippery road to go down, isn't it? We all lose our temper with someone very unpleasant at some time or other, but that doesn't justify murder. We all remain responsible for our actions, no matter how angry we might get."

"Oh, bums to that," she said contemptuously. "If only the legal system was run by women. You men are so bloody rational all the time – or think you are, anyway."

As she took his empty mug away she glanced at the clock. "Here! Aren't you going to be late?"

"I'm not going to the nick this morning," he explained. "I've got an appointment with the ACC."

"Oh," she said. "About that Academy job, I expect?"

"Actually, no," he replied, "or at least, I don't think so. It's all rather curious, actually."

"What's curious?"

"Well, Jim Morris told me that the Academy's being closed down. That in future detectives will have to learn their skills on the job, as it were."

"But that's what used to happen, wasn't it?" he asked, puzzled. "That's why they set up the Academy in the first place, because the old system didn't work."

"Yes, I know. That's the curious thing."

"Well, Jim Morris must have got it wrong," she said dismissively.

"No, that's what I said, and he told me it was on the square. That means that he's a mason, and that he was told by a fellow mason from within the force. They don't usually lie to each other, you know."

Caroline sat down and eyed him with amused despair.

"Hasn't it occurred to you that if you think the danger of being offered this job has passed, then you might pretend to be eager to accept it? And that if this is disinformation then you fall straight into their trap?"

"Oh, Caroline, really! Whose trap?"

"Jim Morris for a start. You've said yourself that he'd be glad to be rid of you, and maybe the ACC's in on it too."

"That was before," he said defensively. "I think Jim Morris is OK with me now. And as for the ACC, well, he could just order me to take the job if he wants to. No, I'm inclined to think that this is kosher. It's just the sort of daft idea the MPC might come up with under political pressure. After all, it addresses the short term issues very nicely, or appears to, and by the time the chickens come home to roost he'll be retired on a nice fat pension and it will be someone else's mess to clear up."

"Why don't you have that discussion with the ACC?" she asked brightly. "Might do your career prospects a power of good, don't you think?"

"Simon," the ACC greeted him expansively as he waved him to a chair, "many congratulations on a job well done."

"Thank you, sir," he replied, "though it turned out to be quite simple in the end – deceptively simple actually. The only problem was that we were all staring so hard in the wrong direction."

"Hm. Was Raffen prepared to kill Howse, do you think?"

"I'm almost certain of it, sir. What would have been the point of disposing of the letter but leaving Howse to blab about it? No, I reckon Raffen went into that room intending to murder Howse, and was naturally surprised as hell to find that someone had done the job for him."

"So why did he lie about that timing point, then? After all, it's not even as if it mattered terribly much. If he knew about his grandfather and Hamilton, then he knew, and that's all there was to it."

"I'm not sure he was lying, sir," Collison said carefully.

"What do you mean?" asked the ACC with a frown.

"I mean I'm not convinced that David Raffen's suicide note was genuine. It's difficult to say as we're not allowed to see the original, but I've been thinking about it, and the more I think about it the less I like it. Look at it this way. I have a conversation with Commander Newby one day in which we agree all the things of which it would be wonderful to have clear evidence. Overnight David Raffen, who has just been interviewed and given nothing away, dies suddenly, and very conveniently leaves a note which tells us everything we want to know. Convenient for Newby too, since it apparently also contained a lot of damaging stuff on security people they already suspected but hadn't been able to nail with anything. He told me himself that it gave him a wonderful excuse to re-open their cases."

"A bit fanciful, isn't it?"

"I don't think so, sir. I think Newby himself gave us a clue when he talked about situations where you know damn well what happened, but can't prove it. I think Newby knew all about the Hamilton murder from Russian defections during the Cold War, but couldn't tell us without compromising some source or other. So he laid a trail for us to find out about it ourselves. Of course, he believed and hoped it would lead us to the Honourable Hugh as the murderer of Peter Howse, hopefully at his father's incitement, which would have led to a very public exposure of all the background facts, including how and by whom Hamilton came to be killed all those years ago. He wasn't to know that the nephew had got there first. After all, if you knew everything that Newby knew then Raffen was indeed the obvious suspect."

"But by the time the suicide note came into existence you

already knew about Hamilton having been murdered," the ACC countered, "and that this made Raffen the obvious suspect for the Howse murder, so even if the suicide note was fake then it wasn't exactly laying a trail was it? You'd already done most of the hard work."

Collison shook his head dubiously.

"I think we were being led by the nose long before then. When Bob Metcalfe went down to Exeter, the archivist told us they'd had two break-ins recently. The first was camouflaged to look like some local yobbos after cash, but I think it was really to take a look at the Christie carbon copies and check what sort of paper and typewriter had been used. The second nocturnal visit was to remove one of the existing copies and replace it with the one which Bob found, as he was meant to find it. The archivist said he didn't remember seeing it before, which was strange given its highly unusual contents, and Bob said that although the collection was locked away by then it was in very ordinary cabinets which could be opened in a couple of seconds by any professional."

"So you think that letter was a fake too?"

"I do, sir, yes. After all, how likely is it that if such a letter had ever been received, the security services would have done absolutely nothing about it?"

"It's an interesting theory," the ACC admitted, "but since it's irrelevant to the outcome of the investigation I think we can safely ignore it, can't we? After all, it's not as if you'd ever be able to prove it anyway."

"But it does bear on David Raffen's death, doesn't it? If

my theory is right, then it makes the circumstances of his death highly suspicious."

"Now you stop right there!" the ACC said very sharply indeed, bringing his right hand down on the desk with a hard smack.

He started intently into Simon's eyes while drawing a deep breath.

"There will be a properly conducted inquest into the death of David Raffen, as is right and proper," he said quietly. "Personally, I have no doubt that it will reach a verdict of suicide. Given what is shortly to become public knowledge about the deceased and his family secrets, that will seem to everybody an entirely natural conclusion, which in fact it is. Neither you nor I is ever going to suggest that it might have been anything else."

"The problem with you, Simon," he went on more normally, "is that you're too bright for your own good."

"Too bright to give Special Branch their desired outcome, anyway," Collison commented sardonically. "You know, sir, it's frightening. If I hadn't suddenly made that connection with the murder weapon then I'd have charged Raffen, and given all his lies and the overwhelming circumstantial evidence he'd almost certainly have been convicted. Hell, we all believed he was guilty, so why shouldn't a jury?"

"Well, he was guilty really, wasn't he?" reasoned the ACC. "OK, he didn't have to commit the final act, but he was intending to."

"I suppose so," Collison conceded, "and we do have him

for concealing a death, theft of the letters, criminal damage for destroying one of them, and probably conspiracy to obstruct the course of justice as well."

"All true," agreed the ACC, "not that you'll ever be able to charge him, I'm afraid."

"How come, sir?"

"I happen to know that Commander Newby is meeting with Hugh Raffen as we speak. It is being put to his lordship that these charges will all lie on file and be brought out and dusted down should he ever be implicated in any way in the publication of his father's memoirs. I believe it's also being proposed that he petition to relinquish his peerage. Bit awkward, otherwise. I think it needs a vote of both Houses of Parliament."

"I see. Well, that would be something, I suppose."

"What the soon to be un-Lord Raffen doesn't know, of course," the ACC went on, "is that the full story of his grandfather's misdeeds is going to be all over the front pages of the newspapers tomorrow, as indeed will you. Whether or not your theory is correct, you're undoubtedly right that it was Special Branch's desired outcome that Raffen be very publicly convicted of the Burgh House murder. The only way they can put everything into the public domain now is to make sure that you are lauded to the skies for having solved not one but two murders, one of which was a particularly baffling cold case with sinister security overtones. The press are going to love it."

He turned over a few pages of his notebook.

"You remember Mo Wallace?"

"The Met's PR man? Shiny shoes and shiny hair?"

"That's the one. I've just been meeting with him before you came. Apparently the Mail are going with "Super Simon Strikes Again". Clever enough, I suppose, if you like that sort of thing. Whereas in the Telegraph you're going to be "Collison of the Yard". I think I prefer that. More gravitas, don't you think? And no reference to your rank, which means it's a soubriquet you can carry with you through the many remaining triumphs of your career. Oh, the Commissioner wants to see you, by the way, to congratulate you in person."

"Speaking of my future career, sir," Collison ventured innocently, "I've been thinking a bit more about that job at the Academy."

"Ah," the ACC said absently, stroking his nose, "not so sure about that any more. Newby wants you for the Branch, you know. There's a Chief Super's position coming up there in a few months. Job's yours if you want it. We might even be able to arrange for you to take Metcalfe or Willis with you."

"Commander Newby did mention that to me actually," Collison admitted. "I'm very flattered, sir, but I'm not sure it's for me. I don't think I have the right ... mind-set, shall we say."

"No need to make up your mind so quickly," the ACC said blandly. "Take a few weeks to think about it. It would look very good on your CV, you know. The present

Commissioner was in the Branch, and so was the one before him."

"I will think about it, sir. Anyway, I still have my case report to write."

"And a paper, I believe?" the ACC reminded him.

On the other side of London at much the same time, Karen Willis entered one of the large, glittery department stores on Oxford Street. She made her accustomed way to the hosiery department and picked up a packet of her favourite stockings. Then, even as the cellophane crackled invitingly in her hand, she gave a start and put them back in the rack, turning instead with a sad shake of her head towards the undiscovered territory inhabited by tights in serried ranks on the displays opposite.

Suddenly, while still only halfway across the aisle, she paused in mid-stride and looked back at the stockings counter as if yearning for lost nostalgic pleasures, and wearing a winsome expression which might best be described as highly ambiguous.

**A WHIFF OF CYANIDE**, the third book in the *Hampstead Murders series*, publishes summer 2017. Please enjoy the following extract with our compliments:

Ann Durham eased herself into the armchair in her hotel room and noticed with distaste that the furniture at such establishments seemed to be growing narrower with each passing year. She rubbed her feet together with little jerky movements until she had succeeded in dislodging her shoes. They were expensive, which was all well and good, but new, which was not, for they were already hurting her. Thank goodness she had brought an older, less aggressive pair with her in her monogrammed designer luggage (aubergine, with the distinctive design of a brand which is often offered less convincingly on beaches in Thailand).

As she tried to settle her substantial thighs more comfortably within the restrictive confines of the chair, she considered her situation, and as she did so a scowl played across her face. It would be chivalrous to record that she had a face which looked as though it and scowls were generally strangers, but quite untrue. On the contrary, the tight line of her pursed lips hinted at the personality of a woman who was perpetually displeased with the actions of others, and not slow in making such feelings known.

The scowl was, however, for once not entirely unjustified, for the circumstances in which she found herself were indeed disagreeable. The doyenne of English crime fiction, a woman whose books had been adapted many times for television and translated into many different languages, she saw her position of natural leadership within the writing profession as being quite naturally accepted without question. Yet suddenly in place of servile acquiescence she found resistance, and even outright rebellion. Where once her wise and gracious leadership had been praised and welcomed, she now heard defiant whispers using ugly, unkind words such as 'tyranny' and 'dictatorship'.

Her mistake, of course, had been in not attending the final meeting of the organising committee, though at the time it had hardly seemed necessary. As Chair of the Crime Writers' Association (a role she had filled for many years) as well as every similar body, she was accustomed to her wishes, once made known, being accepted without question. Her presence in person should not have been required. Yet in the event some she had thought to be her friends, or at least compliant sycophants which was surely much the same thing, had seized the opportunity to rebel while the remainder had proved unequal to the task of facing down the opposition, as she would undoubtedly have done herself had she only been present, and enforcing her implacable will.

Really, she thought, as though she didn't already have quite enough problems to worry about!

It was such a small point, they had pleaded with her

afterwards, trying to justify their betrayal. A simple change of venue, and a decision which had been forced upon them anyway by the unexpected availability of the usual hotel in Bristol. Yet she saw it for what it undoubtedly was: the thin end of the wedge. The inflicting of what was as yet the smallest of cracks in the deepest foundation of her rule, but one which left unchecked would surely spread and risk undoing everything for which she had worked for so long.

Already it had begun. With the change of venue had come a sudden realisation (or at least, that is how it had been presented) that the rooms housing the sessions were larger than had been the case for all those years in Bristol, thus both justifying and necessitating the promotion of the convention to the public at large. She shuddered at the thought. The paying public were of course a tiresome necessity for any provider of goods or services and they were all very well in their place, but that place was in their homes reading her books or watching her television programmes, not thronging the halls of a writers' conference. When she met them at Book Festivals it was hardly a meeting at all in the true sense of the word, simply an hour or so of pre-arranged questions, all phrased so as to allow her to bring out, with all due modesty, her overall wonderfulness, followed by signing books for a gratifyingly lengthy queue of supplicants. The whole point of having had a sensible person like herself in charge of the arrangements year after year had been to avoid exactly this sort of situation; the horror of distinguished writers having to rub shoulders with the hoi polloi – and for three days, no less.

Now there were rumours of an election being held for the post she had held as of right for so long. While publicly she refused even to acknowledge the existence of such deranged fantasies (a stance which was assisted by no interviewer having as yet been so brave as to broach the subject), privately she felt intense irritation and a small but growing sense of foreboding.

While it was of course quite ridiculous that she should be forced into an election for a post which nobody could possibly fulfil anything like as well as she could, given her experience, expertise and warm personal skills, there was always the possibility that such an eventuality might indeed occur. While it was equally ridiculous that anyone might prefer her likely challenger (Tom Smythe – a pretentious little man whom she knew for certain had changed his name from Smith), there was always the chance that collective insanity might strike detective authors as a whole; already she was hearing blandishments such as 'time for a change', and 'a new approach'.

She snorted aloud at the thought of the creator of that dull little Inspector Naesby in Lewes, who plied his uninspiring trade among the antiques dealers of East Sussex, being elevated to a position so far beyond his abilities, to the ultimate detriment of the entire crime writing fraternity. Surely such an outcome was impossible? And yet ....

With a tut of exasperation she resolved to put on her comfortable shoes and head downstairs to stiffen morale among her supporters.

"A little touch of Harry in the night," she murmured purposefully.

At about the same time, Peter Collins was heading into the hotel, somewhat diffidently, since he was still getting used to the idea of being a writer, and this was his first formal outing as such. He introduced himself at the check-in desk and there was a gratifying little buzz of excitement as a plump and jolly young lady said 'oh yes, you're a speaker, aren't you?', found his name badge (a different colour to those on the main registration table, he noted) from a separate cache to the side, and escorted him across the crowded lobby of the hotel; she seemed almost to shoulder people aside as she did so, but perhaps she was just nimbler on her feet than might be expected, Peter mused. Suddenly he felt like a frail craft following in the wake of an ice-breaker. She broke free from the crowd and headed up a flight of stairs, sending a non-stop stream of loud conversational gambits over her shoulder as she did so.

On the first floor, Peter was led through a dazzling collection of books displayed for sale on trestle tables to a separate room which had a handwritten 'Speakers' Room' (with an apostrophe correctly employed, he noted approvingly) sign sellotaped beside the door.

"You can come here anytime," the girl hooted, now a little breathlessly after having combined climbing the stairs with constant chatter. "Now, I'm not sure if there's anyone ... oh, yes, look!"

She seized him by the arm and propelled him across the room with surprising strength towards a rather imposing individual dressed in a three-piece suit cut from dark blue pinstripe, a gold watch chain stretched across his rather ample midriff. Given that everyone else in the throng through which he had just been led was very badly dressed (even by the standards of writers, as he would come to realise as he got to know the breed better), to say that he stood out would be an understatement. He had the air of an old style stockbroker come to advise on the family trust fund.

"Peter, this is Tom Smythe," she said. "Tom, this is Peter Collins. Can I leave you two to get to know each other? I really ought to get back to the desk. Gosh, we've never had a crowd like this before."

Without waiting for an answer she strode from the room. Peter just had time enough to notice that she was wearing a name badge which said "Fiona". He and the other man shook hands in that friendly but wary fashion which writers tend to employ before they have worked out whether you are a competitor or not.

"Can I offer you a coffee?" Smythe enquired, gesturing towards the refreshment table.

Collins's glance took in some plastic cups and a thermos flask, and he declined as graciously as possible.

"This your first time?" Smythe asked.

"Yes, my first time at any book festival, in fact. As a

speaker, that is. Obviously I've been in the audience at quite a few, particularly crime ones."

"Ah, new to the game, eh?" Smythe observed cautiously. "What sort of stuff do you write, then?"

"I've written a book about poisonings, in fiction and real life," Collins explained, "but it hasn't actually been published yet, so I feel a bit of a fraud, actually."

Now that Smythe had established that he was in the presence of a creator of non-fiction, the atmosphere thawed considerably.

"Oh, my dear chap," he said expansively, "you don't need to worry about that. Why, there are people here who haven't had anything published for years. If you're a fraud, what does that make them?"

He laughed in a light, whinnying fashion.

Before Collins could think of anything to say in reply, his arm was grabbed, this time by Smythe.

"But whatever you do," he hissed conspiratorially, leaning closer, "don't refer to it as a book festival. Not if the old trout's around, anyway. As far as she's concerned, and so far as we are for public consumption, it's a writers' convention."

"Oh," Collins said, moving back instinctively and noting with relief that Smythe let go of his arm as he did so.

"What's the difference?" he asked disingenuously, for he understood all too well.

"The public, of course, old boy. At a writers' convention you're just talking to other writers, most of whom are jealous as hell of you anyway, because you're successful enough to be up on stage while they're not. It's just an ego-massaging exercise, with everyone saying how marvellous everyone else is. God knows why, because it's obvious that nobody means it."

"I see," Collins replied. "And a book festival?"

"Ah," Smythe said appreciatively, rubbing his hands together, "now you're talking, old man. The reading public. Lots of punters who've read your books – or just some of them, hopefully – and some of whom will actually buy some afterwards and queue up for you to sign them. That's all writers care about, you know, or should be anyway; selling books. Everything else is just an irrelevance, a distraction."

"Oh," Collins said, feeling it a somewhat lame response, "and who's this old trout you mentioned?"

"Queen Ann, of course. Ann Durham."

"Oh, Ann Durham," Collins enthused. "I'm a great fan of her Inspector Bergmann books. Vienna between the wars is such a marvellous setting, don't you think? An inspired choice, really."

"They're all right if you like that sort of thing, I suppose," Smythe said dismissively, "but what's she done recently? If you ask me, they were just a flash in the pan."

"She wrote six, didn't she?" Collins demurred. "Hardly a flash in the pan, surely? And they were all adapted for television."

"So were mine," Smythe said bluntly, "and I'm still churning them out, though God knows it gets harder and harder with each successive bloody book. But the last

Bergmann book was published – what, twenty years ago? More?"

"More, I think," Collins conceded. "Of course she's written some other stuff since, but I have to concede that none of it was nearly as good."

While he was making this last remark he was thinking furiously about who this Tom Smythe might be, for surely from what he had said he was expecting Collins to know for exactly which televisions series, and thus which books, he was responsible. This might generally have been a safe bet, but in Collins he had encountered, though he did not know it, a man who watched little television and read almost no contemporary crime fiction.

Fortunately, Smythe was warming to another theme.

"On the subject of the old trout, I should mark your card, old boy," he said. "It seems like there's finally going to been an election for the post of Chair. Ma Durham grabbed it some time back and since then has somehow always managed to persuade the committee by sheer bloody force of will not to hold an election but simply to confirm her in the post for the coming year."

"Not really relevant to me, I'm afraid," Collins said quickly, for he hated anything that smacked even slightly of politics, "I'm only an associate member, so I'm not eligible to vote."

Smythe was however not so easily deterred.

"When's your book due out?" he demanded.

"In a few weeks," Collins admitted reluctantly.

"Well, you're OK then," Smythe purred. "Your associate membership automatically transitions to full membership on the publication date, and the vote won't be a for a month or two yet."

"Who else is standing?" Collins asked.

"Nobody officially at the moment because the election hasn't been called by the committee, but I don't mind admitting that I will be throwing my hat into the ring. I'm sort of the senior man as it were once you take Durham out of the equation."

"And how would you propose to do that, Tom dear?" enquired Ann Durham who had joined the group unannounced and unnoticed. "Murder, perhaps?"

**GUY FRASER-SAMPSON** is an established writer, having published not only fiction but also books on a diverse range of subjects including finance, investment, economics and cricket. His darkly disturbing economic history *The Mess We're In* was nominated for the Orwell Prize.

His *Mapp & Lucia* novels have all been optioned by BBC TV, and have won high praise from other authors including Alexander McCall Smith, Gyles Brandreth and Tom Holt. The second was featured in an exclusive interview with Mariella Forstrup on Radio 4, and Guy's entertaining talks on the series have been heard at a number of literary events including the Sunday Times Festival in Oxford and the Daily Telegraph Festival in Dartington.

## THE FIRST THRILLING TITLE IN THE HAMPSTEAD MURDERS SERIES

£7.99, ISBN 978-1-910692-93-6

The genteel façade of London's Hampstead is shattered by a series of terrifying murders, and the ensuing police hunt is threatened by internal politics, and a burgeoning love triangle within the investigative team. Pressurised by senior officers desperate for a result a new initiative is clearly needed, but what?

Intellectual analysis and police procedure vie with the gut instinct of 'copper's nose', and help appears to offer itself from a very unlikely source a famous fictional detective. A psychological profile of the murderer allows the police to narrow down their search, but will Scotland

Yard lose patience with the team before they can crack the case?

Praised by fellow authors and readers alike, this is a truly original crime story, speaking to a contemporary audience yet harking back to the Golden Age of detective fiction. Intelligent, quirky and mannered, it has been described as 'a love letter to the detective novel'. Above it all hovers Hampstead, a magical village evoking the elegance of an earlier time, and the spirit of mystery-solving detectives.

URBANE